**"You need a reason for being here, in case Fulton or your CO catches you on-site."**

"If I could pass under the radar...if everyone could see me as something other than a cop...a guest, maybe, or a new member of staff, they could be inclined to talk. That would make my job easier."

"Not staff," she said contemplatively. "That wouldn't be right."

"Then what did you mean?"

"A guest, maybe," she decided. "That would get you in the restaurant, the bar, the spa, the golf course and stables...everywhere but C Building." Her eyes cleared. "Oh."

"What?" he asked, feeling his stomach muscles tighten as he watched her pupils dilate.

Her gaze trickled down his throat, over his shoulders and down his chest. "It's that simple...and that complicated."

"Throw me a bone here, Colton."

"You need to immerse yourself among staff and guests. You need a cover. Being my boyfriend would guarantee access to pretty much anything."

"Your boyfriend." He heard his tone flatline. It was the worst idea he'd ever heard.

And it was the best idea he'd ever heard.

Dear Reader,

Welcome to Mariposa Resort & Spa, owned and operated by Adam, Laura and Joshua Colton!

I enjoyed writing this first book in The Coltons of Arizona continuity. Red Rock Country is a dream destination and this has been a dream of a project. I loved working with the other authors and our editor to bring Mariposa, the Colton siblings, and their friends, family and staff to life.

Laura and Noah have been so much fun to pit against one another for their common goal of flushing out a killer on the resort. I love an opposites-attract romance—even better that these opposites must engage in a fake relationship in order to catch the bad guy.

Words have never come to the page faster than when Noah and Laura clash for the first time, or when their shared grief over Allison's death binds them together in spite of everything that is so wrong about their relationship (and yet so very right)!

I hope you love The Coltons of Arizona as much as I do. Stay tuned for the second book in the continuity by Patricia Sargeant for Alexis's story.

Happy reading!

*Amber*

# COLTON'S
# LAST RESORT

**AMBER LEIGH WILLIAMS**

**ROMANTIC SUSPENSE**

Special thanks and acknowledgment are given to Amber Leigh Williams for her contribution to The Coltons of Arizona miniseries.

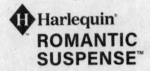

**Harlequin®**
# ROMANTIC SUSPENSE™

Recycling programs for this product may not exist in your area.

ISBN-13: 978-1-335-50265-0

Colton's Last Resort

**Amber Leigh Williams** is an author, wife, mother of two and dog mom. She has been writing sexy small-town romance with memorable characters since 2006. Her Harlequin romance miniseries is set in her charming hometown of Fairhope, Alabama. She lives on the Alabama Gulf Coast, where she loves being outdoors with her family and a good book. Visit her on the web at www.amberleighwilliams.com!

To Beardy and the littles,

I've never written a book faster. It's a testament to your love and understanding that I was able to do so during a difficult time. Endless bear hugs and ice cream kisses for all of you!

And to Patricia, Kacy, Kimberly, Charlene, Addison and our editor, Emma Cole.

It has been lovely working with all of you.

# *Prologue*

Allison Brewer didn't belong in a morgue. She was a twenty-five-year-old yoga instructor with zero underlying conditions. She never smoked, rarely drank, and was the picture of health and vitality.

Detective Noah Steele sucked in a breath as the coroner, Rod Steinbeck, pulled back the sheet. How many times had he stood over a body at the Yavapai County Coroner's Office? How many times had he stared unflinchingly at death—at what nature did to humans and what human nature did to others?

*She looks like she could still be alive*, he thought. No cuts or bruises marred her face. There were no ligature marks. She could have been asleep. She looked perfectly at peace. If Noah squinted, he could fool himself into thinking there was a slight smile at the corners of her mouth. Just as there had been when she'd feigned sleep as a girl.

However, an inescapable blue stain spread across her lips. He could deny it all he wanted, but his sister was gone.

"I'm sorry, Noah," Rod said and lifted the sheet over her face again.

"No." The word wasn't soft or hard, loud or quiet. Noah surprised himself by speaking mildly. As if this were any other body…any other case. His mind was somewhere near the ceiling. His gut turned, and his chest ached. But he let that piece of himself float away, detached. He made himself think like he was trained to think. "What're your impressions?"

"Fulton's already been here. It's his case. And for good reason. You're going to need some time to process—"

"Rod." He sounded cold. He was. He was so bitterly cold. And he didn't know how to live with it. He didn't know how to live in a world without Allison. "Next of kin would be informed of any progress made in the investigation. I'm her next of kin. Inform me."

Rod shuffled his feet. Placing his hands at each corner of the head of the steel table, he studied Allison. "I'm not sure I'm comfortable with this."

"She's dead." Noah made himself say it. He needed to hear it, the finality of it. "If Sedona Police wants me to process that, I need to know how and why."

Rod adjusted his glasses. "Look, maybe you should talk to Fulton."

"She was found at the resort," Noah prompted, undeterred, "where she works."

"Mariposa."

"You were on scene there," Noah surmised. "What time did you arrive?"

Rod gave in. "Nine fifteen."

"Where was she?"

"One of the pool cabanas," the coroner explained.

"Tell me what you saw."

"Come on, Noah…"

"Tell me," Noah said. He knew not to raise his voice. If he were hysterical, it would get back to his CO. He'd be put on leave.

He needed to work through this. If he stopped working, stopped thinking objectively, he would lose his mind.

Rod lifted his hands. "She was found face down, but one of the staff performed CPR, so she was on her back when I arrived. Her shoes were missing."

*That could've been something,* Noah thought, if Allison hadn't had a habit of going around barefoot where she was comfortable, particularly when entering someone's home.

The temperature had dipped into the thirties the night before. *A little cold for no shoes, even for her,* he considered. "What was she wearing?"

"Sport jacket and leggings," Rod explained. "Underneath, she wore a long-sleeved ballet-like top cropped above the navel with crisscrossed bands underneath. It was a matching set, all green."

"What do you figure for time of death?"

"Right now, I'd say she died somewhere between one and two this morning."

*She hadn't gone home to bed,* Noah mused. "Any cuts, lacerations? Signs of foul play?"

"Some abrasions on the backs of her legs."

"Show me."

Again, Rod paused before he walked to the bottom of the table. Lifting the drape, he revealed one long, pale leg with toes still painted pink. Noah tried not to see the unearthly blue tone of the skin around the nails. He craned his neck when Rod showed him the marks on her calves.

"She was dragged," Noah said as he realized what had happened. Why did the air feel like ice? The cold filled his lungs. They felt wind-burned, and the pain of it made his hands knot into fists.

"That would be my understanding," Rod agreed. He replaced the sheet gingerly.

"Before or after TOD?" Noah asked.

"After."

Noah's brow furrowed. "She was killed somewhere other than the cabana and staged there." His voice had gone rough, but he kept going, searching. "Were there any items with her at the scene?"

"Fulton noted there was no purse, wallet or cell phone. She was identified by members of Mariposa's staff."

"Were her lips blue when you got there?"

"Yes." Rod nodded. "Her fingernails and toes were discolored as well."

Noah scraped his knuckles over the thick growth of beard that covered his jawline. "Who found her?"

"From what I understand," Rod said slowly, "it was a staff member. You'll have to get the name of the person from Fulton."

"Who was there when you arrived on scene?" Noah asked curiously.

"There was a small crowd that had been blocked by officers," Rod told him. "Several members of security, one pool maintenance person and all three of the Coltons."

"Coltons." Noah recognized the name, but he let it hang in the air, waiting for Rod to elaborate.

"The siblings," Rod said. "They own and manage Mariposa. Adam, Laura and Joshua, I believe, are their names."

"What was your impression of them?" Noah asked, homing in.

Rod considered. "The younger one, Joshua, was quiet. Laura didn't say much either. She seemed stricken by the whole thing. The oldest one, Adam…"

When Rod paused, Noah narrowed his eyes. "What about him?"

"He did all the talking," Rod said. "He ordered everyone

back and let the uniforms, Fulton, crime scene technicians and myself work. There was no attempt to tamper with the scene. Although I did hear him speaking to Fulton as we readied the body for transport."

"What did he say?" Noah asked, feeling like a dog with a bone.

"He wanted Fulton's word that the investigation would remain discreet," Rod said. "They get some high-profile guests at Mariposa. He didn't want their privacy or, I expect, their experience hindered."

The muscles around Noah's mouth tensed. "A member of their staff is found dead, and the Coltons' first thought is how it's going to affect their clientele? Does that seem right to you?"

"I'm not the detective," Steinbeck noted.

*No*, Noah considered. *I am.* "You'll do a tox screen?"

"It's routine," Rod replied. "As it stands, I don't have a cause of death for you."

"You'll keep me informed?" Noah asked.

"I'll stay in touch."

Noah forced himself to back away from Allison's body. Deep in some unbottled canyon, he felt himself scream.

"Have your parents been notified?"

The question nearly made him flinch. Rod didn't know. No one did. Not really.

It didn't matter, he told himself. He'd loved her, hadn't he? He'd loved her as his own. "She doesn't have parents," he said. "Neither of us do."

"I'm sorry." Rod placed his hand on Noah's shoulder. "I'll take care of her."

"I know." Noah turned for the door.

"Don't get yourself in trouble over this," Rod warned. "Let Fulton handle it. He'll find out what happened to her."

Noah didn't answer. In seconds, he was out of the autopsy room, down the hall, crossing the lobby. Planting both hands on the glass door, he shoved it open.

Cold air hit him in the face and did nothing for the lethal ice now channeling through his blood.

He thought about stopping, doubling over, bracing his hands on his knees.

He could hear her. Still.

*Breathe, Noah. Deep breath in. And let it out.*

Noah shook his head firmly, blocking out her voice. He thought of what Rod had said—about the scene and his impressions of the people there.

He took out his keys, walking to the unmarked vehicle that was his. Opening the driver's door, he got behind the wheel and cranked the engine. The sun was sinking swiftly toward the red rock mountains in the distance, but he picked up his phone. Using voice commands, he said, "Hey, Google, set a course for Mariposa Resort & Spa."

He studied the GPS route that popped up on-screen before mounting the phone on the dash. Shifting into Reverse, he cupped the back of the passenger headrest. Turning his head over his shoulder, he backed out of the parking space.

To hell with staying out of Fulton's way. Someone was responsible for Allison's death. He would find out who.

And he was going to nail the Coltons' asses to the floor.

# Chapter 1

*Ten Hours Earlier*

"**D**ad wants to meet."

Laura Colton stared at her brother over the rim of her thermos. "You couldn't have let me finish my coffee before dropping that bombshell?"

Her brother Adam raised a brow as he eyed the overlarge bottle. "There are three cups of java in that thing. If that's not enough to prepare you for the day, it's time you rethink some of your life choices."

"I demand coffee before chaos," Laura informed him and took another hit to prove her point. She was no stranger to butting heads with her older brother. They worked closely as owners and managers of Arizona's premier resort and spa.

It was their passion for Mariposa that made them lock horns. The resort wasn't simply the business venture that supported them. Before it was Mariposa, it was the respite their mother had sought when the disappointment of her marriage to Clive Colton had grown to be too much. Laura and her siblings' memories of Annabeth Colton were tied not just to the project she had started shortly after the birth of her third child, Joshua, but the land itself.

The three of them had buried her here at Mariposa after her battle with pancreatic cancer.

Laura loved Mariposa. It was more home than her actual hometown of Los Angeles had ever been. When Adam had asked her and Joshua to join him after he'd taken legal control of the resort at the age of twenty-one, neither of them had hesitated. From there, their management styles had been born out of renovations and the desire to make Mariposa their own.

The Coltons had put the once-small hotel on the map. It had been transformed into a getaway for the rich and famous, with twenty-four acres of spacious grounds northeast of Sedona. It now boasted thirty guest bungalows with stunning views of Red Rock Country, a five-star restaurant named after Annabeth herself, a garden, rock labyrinth, golf course, spa, horse stables and paddocks, and hiking trails.

Laura had learned to work with both of her brothers. They were invested in their shared vision, in this life. She could take their ribbing. Just as she could take the fact that she and Adam were both workaholics whose dedication and zeal left little in the way of private lives.

She drank more coffee and tried not to rue the long chain of failed relationships she'd endured, letting her eyes stray to the view from the conference room windows of L Building.

Shadows were long across the rocky vista with its stunning juxtaposition of blue sky and red geography. From its flat ridge top, Mariposa woke briskly. Staff would be going about preparations for the day. The chef at Annabeth would be arranging its signature champagne breakfast. Below the ridge and the bungalows, the horses would be feeding. The helicopter pilot who transported guests from the airport in Flagstaff would be doing preflight checks.

If she had to scrap her plans to be married with children by her late twenties for this, so be it. *There's plenty of time for all that*, Adam liked to say when anyone commented on his lack of a wife or children.

Plenty of time, she mused. No need to worry about the fact that she was tripping fast toward thirty.

Cautiously, she asked, "What does Clive want?"

Adam chuckled a little as he always did when she called their father by his given name. "He didn't say."

She ran her tongue over her teeth. "Is he bringing Glenna?"

"He didn't mention her," Adam said, referring to their stepmother of four years. Laura imagined it seemed odd to him still, too. Clive's string of mistresses hadn't been a well-kept secret. He'd fathered a fourth child outside of his marriage to Annabeth. Dani had come to live with Adam, Laura and Joshua in Los Angeles for a time. Laura had been only too happy not to be the only girl, and the four of them had been all too aware of Clive's neglect.

Laura had never forgotten that, and she'd never been able to forgive Clive for his carelessness or whims. She knew his affairs had been one reason Annabeth had escaped time after time to Arizona. She'd loved Clive, despite his faults and mishandlings. The heartbreak and embarrassment of knowing he had looked for companionship elsewhere…that he had married her for her money…it had been too much for Annabeth to bear.

No, Laura had never forgiven her father, even if Glenna wasn't like the other women. She was close to Clive's age, for one, and beautiful, like his mistresses. Unlike the others, she was mature and independent. She even owned her own business, and it was a successful one.

It didn't mean Laura's father had turned things around. He'd had little to do with his children's upbringing. Annabeth had raised them practically on her own until the cancer had taken a turn for the worse when Laura was just twelve years old.

"I thought we could arrange Bungalow Twelve for him," Adam continued as he shuffled papers in the file spread on the table in front of him.

Laura pursed her lips. Adam was a businessperson, not a bitter man or a hard one. The snub was subtle. Every bungalow at Mariposa was luxurious, but only bungalows one through ten featured a private outdoor pool and were prioritized for VIP guests. She rubbed her lips together, considering. "You don't think he'll notice?"

Adam picked up a pen and made a mark on the latest budget report he'd likely stayed up late last night reviewing. "Notice what?"

Adam wasn't petty either. Neither was she, Laura told herself as she made a notation in the notes app on her phone. "Bungalow Twelve," she agreed. "When are we expecting him?"

"The day after tomorrow."

"And when is he departing?"

"He didn't say that either."

"He can't just come and go as he pleases," Laura pointed out. "We have guests coming in after him, and the concierge and Housekeeping require notice."

Adam lifted his eyes briefly to hers. Even sitting, he looked lanky despite his broad shoulders. His blue eyes matched hers, and his medium-blond hair was never not short, trim and stylish, even when the rest of the world was waking up. People liked to think he'd been born in a suit, and if she hadn't grown up with him, she'd wonder, too.

"I'm sure you'll let him know when he arrives. Let's move on."

Laura made another notation about her father's visit and did her best to ignore the unsettled feeling that pricked along her spine.

"The wedding on Valentine's Day weekend," Adam continued. "I'm assuming everything's on schedule?"

"I spoke to the mother of the bride yesterday," she explained. "They've asked for another three bungalows, as the guest list has expanded."

"A little late for that."

"I said we could do it," she admitted, "as long as they agreed to cap the number there."

He let loose a sigh. "I'll have to adjust the price points. How many more plates is that for the reception?"

"Five adults, four children."

He scrawled and started talking numbers.

"We need to talk about this year's anniversary celebration," she interrupted. Mariposa had opened on Valentine's Day almost twenty-two years ago. "Since the wedding is on Valentine's Day, I propose we move the celebration to Wednesday, the eighteenth."

Adam stopped counting to consider. "That works for me."

"We'll have a bandstand, like last year," she said, ticking items off her list. "Live music, hors d'oeuvres, cocktails and fireworks. And you'll make a speech."

He raised his gaze to hers. "Will I?"

"Yes," she said, beaming. "People like to hear you speak."

He waved a hand. "If I must."

"Good man," she praised and put a check mark next to Adam's Speech on her list.

An infinitesimal smile wavered across his lips. "You enjoy painting me into a corner and patting me on the head when I have no choice but to comply."

"I'm sure I don't know what you mean." She tapped the hollow of her collarbone. "Is that the tie I bought you?"

"Yes," he said after a glance at it.

"It looks very nice," she said. "And I was right. It does bring out your eyes."

His smile strengthened. "Clever girl."

The door to the conference room opened. Laura eased back in her chair as Joshua loped in. He smiled distractedly through dark-tinted shades when he saw the two of them seated on either side of the table. "Greetings, siblings."

"You're late," Adam pointed out.

"Oh, you noticed," Joshua said, unfazed as he pulled out a chair and dropped to it. "How thoughtful of you." He caught Laura's look. "You're not going to tell me off, are you?"

He was so charmingly rumpled, any urge to scold him fell long by the wayside. Joshua was twenty-seven. His dirty-blond hair was perpetually shaggy. When he took off his glasses, his eyes laughed in the same shade as hers and Adam's. At six feet, he was trim and muscular. He couldn't claim to eat and sleep work as they did, but he was just as devoted to Mariposa. He was very much at home in his role as the resort's Activities Director.

"No," she replied.

He pecked a kiss on her cheek. "You're my favorite."

"For the moment."

He leaned his chair back and crossed his legs at the ankles. "What's the latest?"

"Clive is coming," she warned, handing over her thermos easily when he held out his hand for it.

He took a long sip. "And how do we feel about that?" he asked, squinting at Adam across the long, flat plane of the table.

Adam answered without inflection. "Indifferent."

"Oh?" Joshua said with a raised brow. He looked at Laura for confirmation.

Laura cleared her throat. "We're placing him in Bungalow Twelve."

Joshua laughed shortly before setting the thermos on the table between him and her. "I approve."

"I thought you might," Adam said, again without looking up.

Joshua had been only ten when their mother had died. His memories of Annabeth were the foggiest—most of them mere reflections through a vintage-cast mirror. Though he remembered well how Clive had abandoned them to their grief. As the youngest, he'd needed the most stability and guidance. It was Adam and Laura who had stepped into that role—not their father.

"Glenna won't stand being demoted to anything below the amenities of Bungalow Ten," he warned.

"We don't know she's coming," Laura revealed.

"I'm just saying," Joshua said, holding up his hands.

None of them had gotten to know their stepmother well. But Joshua was right. Glenna may keep her thoughts to herself, and she could be perfectly cordial. But she also had a discerning eye and was accustomed to a certain type of lifestyle. One reason, no doubt, she had been drawn to Clive Colton. As CEO of Colton Textiles, he lived in a Beverly Hills mansion she had already refined to her tastes.

Laura sighed. "I'll deal with that if it comes."

Joshua sketched a lazy salute. "I'll have Knox loan you a helmet."

"I have one," she reminded him. Not that she'd need it. She could handle Clive, and she could certainly handle Glenna. She shook her head. "Are we being unkind?"

Her brothers exchanged a look. "In what way?" Adam asked.

"He hasn't been well," Laura reminded them. "The mini-strokes last year and the rumors about sideline business deals going sideways... We could be losing him."

They lapsed into silence. Joshua reached up to scratch his chin. "Is it not fair to say I feel like I lost him a long time ago?"

She studied him, and she saw the ten-year-old who'd needed a parent. His hand clutched the arm of the swivel chair. She covered it with her own. "It is fair," she assured him.

Adam had shielded his mouth with his writing hand. He dropped it to the table, the ballpoint pen still gripped between his fingers. "Mom left the resort to us in her will not just because she wanted us to have a piece of her and financial security. She left it because she knew the house in Los Angeles wasn't a home. She left us a place we could belong to. Dad never provided that for her or us. She made sure after she was gone we wouldn't need to rely on him, because she knew all he would ever do was disappoint us. Like he disappointed her."

"She left us fifty percent of the shares in Colton Textiles, too," Joshua added. "If it'd been him...if he had gone first... would he have done the same?"

Laura shook her head. "I don't know." But she did, she realized. She knew all too well.

Adam dropped the pen. He folded his hands on the table-top. "If we have an opening, we can slot him into one of the VIP bungalows. Would that ease your conscience?"

Laura considered. She opened her mouth to answer.

A knock on the door interrupted.

"Come in," Adam called.

The panel pulled away from the jamb. Laura felt the tension in the room drain instantaneously as Tallulah Deschine peered into the room. The fifty-year-old Navajo woman was head of housekeeping at Mariposa. She'd been with the Coltons since the renovation. In the last decade, she'd become more of a mother to them than a member of staff, and she was one of the few workers at the resort who, like Adam, Laura and Joshua, lived in her own house on property. "I'm sorry to intrude."

Joshua sat up straighter. "No need to apologize, Tallulah. Come sit by me." He pushed out the chair next to his.

Worry lines marred her brow. "There's a situation. Down at the pool."

"What kind of situation?" Adam asked, his smile falling away in a fast frown.

Tallulah's attention seized on Laura. She opened her mouth, then closed it.

Laura saw her chin wobble. Quickly, she pushed her chair back. "What is it, Tallulah?" she asked softly, crossing to the door. She heard Adam and Joshua get up and follow suit. "What's happened?"

Tallulah's eyes flooded with tears. She spoke in a choked voice. "The maid, Bella… She noticed one cabana was never straightened after hours last night. When she went inside to do just that, she found someone there."

Adam touched her shoulder when she faltered again. "Someone who? What were they doing there?"

"Oh, Adam." Tallulah shook her head, trying to gather herself. "Bella thought she'd fallen asleep there, so she tried waking her up. She couldn't. There's something *really* wrong…"

"Who is she?" Laura asked. There was a hard fist in her stomach. It grew tighter and tighter, apprehension knotting there. "Tallulah, who did Bella find in the cabana?"

"It's Allison," Tallulah revealed. "The yoga instructor. Knox knows CPR. He's trying to bring her around—"

"Did you call 9-1-1?" Adam asked, his phone already in hand.

"Alexis made the call."

"EMTs should only be ten minutes out," he assured her.

Joshua pushed through the door. "If she's not breathing, that's not enough time."

Laura tailed him. He'd already broken into a run. She didn't catch up with him until they came to the end of the hall.

If Allison wasn't asleep in the cabana…if she wasn't breathing… What did that mean?

Laura hastened her steps and nearly ran into Alexis Reed, the concierge, and Erica Pike, Adam's executive assistant, in the lobby.

"What's going on?" Alexis asked urgently. "Is Allison okay?"

"I don't know," Laura said. Joshua didn't stop. He hit the glass doors. They swung open. She followed him out into the mountain air. Her heart was in her throat as they raced to the pool area.

The drapes on the farthest cabana were still closed. The pool maintenance person, Manuel, stood outside with his hat in his hands. Their head of security, Roland, stepped out, expression drawn.

"How is she?" Joshua asked. "Did Knox bring her around?"

Roland shook his head.

Laura fumbled for speech. "What?"

Joshua swept the curtain aside.

Laura moved to follow him, but Manuel brought her up short. "I don't think you should go in there, Ms. Colton."

She shook her head. "Why? What's wrong with her?"

Roland took a breath. "I don't know how to say this, but I don't think she'll be coming back around."

Laura couldn't wrap her head around the words. She slipped past Manuel and Roland, ducking through the parting of the drapes. Her footsteps faltered when she saw Joshua and Knox Burnett, the horseback adventure guide, leaning over the still, white face of the woman lying supine on the outdoor rug. Neither of them moved. "Why did you stop?" she asked Knox. "Why aren't you helping her?"

"Laura…" Joshua mumbled. "You need to go."

She crouched next to him. Her hand lifted to her mouth when she saw the tint of Allison's lips.

Knox's face was bowed in an uncharacteristic frown.

Even as she denied what she was seeing, she looked at him. "Why did you stop?" she asked again.

He was panting, his long hair mussed. His face inordinately pale, he said, "She's cold. So cold. I couldn't get a pulse. She never had a pulse…"

Laura looked down at Allison's face. Her dark eyes stared, unseeing. "Oh, God," she said with a shaky exhalation.

Joshua's fingers closed over hers. He spoke in a whisper, as if afraid Allison would hear. "She's gone."

# Chapter 2

Laura frowned at the water glass on the table in front of her. She wished for her thermos. Hell, she wished this interview could take place at L Bar. The bartender, Valerie, knew Laura's drink of choice.

*Allison*, she thought. *Oh, God. Allison...*

Detective Mark Fulton of the Sedona Police Department sat across the table. He hadn't allowed either of her brothers to join her. They had each been questioned separately, as had Bella, Knox, Tallulah, Manuel and Roland.

"I understand you were the one who initially hired the deceased," Fulton commented.

She studied the small corona on top of his shiny, hairless head, a reflection from the wide chandelier above them. Forcing herself to look away, she traced the pattern of his tie with her gaze—circles overlapping circles in various shades of blue, each edged with a thin gold iris. "Allison," she said. She swallowed. She hadn't let herself cry.

Not yet. She'd been surrounded by people—her brothers, the staff, the guests—since the discovery of Allison's body.

Her voice split as if the strain of not crying had injured her vocal cords.

"Sorry?" Fulton said, looking up from his notepad distractedly.

"Her name is Allison," she told him. He needed to stop calling her *the deceased*. It sounded discordant, inhumane.

"Of course," he allowed. He spared her a brief smile. "You hired Allison. Ms. Brewer. Is that correct?"

"I did," Laura answered. "Two years ago last September."

"And when did you see her last?" he asked.

Laura thought about it. "Yesterday. She teaches… I mean, she taught a yoga course in the meditation garden at the rock labyrinth at sunset. I saw her coming back from that around dusk. It was between six and six thirty. I was on my way to check on our chef at Annabeth. He had to have stitches the day before. He cut himself during the lunch rush. I wanted to make sure he was okay to work through dinner. I saw Allison walking from the meditation garden toward C Building, which is where the staff locker rooms, break rooms and café are located. It's also where they park their cars when they arrive for work in the morning."

"Did you speak to her?"

"I did," Laura said with a nod.

"How would you describe her demeanor?"

Laura frowned. "I'm not sure what you mean."

"Did she strike you as happy, tired, angry, upset…?"

It took a moment for Laura to settle on the right description. "She was upbeat. Allison was always upbeat. Even when she was fatigued, which I imagine she was after a full day of classes. She does guided meditation for guests and for anyone on staff who wants to join after hours. One reason I was so excited about hiring her was because she had wonderful ideas for improving the wellness of not just Mariposa's guests but the resort as a whole. She wanted fellow members of staff to have the opportunity to rest and recharge."

"That was generous of her."

Laura nodded. "Allison was always generous with her time and attention. Everyone liked her."

"What did you speak to her about when you saw her yesterday evening?"

She narrowed her eyes, trying to recall the exact words of the conversation. "She wanted to grab dinner and was looking forward to a few moments to herself in the break room before the guided meditation with the staff. Sometimes, she liked to join the stargazing excursion after dinner. She was excited about seeing last night's meteor shower before she went home to Sedona. She had a house there."

"Would you mind telling me what she was wearing at the time?" Fulton asked.

Laura fumbled. She thought again of Allison lying between Knox and Joshua. Her blue-tinged lips. Her blank stare.

Something wormed its way up Laura's throat. The taste of acid filled her mouth. She had to force herself to swallow it back down. "Workout clothes. The same ones we… we found her in this morning."

"Was she wearing shoes last night?"

She narrowed her eyes at him. "That's an odd question, Detective. Do you mind me asking how that's relevant?"

"I'm just trying to get a full picture of the deceased… I mean, Allison…in the hours leading up to her death."

He said it gently. Even so, *her death* sounded so final. Laura reached up for her temples, feeling off balance. "Ah… I believe so. Yes. She wore flexible, lightweight footwear between classes. For the classes themselves, she preferred to go barefoot." Laura remembered the tiny lotus tattoo on Allison's ankle. Her eyes stung. "Do you mind me asking, Detective, if you have any idea *how* she died? It just seems strange for someone so young to just…"

Fulton nodded away the rest. "That's why I'm trying to go through all the details. It will help me understand what happened to her."

"Did she have a heart attack?" Laura asked. Even that seemed nonsensical. Allison was so healthy. She was vegan, preferring to bring her own meals instead of having them prepared by others. "It could have been a stroke, I suppose. Or an aneurysm?"

"Again, Ms. Colton," Fulton said in as kind a voice as he could muster. "I assure you. I will do everything I can to figure out what happened to your employee."

Employee? Allison was her friend. Laura opened her mouth to correct him, but she faltered.

"Was there anyone on staff who Allison didn't get along with?" Fulton asked.

"No. As I said, everyone liked Allison."

"What about guests? Have there been any disgruntled students from her yoga or meditation classes?"

"No," she said, finding the idea ridiculous. "None."

"In two years, she never had a dissatisfied student?"

"Not one," Laura said. She would have known. Allison would have told her.

"Did she have a personal relationship with any of the guests?"

"What do you mean by that?" Laura asked.

"Was she closer to any particular guest?" he elaborated. "Beyond the classes. Maybe one she got to know during the stargazing excursions."

Laura frowned. "Allison would never overstep. She knew where to draw the line. She was the perfect mix of friendliness and professionalism, and she never would have thought of mixing business with pleasure, if that's what you're implying."

"You're sure of this?"

She met his level stare. "Yes."

He made several notes before he asked, "Do you know anything about her personal life? Was she involved with anyone on staff?"

"No, Detective. Relationships among staff members aren't encouraged."

"No one on staff seemed especially interested in Ms. Brewer?"

"I don't think so," Laura said. "There was a flirtation with our adventure guide, Knox Burnett. But Knox flirts with everyone."

"What about outside the resort? What was her personal life like in Sedona?"

"She was in a relationship when she first came to the resort," Laura remembered suddenly. "But it ended a few months after she started."

"Did she seem upset?"

"She enjoyed being single again. Prioritizing herself was important. She enjoyed living alone." She came to attention as something occurred to her. "Oh my God! Have you told her family? She didn't talk about her parents, but there was a brother she was close to. She talked about him regularly. Does he know? Should we have contacted him already? I'm sure she put him down as her emergency contact."

Fulton held up a hand. "We have contacted her next of kin. You don't need to worry about that."

"Still, I'd like to extend the condolences of the family and staff," Laura explained. "There must be something we can do."

"I'd be happy to get you in touch, if you like."

"I would," she said. "Very much."

"I'll have that information sent to you as soon as possible," he stated. "One more question, and I'll let you get back to your day. Can you tell me about your whereabouts between one and two o'clock this morning?"

She felt heavy in her chair, as if gravity were exerting more force than necessary. "Is that when Allison died?"

"Yes, ma'am."

"Why do you need to know my whereabouts?"

"It's simply a matter of routine."

"I was in bed," Laura explained. She'd gone to bed early, her large tabby cat at her side.

"Can anyone corroborate that?"

"No." Was her word not enough? "I took off my smart-watch to charge it. I'm sure there's a time stamp, probably around 11:00 p.m. My alarm goes off at 5:30 a.m."

"Your brother informed me there are no security cameras on the property."

"No. The privacy of our guests is very important at Mariposa."

"He said that, too. I just hope it doesn't make matters more complicated for you."

"Why would it?" she asked.

He closed his notepad and pushed his chair back from the table. "I think that's all I have for now. Thank you for sitting down with me. If I have any more questions, I'll let you know."

If he had any more questions for her? She was the one with all the remaining questions, and none of them had been answered. She sat frozen as he rounded the table. Before he could reach for the door, she snapped to attention, standing suddenly. "Detective?"

He stopped. "Ma'am?"

"You will keep my brothers and me informed of any

developments?" she requested. "We all cared about Allison a great deal."

"I will," he agreed. "Have a good day."

She waited until he was out the door before she sank to the seat. Her legs weren't steady enough to stand on.

She should've asked why Allison's lips had been blue. Would Fulton know how long she had been in the cabana?

Had she suffered? Was she scared? How long had she been alone and frightened?

How could this happen? What was she going to do now? How was she supposed to go about their day as if nothing had happened?

Laura's posture caved. She rarely let it, but she folded under the weight of shock and pressed her fingers to her closed eyes.

She hadn't lost anyone close to her since her mother's passing and hadn't forgotten how it felt—the staggering weight of bereavement. It was impossible to forget. But she hadn't expected... She hadn't been prepared to feel it all again.

The shock was wearing away fast. Once it was gone, the grief would sink in. And it wouldn't give way to anything else. She pressed her hand to her mouth, choking it back.

She was afraid of it. Grief. How it gripped and rent. As a child, it had come for her on wraith wings, real but transparent. She hadn't been able to see it, but it had held her. It had hurt her. And it had transformed her into something she hadn't recognized.

Panic beat those wings against her chest now. Her pulse rushed in her ears. She tried to breathe, tried to think through it, but it didn't allow her to.

It was already taking hold.

She'd seen it coming before. Her mother had warned her

there wasn't much time. She had told all her children what to expect at the end of her cancer battle. She had prepared them and armed them for the hard days to come.

This wasn't the same. And yet it was.

She thought of her brothers waiting outside the door. Coming to her feet, she walked the length of the conference room. She paced until the panic subsided—until her breathing returned to normal and her heart no longer raced.

Adam might be the oldest, but her brothers had looked to her in the past. For strength. For stability. When their mother died, she had stepped into Annabeth's power—to carry them, to ground them and to keep them together.

They were grown now, but they would look to her, still. They would need her to handle this…and they would need to lean on her. And so would the staff.

She dried her eyes, fixed her makeup and made herself down the entire glass of water in front of her.

A knock clattered against the door. She checked her reflection in the window before she said, "Yes?"

Alexis stepped in. "Hey. How are you holding up?"

Laura made herself meet her friend's gaze. "I'm fine."

Alexis raised a brow. "You want me to pretend that's true?"

"I'm going to need you to," Laura requested.

Alexis nodded. "Okay." She, Allison and Laura had gotten to know each other well. Besides Tallulah and Laura's brothers, redheaded, smiling Allison and dark, no-nonsense Alexis were the members of staff Laura felt closest to. In some ways, they had been her saving grace over the last few years. There were things she couldn't discuss with Adam and Joshua. Just her girls. The three of them had made Taco Tuesdays at Sedona's Tipsy Tacos a weekly escape from the pressures of the hospitality business. Laura lived and worked at the resort. Alexis and Allison had taught her that getting away, even for a few hours, could be crucial for her well-being.

"How about you?" Laura asked. "How are you handling this?"

Alexis's hazel eyes raced across the length of the table, as if searching for the answer there. "I think I'm still processing."

"It's a lot."

"Yeah, and it doesn't make sense, Laura."

"No," Laura agreed.

Alexis glanced over her shoulder before closing the door at her back. She leaned against it. "That detective. Did he say whether she was attacked in any way?"

Laura had to stop and take another steadying breath. "You think someone hurt her?"

"She can't have just died."

Fulton's final battery of questions came back to Laura. She shivered and rubbed her hands over her upper arms. "But who would do such a thing? Who would want to hurt her?"

Alexis's brow furrowed. "I don't know. But it won't take long for the police to find out exactly what killed her. And I have a feeling they're not done questioning everyone."

Laura thought of that, the implications... "Murder doesn't happen at Mariposa. It never has."

"Maybe not," Alexis said, subsiding. "Look, if you need to go home, Erica and I can cover for you."

"No," Laura said quickly. "You're working through this. Adam and Josh are working through this. I'm going to do the same. We have to get through the day."

"Knox is shaken up pretty badly," Alexis told her. "He should go home."

Laura nodded. "Right. I'll handle that." It would give

her something to do, someone to take care of for the time being. "I'll check back in with you in a little while."

Sadness leaked across Alexis's features. "Oh, Laura," she said as she grabbed her into a hug.

"I know." Laura fought the knot climbing back into her throat. "What are we going to do without her?"

# Chapter 3

Laura knew her presence at Annabeth that evening was re-assuring to people. She just wished she was able to reassure herself as she made a point of going from table to table.

For years, she'd watched her mother do this. The real Annabeth had exuded just the right mix of politeness, grati-tude and grace to put even the most harried guest at ease. Laura tried to emulate that. She channeled her mother's energy and hoped people bought the illusion.

Under the surface, her duck feet churned. She prayed the diners missed the sweat she felt beading on her hair-line and the devastation she knew lurked behind her eyes. Joshua was doing the same at L Bar while Adam did his best to bolster the staff.

Allison's death had hit the heart of the resort.

Laura hadn't found a chance to pull Adam or Joshua aside to ask if Fulton had presented the same questions to them or how they had handled them. Alexis's warning came back to her as she noticed the table with a Reserved card standing empty near the window. The police weren't done asking questions if foul play was involved.

Lifting a hand, Laura flagged the nearest server, a young woman named Catrina. "Isn't this Mr. Knight's table?"

"The actor?" Catrina nodded. "Yes. He normally comes in around six."

Laura checked her watch. "He's running behind. Have someone place a call to his bungalow, please, and see if he'd still like to dine here tonight. If he's decided against it, there are people waiting who can be seated here."

"Yes, Ms. Colton," Catrina said before hurrying off.

"Laura."

She turned to find Erica Pike. The executive assistant stood eye to eye with Laura at five-nine, and her long brown hair was pulled up in a loose bun. Glancing at the table, she asked, "Is everything okay?"

"I was just wondering why CJ Knight hasn't shown up for his six o'clock table," Laura said.

"Oh." Erica's spine seemed to stiffen. "He checked out."

"Checked out?" Laura repeated. "When?"

"Early this morning," Erica explained. "I thought you knew."

"No," Laura said. "A lot's happened."

Erica nodded, her green eyes rimmed with shadows. "I know. Poor Allison."

Laura tried to think about the situation at hand. "Mr. Knight had spoken to me about extending his stay in Bungalow One for a week or more. Why the change of heart?"

"He didn't say," Erica replied. "Roland asked me to find you. The detective from the Sedona Police Department is back."

"So soon?" Laura said and missed a breath.

"A security person from the gate escorted him to C Building," Erica told her. "He's waiting in the break room."

The police were back with more questions, just as Alexis had predicted. Laura offered a soothing smile to a passing patron before striding toward the exit, doing her best not to rush.

C Building was built in the same style as L Building and the bungalows, but the interior was spartan. Music piped softly from speakers. A fountain in the center of the atrium burbled and splashed pleasantly. Both had been Allison's ideas. Extending the same sense of calm ambience to the employees' building that guests enjoyed everywhere else had brought the Mariposa environment full circle.

Tears stung Laura's eyes again. Allison had left a large footprint on Mariposa. She'd made it better for everyone.

Laura faced the closed doors of the break room. Halting, she took a minute to breathe and get her emotions under control. She couldn't seem to still the little duck feet paddling under the surface. To make up for it, she encased ice around her exterior. Donning her professional mask felt as natural, as fluid, as freshening up her lipstick.

She pushed the doors open and stepped in. "Detective Fulton…"

The man who stood from a chair at one of the small bistro-style tables was not Detective Fulton.

She blinked in surprise. He was younger, taller, more muscular. His build distinguished him. He carried himself more like a brawler than a police officer. He had brown hair that grew thick on top and short on the sides, a full beard and mustache. A bomber jacket lay across the table. His black button-down shirt was tucked into buff-colored cargo pants, his belt drawn beneath a trim stomach with a bronze buckle. The pants looked almost military. So did his scuffed boots. He'd rolled his sleeves up his forearms while he'd waited, revealing a bounty of tattoos.

*No*, she decided. This definitely didn't look like a detective. While his attire might have been military-inspired, he didn't carry himself like a military man. More like a boxer. Shoulders square. Hands balled, ready to strike. His hair and ink made him look like a rock star.

He wasn't restful on his feet. He shifted from one to the other, twitchy. His direct stare delivered a pang to her gut, a quick one-two. It was dangerous. Deadly.

Not a rock star, she discerned. A criminal.

She took a step back. "Who are you?" she demanded. The building was empty. The bulk of the staff was in the meeting with Adam at L Building. There was a phone on the desk in the atrium. She placed one hand on the parting of the doors. Should she make a run for it?

That direct stare remained in place. It felt like an eternity before one hand unclenched and sank into a pocket. A badge flashed when he pulled it out. "Detective Noah Steele. Sedona PD."

She wanted to examine the badge. It looked authentic from a distance, but she hadn't studied Fulton's all too closely when he'd arrived this morning. She wished she could go back and implant the image on her mind so that she at least had something to compare to.

"What do you want?" she asked, forgetting her professional demeanor. Her feet itched to run.

His expression didn't change. Neither did it lose its edge. "Are you Laura Colton?"

"There was another man here earlier," she told him. "Another detective. Mark Fulton. He said he was the lead on the case."

His gaze narrowed. She swore she'd seen a rattlesnake do that once on the hiking trails. Part of her tensed, waiting for the buzzing sound of the rattle.

"So, what are you doing here?" she challenged. "Are you really even a cop?"

"Lady, you'd do well not to insult me at the moment."

She dropped back on one heel and crossed her arms. *Lady?* "Should I call Security and have your identity certified by them?"

"It was Security who dumped me here, away from everybody else," he retorted. "Take it up with the meatball at the gate if you don't like it."

Erica did say that security personnel had escorted the detective to C Building. She frowned, opening her mouth to apologize.

He cut in, "You didn't answer my question. Are you Laura Colton?"

"I am," she said and watched, perplexed, as his eyes darkened and his fists clenched again. "It's been a long day...Detective. I'm sorry for the misunderstanding."

"A long day," he repeated, low in his throat. He let out a whistling breath. Was that his excuse for a laugh? Mirth didn't strike his expression. If anything, it tensed. "*You've* had a long day?"

"Yes," she said. She had the distinct impression that he was mocking her—that he disdained her. The level of malice coming off him was insupportable. She'd just met him. What could he possibly have against her? "I'm sure you're aware one of Mariposa's employees was found this morning...dead." She swallowed because her voice broke on that unbelievable word. "Isn't that why you're here?"

He came forward, stepping quickly between the tables. "You're damn right that's why I'm here."

She dismissed the inclination to put her back up against the door. There was a gun in a holster on his hip, she noticed. Her pulse picked up pace. He had no reason to hurt her. None whatsoever. And yet he looked capable of murder. "*Why* are you so angry?" she demanded.

"Why is your family so determined to keep Allison Brewer's death quiet?" he challenged.

She searched his eyes. They were green. Not leafy green, or algae, or even peridot. They were electrodes. Vibrant, steely, stubborn. She saw downed power lines, snapped electrical cables, writhing and sparking—about to blow her world off the grid.

She had to focus on the music, flutes and pipes, something merry and soothing Allison would have loved, to maintain a sense of calm. "What are you talking about?" she asked.

"Your brother Adam told officers at the scene this morning that Allison's death should be kept quiet," he seethed. "You'll tell me why. Why do you and your brothers want this buried? What happened to her?"

"You're acting like there's some sort of cover-up."

"Is there?"

She would have laughed if he were someone...*anyone* else. "No. This is a resort. People come here for privacy. To get away from the world."

"So close."

"What?"

"Close the resort," he said. "Let the police come in and investigate properly."

"There are over eighty people booked at Mariposa through this week alone," she explained.

"If you really care about Allison—"

She stepped to him, fears squashed as her ire rose. "Allison Brewer was my friend. She was one of my closest friends. And I will *not* be accused of covering up her death. Who are you to march in here and accuse me of that?"

If she'd expected him to cower, she was sorely disappointed. He closed the marked bit of space between them, lifting his chin. "If you're so close to her, why has she never mentioned you before?"

He spoke in present tense, just as she had even after witnessing the coroner carrying Allison's body away under a sheet. His fury…his near lack of control. It was cover for something else.

Adam had done this, she realized. After their mother's death. He'd been angry, precarious, until he'd learned to put a lid on it. Until he'd developed control and that laser focus that was so vital to him. "You knew her," she realized. "You knew Allison."

He blinked, and the tungsten cooled. Going back on his heels, he moved away.

She watched him rove the space between tables and chairs, his head low.

Allison hadn't had a type, Laura recalled. But Laura couldn't see her with someone this high-strung. Someone this lethal. She had, however, spoken of her brother often— her foster brother. *As thick as thieves*, Allison had said regarding the two of them.

Laura's brow puckered. "Your last name is Steele."

He turned his head to her, scowling. "So?"

"You don't share a last name," Laura pointed out.

He cursed under his breath. Was he mad that she'd made him so quickly?

"Are you really a detective?" she asked, bewildered.

"Of course I'm a detective," he snapped, pacing again from one end of the room to the other. "Why else would I be here?"

"Other than to accost me and my family?" she ventured. "You act like we're culpable."

"Everybody's culpable," he muttered.

Her eyes rounded. "So…there *was* foul play involved in whatever happened last night?"

He stopped roving. His palm scraped across his jaw, the Roman numerals etched across his knuckles flashing. "Nothing else makes sense."

"Murder at Mariposa doesn't make sense," she said. "The people here aren't prone to violence."

He dropped his hand in shock. "You actually believe that?"

She didn't answer. His mockery locked her jaw.

"Here's a news flash," he said. "Most people are inherently violent."

"If you actually believe that," she countered, "then I'd say you have a very narrow view of humanity. And so would Allison."

He flinched. "Someone at your resort killed my sister, Ms. Colton," he said. "I'd advise you to watch your back, because I won't rest until I have proof."

The quiet warning coursed through her. She sensed, if this man had his way, Mariposa would be reduced to rubble before he was done.

# *Chapter 4*

Goddamn it. She had to be beautiful.

Inside C Building, Noah watched Laura Colton and her brothers through the glass doors of the atrium. Legs spread, arms crossed, he listened to harp strings and water cascading cheerfully from the fountain to his left, trying to read the exchange. Trying to discern what was on her face.

He didn't have to. He recognized it, and it drove a knife through him. She was grieving. The tension around the frown lines of her mouth were indicators, just like her heartbreakingly blue eyes drawn down at the corners. She eyed him, too, through the glass doors as Adam and Joshua Colton stood on either side of her, debating what to do about the situation.

Although he gathered sadness and confusion from her face, she didn't waver. She was a winking star at the edge of the galaxy—remote, out of reach and somehow constant.

His shoulders itched. He didn't roll them, but the urge bothered him. It raised the hair on the backs of his arms and neck. The supernatural sense strengthened as she continued to stare.

He could be constant, too—like a roadblock. An obstacle. He would stop traffic. He would dent fenders. He would do anything to find out what had happened here.

It didn't matter if it made waves for these people. Nothing mattered except Allison.

He hadn't been there. The hopeless thought burned on the edge of his conscience. It burned and smoked, and he hated himself.

He hadn't been there for Allison. Not in the last few months. Not like he should have been. He'd been distracted by work, his closure rate at the SPD and the rise in homicides around the area.

And now Allison was dead. If it wasn't someone else's fault, it was his.

He was responsible…until he found who was to blame.

He couldn't live with her death on his conscience. That sweet little girl. She'd had no one, and he'd promised her. He'd *sworn* he would be there for her—until the last breath.

That last breath was supposed to be his, not hers. It wasn't supposed to be her. It should be another person lying under a sheet at the coroner's office.

He'd known she was too soft for this world—too pure. Too good. And, like a son of a bitch, he'd neglected her.

Her voice came to him. *I'm an adult. Noah, you don't have to chase my monsters out of the closet anymore.*

*Are you sure about that?* he'd challenged.

She had laughed, dropping her head back and belting. Allison never did things halfway, especially when they brought her joy. She'd taken his hand as she'd said, *There are no more monsters. We're free of them now.*

He was the monster, he realized. He was a monster who'd abandoned her to the real world, and she was dead because of it.

As if she could read his thoughts, Laura Colton shivered. She broke the staring contest by turning to gaze at her younger brother, folding her arms around herself.

She was cold, he mulled. Of course she was cold. She was standing outside with the barest of snow flurries falling at a slant from the north. Her white dress was long-sleeved, with a leather belt cinched at the waist and a rustic blue handkerchief tied elaborately at her throat in a Western knot. The handkerchief wasn't meant to keep out the cold. It was silk, for Christ's sake. The dress may have been long, but there was a slit on one side.

As she shifted, he saw a flash of creamy skin. Her boots, the same blue as the handkerchief, with custom floral tooling, rose to just below the knee. Her shoulder-length blond hair swung as the wind flurried and spiraled. She shivered again, visibly.

Noah clenched his jaw. *Morons*, he thought of her brothers. Couldn't they see she was cold? Couldn't *one* of them loan her a jacket?

Adam caught on first. He swung his jacket off in a quick motion and draped it across the line of her shoulders.

*Not enough*, Noah chided even as Laura acknowledged the gesture by touching Adam's arm just above the elbow. Joshua braced his arm across her shoulders and huddled her against his side. He rubbed a hand up and down her arm for friction.

Good, Noah thought. Maybe he could stop feeling sorry for her long enough to separate the woman from the adversary.

She was beautiful. So what? He'd seen icebergs. He'd seen one calve and flip over, churning the sea like a bubbling witch's cauldron, exposing its breathtaking glass underbelly. Unspoiled, untouched. Secret and forbidden.

Laura Colton was that kind of beautiful. And damned if it was going to distract him.

Icebergs were roadblocks, too. Sure, they contained multitudes, and they were frigging fascinating to boot. But they could be upset. They melted. They flipped. And when they flipped, their spires crumbled.

*I won't let you get in my way*, he determined as her heart-breaker eyes seized hold of him again. Frost wove delicate swaths around the edges of the door pane, framing her.

Friend? Allison had never mentioned her. He was sure of it. If he wasn't sure, it was because he had forgotten.

He couldn't bear to think that he'd forgotten.

*You forgot the last lunch*, a voice in his head taunted.

He and Allison normally met for lunch on the first Friday of every month. Tipsy Tacos, the little cantina close to her place that served vegan options alongside the ones with meat he preferred, was her favorite restaurant.

*It's perfect, isn't it?* she'd practically had to yell over the mariachi music, her dark eyes laughing.

Noah dug his phone out of his pocket. He unlocked the screen, then scrolled through his texts. Her messages popped up on-screen.

There was one from a week ago.

Allison: TGIF! Music fest this weekend?

Noah: TGIF. Gotta work overtime. Don't go home with a stranger. Call me if you need a ride.

Allison: Will do!

Then a week before that…

Allison: Did you read the meditation book I gave you?

Noah: Covered up in work. I'll get to it.

Allison: Promise?

Noah: Promise.

Emojis had followed. Then the exchange before that dated two weeks past.

Allison: Thinking of you.

Noah: Thinking of you, too. You ok?

Allison: Worried about you. Let me book you a massage. You need you time.

Noah: I'm fine. Don't go out with that guy again. He's bad news.

Allison: LOL. He said the same about you.

Noah: Never trust a guy in an El Camino.

Allison: I miss you!

Noah: Miss you, too. Sorry about lunch.

Allison: It's NBD. I know work's crazy. Hugs!

Noah: Hugs to you.

Noah winced as he scrolled through the next exchange.

Allison: I'm at the cantina.

Noah: Damn. I'm across town. Had to make an arrest. I'm sorry, Al.

Allison: It's ok.

Noah: I'll pick you up.

Allison: It's nice out. I can walk.

Noah: Let me know if you change your mind.

Allison: Will do.

A smiley face capped the message.

He looked for subtext. He searched for anger on her part. Blame. Disappointment. Anything to beat himself up with. As ever, he found nothing. Just happy, look-on-the-bright-side Allison.

The only other person who'd loved him like this…who'd worried about him like this and looked out for him…was his mother. Before she was killed and he had gotten dumped into the system.

He'd let her down. Even if Allison didn't know it, he'd let her down.

He had to live with that. He had to live with the fact that there would be no more text messages at 10:00 p.m. telling him to *relax…unwind…life's short…live well…*

Forcing himself to swallow, he took stock of his emotions. He felt raw, unspooled. He'd gone at Laura Colton too hard. If she really was Allison's friend, did she have a litany of cheerful, forgotten text messages that broke her heart in hindsight, too?

There was movement, he noticed. He stuffed the phone

back in his pocket as a security guard moved into the Coltons' circle. He placed a hand on Joshua's shoulder. They all turned to listen. Joshua nodded and walked away.

Laura and Adam spoke quietly, nodding back and forth before moving toward the door.

Maybe he should apologize to her, Noah thought. He could have waited to question the Coltons, done some digging into them and Mariposa first… But he hadn't been thinking with his head when he'd left Allison at the coroner's office.

He'd done this before with his mother. There had been grief, and he'd been alone then, too. Nobody had cared about him, much less commiserated with him. He didn't know how to expose the hurt and had no idea how to talk about it. The shock of Allison's death had put his fists up and his head down like a brawler.

He'd swung at Laura Colton, Noah reflected as Adam escorted her into C Building to face off with him again. Noah did his best to relax his stance. *Breathe*, Allison said in his ear as Laura's gaze climbed back to his.

"It was a mistake," he said without taking a beat to think about the wording. He backtracked. "Yelling at you in the break room. It shouldn't have happened. I apologize."

Her hands balled together over the parting of Adam's jacket. After a moment, she nodded shortly. "I accept your apology."

"That doesn't resolve everything that happened here this evening," Adam said evenly. "I intend to call the Sedona Police Department for some clarity on the situation. They wouldn't let you lead this investigation if Allison was a relation of yours, which is why Fulton was the detective on scene this morning. Not you. Does your commanding officer know you're here now?"

Noah studied Laura and her cold, white-knuckled hands.

Then he asked the man, "If it was your sister, what would you do? Would you sit around, bury your head in the sand, hoping somebody else figures out what happened to her? Or would you use every skill, every resource at your disposal, to make sure what happened to her is brought to light?"

Adam tilted his head. "I understand why you're here, Detective. As a brother, I sympathize, and I'm deeply sorry for your loss. If I didn't have Laura…" His shoulders lifted, then settled as he deflated. "I wouldn't be standing here."

"Adam." Laura spoke her brother's name in a whisper. She raised her hand to his arm as she had outside. This time, she held it.

"But the fact remains that we don't know what happened to Allison, precisely," Adam went on. "We don't know that anyone at Mariposa is responsible or if she died of natural causes. That's for the coroner to decide, yes?"

Noah jerked his chin. "Yes."

"So you'll agree that your demand we close the resort is premature at this point?" Adam ventured.

"What happens when the coroner's word comes down?" Noah asked. "What happens when we're certain it was homicide? What then?"

"If that's the case," Adam said carefully, "we'll reevaluate. But I see no reason to close Mariposa."

"You're worried about your bottom line," Noah growled.

"No, Detective," Adam said coolly. "I'm worried about the same thing Allison was, too, every day. The privacy and comfort of our guests."

"You sure it's not the Colton reputation?" Noah countered.

Laura unfolded her hands. "It's late, and the snow's coming in. I'm sure you'd like to get home, Detective Steele, in case the roads become impassable. Why don't we all reconvene after the coroner decides on the manner of Allison's passing, then proceed from there?"

She said it in such a way, Noah felt every argument die.

He didn't want to go home. At home, it would be quiet. He'd have nothing to distract him from the voices inside his head that said Allison's death was on his hands. "Fine."

She offered something of a smile. It wasn't the real thing. Her eyes weren't involved in it. "I'll walk you to L Building."

"That's unnecessary," Adam cut in. "I'll walk the detective back to his vehicle. You go home, Laura. It's cold."

"I'll be fine," she assured him. "I'd like a moment with Detective Steele." When Adam only frowned at her, she added, "Alone."

Adam exchanged a look with Noah, one that warned he'd better tread carefully.

Laura started to remove his jacket. Adam stopped her quickly. "Keep it. And promise to go home as soon as you see him out. You need to get off your feet."

"I will," she vowed.

"A promise is a promise, LouBear," he reminded her. He dropped a kiss to her brow.

The sentiment rang through Noah's head. *A promise is a promise.* He hated himself all the more. Before she could open the door, he reached for the handle.

"Thank you," she said before ducking back out into the cold.

"We'll see each other again, Detective Steele," Adam said in closing.

"You can count on it." Noah left the statement hanging in the air like an anvil. He zipped his jacket as he and Laura followed the well-manicured path back to L Building.

She walked in long strides. "Normally, I love the snow. Tonight, it just makes me sad."

"Allison loved snow." He closed his mouth quickly. He hadn't meant to say it.

"She did," Laura said. "I remember the first winter she worked for us. There was so much that year, she had to move classes inside. She liked watching the snowfall from the windows at Annabeth. She said it was like being trapped in a snow globe."

That sounded like Allison. The black hole in Noah's chest opened further. He felt gravity reeling him in toward it. He hoped it would wait until he was alone to absorb him.

"I need to apologize, too," she revealed.

"For?" he asked.

"I misjudged you," she explained. The cold stained her cheeks. "Back in the break room. I didn't think you were with the police."

"What did you think I was?"

"A criminal." She winced. "I don't like labeling people. But I labeled you right off the bat. And I'm sorry for it."

He didn't know what to feel, exactly. He glanced down at his hands where Roman numerals riddled his knuckles and a spider crawled up the back of one hand. The etchings on the other made it look like a skeleton hand with exposed joints and bones that went all the way up his fingers. On some level, he could understand. He'd spent a fair amount of time undercover because he was good at inserting himself into a certain crowd.

He remembered how in the break room she'd all but backed herself up to the exit door when he'd approached her. Had she thought he was going to hurt her…take her jewelry…worse? A growl fought its way up his throat. He choked it back, along with everything else, and punched his hands into the pockets of his jacket. "I don't expect you to lose sleep over it, Ms. Colton."

"It's Laura," she said as they came to the doors to L Building. She turned to him, the golden light over their heads crowning her. "We're probably going to be seeing a lot of each other. And we both knew Allison. So Laura will suffice." She stuck out a hand for him to shake.

He stared at it. Then her. There were snowflakes in her hair. If someone gave her a scepter and horse-drawn sleigh, she would be a glorified ice princess.

Unwilling to let her shiver a moment longer, he closed his hand around hers. It felt like ice, and it was as smooth as the surface of a mink's coat. He took his away quickly, unwilling to watch his tattoos and calluses mingle with her fancy digits. He pulled the door open for her.

She cleared her throat. "I'm going to miss her, too."

Whatever he could have said was trapped beneath his tongue.

Her lashes lowered, touching her cheeks, before she lifted them again. "As soon as you make the arrangements, I'd like to know. I'd like to say goodbye."

Arrangements. The portents of that barreled down on him. He was Allison's next of kin, her only relative. It was up to him to plan her funeral.

He couldn't bury her. He couldn't even contemplate it. She didn't belong in the ground any more than she belonged in a morgue.

An unsteady breath washed out of him.

Her hand came to rest over his. "I can help you. I've helped plan a funeral in the past. I was young, but I think my brothers and I managed to pull it off well enough. If you need help—"

"It's fine." He barked it, desperate to be away from her

so he could unleash the panic and anguish building up inside him. He held the door open wider. "Good night, Ms. Colton."

Her lips firmed. She strode inside. He watched her long after the door closed. He watched through the glass until she disappeared down the hall, the tail of her white skirt the last thing to disappear. The lights went off seconds later and he was left staring at his own reflection.

*A funeral.*

Another breath wavered out, vaporizing in front of him. He pinched the bridge of his nose, hard. That black hole had him by the balls.

He'd go home, he decided. And when he got there, he'd drink himself into a stupor.

# *Chapter 5*

Laura opened the door to her bungalow the next morning to find Joshua on her front stoop. His messy hair hid underneath a burnt-umber ski cap with Mariposa's pale yellow butterfly logo. Ice crunched under his boots as he moved his toes rapidly to keep them warm. "I brought pastries," he announced.

She eyed the long white box in his hands. "You mean you brought the bakery?"

"Had it delivered," he boasted. He handed her a large cup. "With coffee."

The way to a man's heart might be through his stomach, but Laura was convinced the way to a woman's was by crossing cell membranes with caffeine. She wrapped her hands around the to-go cup, absorbing the heat through the gloves she'd donned. "It's no wonder every man I meet is a disappointment." Tipping the cup to him in a toast, she added, "You are the standard."

He offered his arm. "Watch your step. It's slippery."

She trod carefully until they reached the golf cart he'd parked in front of her house. "Have you spoken to Knox?"

Joshua got behind the wheel. He waited until she was seated, tucking her long skirt around her legs before he released the brake and shot off. "I checked on him last night. He's okay. Still shaken up. Hell, I am, too."

"Did you tell him he doesn't have to come in today? Carter's already agreed to cover for him. The horseback excursions will be canceled because of ice and snowmelt."

Joshua nodded. "He agreed to take the morning off, but he wants to come in after lunchtime. He said working with the horses will help him through things."

Laura could understand that. As the golf cart careened around the corner, she stopped the doughnut box from slipping across the seat. She opened it, then indulged, choosing a chocolate éclair. Nibbling, she balanced the pastry in one hand and her cup in the other. "I don't know if I should tell you this."

"Well, now you've got to." He nudged his elbow into her ribs playfully. "Spill it, ace."

She watched the gardens whoosh by. White coated everything. Mariposa looked enchanting under a crystal frost.

Underneath, was some part of it—or someone inside of it—deadly?

She shuddered, blamed the cold, then polished off the éclair. "She had a crush on you."

"Who?" When he glanced over, she canted her head tellingly. He gawped. "Allison?"

Laura sighed. "She wasn't the type to hold back. But she worked with you. She valued her job. So she sat with her feelings." Reaching over, she cupped his chin in her hand, helping him to close his mouth. "I promised her I wouldn't tell. But I think you two could have made each other happy, at least for a time, and... I don't know. All this reminds me not to waste time if you know what's right for you."

Joshua looked shocked, bereft and everything in between.

He jerked the wheel onto the scenic path, along the wall that fell away from the ridge where Mariposa dwelled. She looked out over the countryside. Snow, red rocks and the Sonoran Desert clashed to make the view that much more spectacular. "We're going to be okay. Right?"

"We've done this before."

She nodded. The three of them had weathered quite a few storms together. "Should I have kept my promise? Should I not have told you?"

He shook his head. "I liked Allison. I liked her a lot. But I have rules, same as she did."

Joshua liked to have fun, but he didn't date anyone in-house. Mariposa was as sacred to him as it was to Laura and Adam, and that included every single person under its umbrella. "I didn't mean to make this harder for you. I just didn't get much sleep last night, wondering whether you two missed out on something special. She was special, Josh."

"I know." His Adam's apple bobbed. He reached for her hand and clutched it. "It's going to be okay."

She had told him that after their mother's death, every night he'd cried himself to sleep. Eyes welling, she turned them away, feeling his fingers squeeze hers. "It's coming up on that time of year."

He kept driving, pushing the golf cart as fast as it would go. If Adam saw him driving like this on the guest pathways, he would chastise him for it. Laura said nothing, however. When Joshua didn't reply, she added, "The anniversary."

"I know."

Every year on the anniversary of Annabeth's death, the three of them took the day off. They'd disappear for a day, first bringing mariposas to her grave, then embarking on a hike. The date coincided with the bridge between winter and spring. Snow gathered in places along the trail. Snowmelt tumbled down passes, rushing for valleys. And early spring growth punched through the bedrock, clawing for purchase like hope incarnate.

They never spoke much on the hike. They never took photos to capture the day. And while Joshua was a more proficient hiker than both Laura and Adam, he never left them behind. They didn't turn back for the resort until they reached the high point—Wrigley's Rough, a jagged fall of rocks with a view of the architectural site of the ancient ruins of the Sinagua people. From the top, they could see every piece of land Annabeth had left them.

Laura couldn't help but think that this year, the anniversary would be especially hard to navigate.

They pulled up to L Building. "Adam doesn't like when you park here," she reminded him.

"It's freezing," Joshua said, engaging the brake. "I'm not making you walk from C Building. Hey," he said before she could step out of the vehicle. "We really are going to be okay."

She adored him for saying it. "When I figure out when the service will be, would you like to go with me?"

"Of course," he agreed. "Are you ready for what comes next?"

"What comes next?" she asked curiously.

"Drink," he advised as they walked to the door that led to their offices at the back of the building. "I got you the big gulp for the meeting with Dad."

She raised her face to the clouds. "Oh," she said.

"You forgot."

"I forgot," she admitted. Pressing her hand to her brow, she shook her head. "It completely slipped my mind."

"That wasn't something else keeping you awake?"

"I didn't think about it at all." She groaned. "Oh, Josh. He's going to waltz in, being all Clive, and I've had no sleep, no prep..."

He nudged the coffee toward her mouth. "Drink, ace."

"Right," she said, tipping the to-go cup up for a steaming swig. She quickly covered her mouth with her hand. "Lava."

Erica waited for them near the closed door of Adam's office. "Good morning," she greeted them. "Your father's flight gets in soon. The helicopter will pick him up around eight thirty. He asked for a meeting in the conference room at ten."

"How does Adam feel about him running the schedule?" Joshua asked.

Erica arched a brow in answer.

"Oh, boy," Joshua muttered. He offered the box of doughnuts to Erica. "Lady's choice."

Erica eyed the contents when he opened it. "I want the one with the sprinkles."

"Excellent," he said, using a parchment square to pinch the corner of the pastry and hand it to her.

"Thank you," she said, cradling it.

"Did you get in touch with CJ Knight's people?" Laura asked. She didn't miss the way Erica tensed, just as she had the night before.

She shook her head, lowering the doughnut. "No. Do you still want me to reach out?"

"Yes," Laura said. "I'd like to know why he vacated Bungalow One so suddenly. He's a valued guest. If his departure had anything to do with the resort, we could offer incentives to bring him back. I have his manager's number. His name's Doug, I think."

"Doug DeGraw," Erica confirmed. "He rarely leaves CJ's side."

Laura frowned at Erica over the lid of her to-go cup.

"What is it?" Erica asked, alarmed.

"Nothing," Laura said. "That'll be all. Thank you, Erica." As Erica moved down the hall, Laura grabbed Joshua by the collar and pulled him into her office.

"Hey, what—"

She shut the door, closing them in. "She called him CJ."

"So?"

She frowned. "Josh, when was the last time you called a guest by his or her first name?"

He thought about it. "Over the summer, maybe. There was that competitive rock climber. The blonde one with the killer— Oh!" He took a step back, holding up a hand. "Wait a minute. You think Erica and CJ Knight…"

"I don't know," Laura replied. "But Erica is a professional. And calling one of our VIPs by his first name was a sight less than professional. You should look into this."

"Me?" he asked, aghast. "Why me?"

"Because the majority of people, including Erica, don't just respect you. They love you. You also have a tendency to meddle in other people's affairs," she stated.

"I do not."

She placed her finger over his mouth to quiet him. "Please. For me."

He frowned, then tugged off his hat and ran a rough hand through his hair. "Fine," he said reluctantly. "But I'm not comfortable with this. What are we going to do if something did happen between Erica and Knight?"

"I don't know," she said. "She's the best executive assistant we could ask for. And I doubt CJ Knight left because of Erica, even if they crossed the line. They could just be friends. If she is close to him, she may have more insight into why he left or if he plans to return. Adam's worried about any hint of wrongdoing coming off Allison's death. Celebrity guests get nervous when bad press starts to circulate. And if word leaks to the media that someone like CJ Knight left Mariposa—"

Joshua nodded off the rest. "I get it. Damage control. I'll talk to Erica."

"I appreciate it," she told him. "Truly."

"I've always got your back, ace," he murmured. "You know that. And, for the record, I didn't sleep last night either. If you toss and turn again tonight, call me. If we're going to be awake, we might as well talk each other through it. Or drink about it."

She raised her hand to his lapel, flipping it the right way out. Smoothing it, she offered him a small smile. "I like that idea."

Someone knocked on the door. Before she could answer, Adam stepped in. "You heard?"

"About our ten o'clock?" Laura asked. "Erica told us."

Joshua lifted the pastry box. "Doughnut?"

Adam frowned over it. "Jelly-filled?"

"Lemon or raspberry?"

"Lemon," Adam said and took the parchment around the doughnut when Joshua offered it to him. "Thanks. By the way, I called Greg. He'll be sitting in on the meeting."

Joshua gave a little chuckle.

"I missed the joke," Adam said critically.

"You're the one who wants our attorney to sit in on a family meeting," Joshua pointed out.

"Why is that?" Laura asked.

Adam shifted his jaw. "I have a feeling Greg should be a part of this."

Laura trusted Adam's instincts. Still, there was another matter. "Clive won't like it. It'll put his back up."

"So will the fact that you still call him Clive," he noted.

"Have you heard anything about Allison's case?" Joshua asked.

"No," Adam said. "I couldn't sleep last night, however—"

"Disturbed, party of three," Joshua inserted.

"—and I had a thought," Adam continued, ignoring him. "I'd like to set up a fund for her family to help cover funeral costs."

"Adam," Laura breathed. "That's a wonderful idea."

"I second that," Joshua said. "And she should have a plaque to go in the meditation garden. It was her idea, her design. It should be in her name."

"Just like the restaurant is in Mom's," she mused. "Of course."

Joshua's phone beeped. "That's Carter. I offered to help him with the morning work down at the stable. I'll be back for the meeting."

"Preferably on time," Adam called after him.

Joshua tossed a wave over his shoulder and shut the door behind him. Adam looked at her. "Since Detective Steele is the only relative so far who's contacted us, do you think we should send the offer through him, or would you be more comfortable speaking with her parents directly?"

"He's her foster brother," she explained. "I don't think her parents are in the picture. She never spoke of them. Only him. And, you should know, last night, I got the sense Detective Steele was overwhelmed by the idea of planning a funeral for her. I offered to help. He refused. Judging by his behavior, I'm not sure he'd be willing to take on financial help."

"Was he a jerk to you, Lou?"

"Hey," she said with amusement, measuring the width of his straight-backed shoulders. He was wearing his best suit today and his muscles were knotted, ready, beneath it. "Easy there, knuckles."

"He threatened you in the break room," Adam reminded her.

"He threatened all of us," she amended. "And underneath..." She sighed, remembering. "My God, Adam. He looked broken."

"I don't envy him," Adam muttered.

"I'll speak to him about the fund," she said.

"Are you sure?" he asked. "Erica can see to it."

"I know she can," Laura said. "But this is personal."

Adam conceded. "Are you ready for Clive?"

Laura eyed the to-go cup she'd set on her desk. "Ask me again after coffee."


At sixty-one, Clive Colton looked shrunken. He still had his spine. Admitting weakness was distasteful to him. But now he cut a less imposing figure, more compact and slightly stooped compared to his once-distinctive six-foot frame. More salt than pepper tinted his hair. His suit was conservative, tasteful and impeccably bespoke.

He hugged her upon entering the conference room, just as he embraced Adam and Joshua. The latter pulled away after a brief clutch. The hug wasn't about warmth or familiarity. It was for form's sake, something Joshua didn't give a fig about.

Greg Sumpter, the siblings' private attorney, shook hands with Clive. "It's been a long time, Clive."

"Sure," Clive said, his smile falling away. "How are you, Sumpter?"

"Oh, just fine, thank you," Greg replied jovially. Tall, fit, Greg was dressed casually. No suit or tie for him. He wore his collar open. His relaxed demeanor, paired with his legal savvy, had appealed to Adam, Laura and Joshua right away. He visited the resort often, not just for business, but to check in personally with the three of them and to see Tallulah. He was forty-eight and unmarried, and Laura knew he had a one-sided love for their head of housekeeping.

"I didn't expect to find you here," Clive told him.

Adam spoke up from the head of the table, where he stood behind his usual chair. "I asked Greg to join us."

"Why is that?" Clive asked.

Greg answered quickly. "He thought you and I could play a round of golf later. It snowed last night, but it should melt off quickly. Do you still get out on the course?"

Clive lifted a shoulder. "Now and then. Can't swing it like I used to."

Joshua groaned.

"We'll tee off this afternoon," Greg said. "How's that sound?"

"Fine," Clive said, pulling out a chair for himself.

Greg sent Adam a wink before taking a seat. Laura folded into a chair between her brothers, smoothing her skirt over her legs. "What do we owe the pleasure of a visit?" she asked Clive directly. "You didn't bring Glenna with you?"

"Not this time," he said, running a hand down his tie.

"And your health?" Adam mentioned. "How are you feeling?"

"Spry enough," Clive said, cracking a smile. That smile had caught the imagination of his wife and mistress and the other women he'd taken a shine to through the years. "Thanks for asking."

"Would you like coffee?" Laura offered. "Tea?"

"Mylanta?" Joshua muttered, earning a nudge from Laura.

Clive didn't seem to hear him. "No. Thank you, though, Precious." His grin broadened. "Anybody tell you lately you look just like your mother?"

"No," she answered.

"Pretty as a picture," he said proudly. "Just like Annabeth. She was stunning. Before the cancer did its bit—"

"What did you call this meeting for?" Adam interrupted as Laura tensed and Joshua muttered under his breath.

"Are you in a hurry, son?" Clive asked.

"We've got meetings scheduled for the conference room at eleven thirty and after lunch," Adam told him. "Spring means nuptials, and Mariposa has become the place for destination weddings."

"Congratulations," Clive said. His eyes were drawn to the view from the windows. "You've built something impressive here. You were so young when you took it on. I didn't think you'd last long in Arizona. Now you've got something to be admired."

"Yes," Adam replied.

Laura's tension refused to drain. Adam had been right to invite Greg. There was something Clive wasn't saying.

They waited him out. He swiveled back to the table. "I've come to ask for your help."

"Our help?" Joshua asked.

Adam rolled over his brother's incredulity. "Are you in trouble?"

"No, no," Clive said, waving a dismissive hand. "Nothing that drastic. The company's just seen better days, is all."

"What could we do?" Laura asked.

"I understand the resort's made some significant gains," Clive said. "I also understand that you've got plenty of capital at your disposal."

"How do you know that?" Joshua asked.

Clive chuckled. "If there's one thing I understand, son, it's business."

"A business you stole from Mom's inheritance?" Joshua parried.

Clive stared at him. "Colton Textiles is in my name, son. Not your mother's. And I'm not sure I care for your tone."

"This is me playing nice," Joshua informed him. "And you may come from money, but you never made your own. You play with everybody else's. You married Mom for hers. If not for her, you wouldn't have a leg to stand on."

"Josh," Adam cautioned. "Maybe you should take a walk."

Joshua looked at his brother. "I have a right to be here, and somebody has to speak for her."

A headache was brewing behind Laura's left temple. She wished for coffee. "It's okay," she said to Adam. "Let him speak for her."

Adam relaxed gradually. He addressed Clive again. "What did you have in mind?"

"A loan," Clive revealed.

"How much?"

"Two fifty to start."

Joshua scoffed. "Two hundred and fifty thousand?"

"If that doesn't get the company back on its feet, then another," Clive added. "This is your inheritance, too, don't forget. My legacy to the three of you. You each have a stake in Colton Textiles. Adam, you especially."

Laura thought about it. Colton Textiles was a fine-fabrics

importer. When Annabeth had died, she had left shares to each of her children. Adam had eighteen, and Laura and Joshua each had sixteen. Clive had wound up with the lion's share.

"Don't do this, Adam," Joshua implored. His eyes burned.

Adam considered. "That's a lot of money."

"You'll make it up in no time," Clive said smoothly. "And it's a loan. You'll have a return on your investment in due time. With interest."

Laura shook her head. "You can't expect us to decide on the spot. We'll need to discuss it and come to an agreement. Together."

"The three of you?" Clive questioned.

"That's how things are done around here," Adam informed him.

Clive eased back in his chair. "Good for you, kids. Good for you."

Did Laura imagine his condescension, or was it real? Her father wasn't just the face of Colton Textiles. He was a chameleon who could easily mask his true feeling and intentions when it suited him.

When there was something he needed to hide.

Adam rose and the rest of them followed suit, Clive coming to his feet at last. "We should have a decision for you soon."

"Tomorrow," Clive requested as they hovered around the door. "By the end of business hours. If I'm to make gains, too, I'll need that money as soon as possible."

Adam gave a nod. "Fine."

"How 'bout you and Laura join me for lunch?" Clive asked, putting his hand on Adam's shoulder. "Just the three of us. I hear your restaurant's five stars. What's it called again?"

"Annabeth," Joshua retorted.

Clive smiled, nonplussed. "Of course it is."

"I'm due in Flagstaff at lunchtime," Adam explained.

"Laura?" Clive looked to her, expectant.

No plans came to her mind. "All right."

"Splendid," he replied. Reaching out, he gave her chin a light pinch. "Are you still seeing Quentin Randolph?"

The name struck her off guard. "No. How…how did you know about Quentin?"

"I knew him before you did," he said. "I told him about Mariposa. And about you."

She stared, unable to believe a connection between her father and the man who had grossly betrayed her was possible. "He never mentioned you."

"A shame it didn't work out," he said. "You were quite the power couple. What happened this time?"

He'd turned out to be just like Clive—a chameleon. She ignored the question and moved to the door to open it.

Joshua beat her to it. "I need some air," he muttered to her.

"Same," she whispered.

"There's something sketchy going on," Joshua said. He pointed to Laura. "You know it. And I know it."

Adam crossed his arms. "Why do you think I had Greg sit in on the meeting? I knew there was something off when Dad called initially."

Next to him, Greg planted a hand against the wall in a relaxed stance. "I can look into him. See what's really going on with Colton Textiles."

"If he needs that kind of money, it's bleeding," Joshua said. "It's bleeding badly. And if he needed money, why didn't he go to Glenna? She's got plenty. Why did he come all this way?"

Laura chewed over it. "He was right about one thing. We all have a stake in Colton Textiles. It was Mom's company, too. It's as much a part of her legacy as Mariposa. If it is bleeding, could we really just watch it die?" Wouldn't that be like watching a part of Annabeth die all over again?

Adam turned to Greg. "Can you look into it by tomorrow afternoon?"

"I'll make the necessary calls," Greg said. He pulled a face. "I may miss my tee time with the man of the hour…"

Joshua cracked a smile for the first time since Clive's arrival. "Aw, shucks."

"Let us know what you find out," Laura said. She hugged him. "And thanks for sitting in. If you don't go soon, you'll miss lunch with Tallulah."

Greg grinned. "You know me too well."

"She's taking her lunches with the kitchen staff now," Joshua pointed out, "since her nephew, Mato, got hired on as sous-chef."

"Thanks for the tip." Greg gave the men a salute before strolling off.

Joshua waited until he was out of earshot. "He's loved Tallulah as long as we've known either of them."

"Yes," Laura said with a soft smile.

"I don't know if I could wait that long," Joshua confessed, "for someone to decide whether she wanted me."

"Yeah, you're much more of the now-or-never type," Adam drawled. "Or now *and* never. Never being next week when you decide you've had enough."

Joshua pursed his lips. "Is that any worse than the kind of man who's married to his desk?"

"Enough," Laura said. "Both of you."

"What was all that business about Quentin Randolph?" Joshua asked. "Clive was the one who set you two up?"

"No," she said automatically. She didn't want it to be true. The idea made her feel ill.

Adam's phone rang. He took it from his pocket. "I have to leave for Flagstaff shortly." He glanced up at Laura. "You can cancel lunch. Dad can dine alone."

"I'm not afraid of him," she claimed.

"I never said you were, Lou," he told her.

"You don't owe him anything," Joshua chimed in.

"I'll be fine," she explained. "Maybe I can get some more information about Colton Textiles out of him."

Joshua sighed. He patted her on the back. "Good luck with that, ace."

# Chapter 6

The following afternoon, Noah flashed his badge at the man in the Mariposa security booth. The uniformed guard waved him in. He steered his car into the same lot he'd parked in two nights prior. Then he followed the path to L Building and ventured into the open-air lobby.

The clerk at the front desk's name tag read Sasha. She smiled, waving him forward. "How can I help you?"

"Laura Colton." Noah didn't know why her name was the first thing out of his mouth, but there it was.

Sasha picked up the phone on the desk. "Do you have an appointment?"

"She's expecting me," he said, sidestepping the real question.

"Name?"

"Steele."

"Just a moment."

After placing a call, she revealed, "Ms. Colton is at L Bar. Go through the doors here and take a left."

Moving briskly, Noah heeded her instructions. He found himself inside an impressive room. On one side, liquor-stocked shelves sprawled from floor to ceiling. The bartender moved tirelessly from one patron to the next. Music played at just the right volume, not too soft, not too loud.

Here, the atmosphere felt easy, not stodgy, like he'd expected.

He saw her at the same time she saw him. Laura's dress flowed around her, long and red with turquoise necklaces stacked above the V-necked bodice. Her boots were black leather to match her wide belt. Large earrings dangled from her ears. She'd swept the strands of hair that framed her face back in a subtle half-do.

She looked perfect. Noah felt his joints lock up in response.

What was it about this woman?

She walked to him slowly, offering a nod to a patron who acknowledged her in passing. "Detective Steele," she greeted him. "Back so soon?"

He could see the apprehension lurking behind her icy blues. "Is there a place we can talk?"

"Detective Fulton didn't mention an update in the case," she said. "Is that why you're here?"

The envelope from Steinbeck weighed heavily in Noah's pocket. "Is there somewhere we can talk?" he asked again.

She looked around and seemed to decide that the bar was not the place to have this conversation. "Follow me."

She led him to a back hallway with windows where paintings would have been in any other setting. The Coltons' resort decor leaned heavily on their natural surroundings.

She swept keys out of the small jeweled bag she carried and unlocked one of the closed doors. "Have a seat," she said as she pushed the door open and switched on the light.

Her office, he decided. With its buttery-leather ergonomic desk chair and the wide crystal vase overflowing with fresh desert blooms, how could it be anything but?

"Coffee?" she asked as she rounded the desk.

"No." He didn't sit, although the plush chair looked inviting. Was that a real cowhide or just for show?

She remained standing, too. "Well?"

He pulled the envelope from his pocket and handed it across the desk. "Coroner's report."

She held it for a moment, then turned it over. The flap wasn't sealed. She pulled it back, then pried the report from its pocket. Unfolding it, she gathered a steadying breath in through the nose.

He watched her eyes dart across the page, reading Steinbeck's findings, and knew the exact moment she learned the truth. She raised her eyes to his in a flash of disbelief before staring at the paper again. "She died of an overdose?"

"Of fentanyl," he said grimly.

She shook her head. "That can't be right. That would mean…"

"Somebody drugged her," he finished, advancing another step toward the desk. "The coroner showed me the entry site. The needle went in above her left hip."

The page and envelope fluttered to the surface of her desk. Her hands lowered, limp, to her sides. "You were right," she breathed. "How is that possible?"

"She was killed," he reiterated. "At your resort. And you're going to let me find who did it. That was the deal."

Fumbling for the arm of her chair, she sank into it.

He gripped the edge of the desk, fighting impatience. Fighting the inclination to circle the thing and put his hands on her. Whether it would be to help her snap out of it or just to see if she would let him, he didn't know. "Look, my CO doesn't want me on this. He asked me to back off. Stay home. Wait for Fulton to tie up the case."

"Something tells me you're not going to do that," she said wearily.

"If I had your cooperation," he replied, very close to begging, "if I had your permission, I could dig through back channels. I could find what's under the surface. The underbelly."

Her throat moved in a swallow. "This morning, I would've argued that Mariposa doesn't have an underbelly. But this…" She touched the edge of the autopsy report. "Who could have done this? Who here could be capable…?"

He went around the desk. Instead of touching her, he gripped the arms of the chair. He pushed himself into her space and watched her eyes go as round as pieces of eight. "I'll help you. I won't rest until the person responsible is behind bars. But you have to help me."

She bit her bottom lip carefully. It disappeared inside her mouth as she searched his eyes. Her guarded expression closed him off and he was certain the answer would be no.

Her lip rounded again, pink. Perfect, like the rest of her. She canted her head to the side. "You need a reason for being here," she said. "In case Fulton or your CO catches you on-site."

She was…saying yes? He missed a breath. "If I could pass under the radar…if everyone could see me as something other than a cop…a guest, maybe, or a new member of staff, they could be inclined to talk. That would make my job easier."

"Not staff," she said contemplatively. "That wouldn't be right."

He frowned at the tattoos on his hands. They were right there for her to see. "What, you don't hire criminals?"

"That's not what I meant," she said defensively.

"Then what did you mean?"

"A guest, maybe," she decided. "That would get you in

the restaurant, the bar, the spa, the golf course and stables…
everywhere but C Building." Her eyes cleared. "Oh."

"What?" he asked, feeling his stomach muscles tighten
as he watched her pupils dilate.

Her gaze trickled down his throat, over his shoulders and
down his chest. "It's that simple…and that complicated."

"Throw me a bone here, Colton."

"You need to immerse yourself among staff and guests.
You need a cover. Being my boyfriend would guarantee access to pretty much anything."

"Your boyfriend." He heard his tone flatline. It was the
worst idea he'd ever heard.

And it was the best idea he'd ever heard.

She was right. Being Laura Colton's paramour wouldn't
just open doors. It would make people openly curious about
him. Those people would lower their guard enough…maybe
be clumsy or trusting enough to let something slip. To let
him in.

The possibilities came tumbling down as reality set in
again.

Who the hell was going to believe that she would date
*him*? She ruled this high-class joint. She was Mariposa's
princess. He lived on a city salary, drove a decade-old city-
issue sedan that ran rough in the winter, and he had no family left to speak of.

Who would buy that Laura Colton would choose to slum
it with Noah Steele?

He backed off. "Yeah, that's not gonna work."

"Why not?" she asked his retreating back. She gained
her feet again. "If someone here killed Allison, they have
to be found. They have to be brought to justice. What if
they strike again? What if someone else is killed? I have to

protect the rest of the staff, the guests, my family… You're the man to help me do that. Not Detective Fulton."

Fulton had cop written all over him while Noah…didn't. "I don't exactly fit into the woodwork around here either. I'm not the country-club type."

"I told you I don't like labels, and we get many people here of different backgrounds, Detective."

"I bet I don't know a single person who could afford a night in one of your bungalows. What's the going rate these days?"

"For a night?"

"Yes."

She paused. "Five thousand."

A strangled laugh hit his throat. "Holy sh—"

"That includes food and all resort amenities except alcohol, spa packages and special excursions," she explained. "Our guests are happy to pay the price because they know it means we take care of their privacy and security while they're here. They can immerse themselves in the resort and landscape."

"And there are no cameras anywhere," he recalled.

"No."

He cursed. "That's going to make my job difficult."

"All staff members also sign nondisclosure documents when they join the Mariposa team," she warned.

"Then you're wrong," he said, crossing his arms. He eased back against the wall, tipping his head against the plaster. "It's the perfect place for a murder. And I bet Allison's killer knew it."

"That doesn't make me feel any better."

"I'm not here to make you feel better," he reminded her. "I'm here to catch a killer."

She drifted into thoughtful silence. Finally, she came

around the desk. "What if you weren't Noah Steele from Sedona? What if you were Noah Steele, the politician's son?"

"Do I look like a politician's son to you?"

"You could be the son of a shipping magnate. Or you could be an entrepreneur."

"I knew I should've packed my sweater-vest."

Defeated, she sat on the corner of her desk. "You're not making this easy."

He swallowed the inclination to apologize to her. Again.

Her chin snapped up. Her stare roamed his boots, his hair. As she perused him, it made him come to attention. "What're you doing?" he asked, bracing himself for whatever thought bubble she'd conjured.

Prospects flashed across her face. They practically glittered. "When I first saw you, I thought you could be a rock star."

"I can't carry a tune."

"You don't have to," she said. She crossed to him. "You're not here to entertain. You're here to get away from shows. Touring. The loud party atmosphere. You're here to disconnect. Recharge. It's a commonality many of our guests share, so you'd have a good jumping-off point for conversation."

She was close enough he could see the beauty mark she'd tried to hide under her concealer. It lived, camouflaged, near the corner of her mouth. "And what band am I supposed to be from?"

"I don't know. You could be a cover band, a good one that tours nationally. And you don't have to be the front man. You could be a bass player. A drummer."

"Maybe I just got out of rehab," he muttered, his voice imbued with sarcasm.

"The people who know me will never buy that I'm dating an addict."

"Speaking of people who know you," he said, "Adam knows who I am. He won't buy any of this."

"Adam will have to know," she agreed. "Josh saw you through a window two nights ago. If he remembers you, we'll let him in on the scheme. If not, then I'll tell him. I prefer not to."

"Why?"

"Because he can be terrible at keeping secrets," she admitted. "I love him, but he wears his heart on his sleeve. When would you like to start?"

They were really doing this—this fake dating thing? He took a long breath. "As soon as possible if I'm going to make headway."

"Tomorrow morning, then. Be here at nine. We'll have a champagne breakfast at Annabeth. That way, I can start introducing you as—"

"The boyfriend." He shook his head. "If I saw you and me together, I wouldn't buy it."

"Not everyone's a detective," she said. "Most people take what they see at face value. They don't analyze. If we play it off right…if we're convincing…then you have free rein over Mariposa for the foreseeable future."

"You'll need to tell big brother," he warned. "Tonight. He'll need to play along, too. I have a feeling he won't approve."

"Let me worry about Adam." She hesitated. "You should come earlier than nine. Can you be at my place at eight? To be convincing as a couple, we'll need to establish history. Basic facts like where we met, how long we've been dating and so on."

"Why not now?" he asked. Last time they'd been together like this, one-on-one, he'd been desperate to get away from her. Now the space between them was no longer a minefield of fresh-turned grief. It felt…warm and, yes, precarious. But he wasn't alone. Here, with her, he wasn't a victim to his thoughts and the self-blame that had plagued him since finding out Allison was gone.

Laura drooped like a flower without water. "I have a meeting tonight. It's a family matter. My…father's in town."

Why did she pause before the word *father*? He still knew very little about the Coltons and Mariposa. He could use the time tonight to research. "Eight o'clock."

"I'll tell Roland you're coming. You won't have trouble getting in." An indentation appeared between her brows.

"What?" he asked.

"I'm sorry," she said, shaking her head. "I didn't know how to say goodbye for a second."

Amused, he wondered what path her thoughts had gone down. "No one's looking. I think a handshake will do, Ms. Colton."

"Of course." She offered her hand. "And no need to call me Ms. Colton anymore, remember?"

He gripped her hand softly. Cradled it. What else did someone do with a hand like hers? "Laura," he said, hearing how it left him like a prayer.

The other night, he'd dropped her hand like a hot potato. Now he made himself hold it. He made himself picture it— her and him. Together. If he was going to convince anyone else they were an item, he had to convince himself first. For one dangerous moment, he let himself imagine pulling her closer. He imagined holding her, the smell of her hair, pressing his lips to the curve between her neck and shoulder, running his hands up the length of her spine…

He imagined the shape of her under his hands, how a woman like her would respond to his touch...

"Noah," she replied.

Heat assaulted him. Before he could hit the safe button, a vortex of flame swept him up. It refused to spit him back out.

Noah took a step back. The doorknob bit into his hip.

Shaking her hand had been too much? What was he going to do tomorrow when they had to convince Laura's family, friends, employees and guests that they were a couple? Flame-retardant gear wouldn't keep him safe from this inferno.

Allison's death had ripped his defenses wide, exposing him.

He couldn't let Laura Colton take advantage of the fact.

"Good night," he said shortly.

"Good night," she returned, and the slight smile on her face stayed with him long after he left.

"Have you lost your mind?"

Laura stood her ground. "It's a good plan, Adam."

"He's the wrong cop," Adam reminded her. "He's emotional. According to his commanding officer, he's not even supposed to be anywhere near this."

The guy in her office hadn't seemed emotional. Determined? Yes. Standoffish? Absolutely. Underneath, Laura was certain Detective Steele—*Noah*—had to be hurting. But his clear-cut focus had struck her, inciting her own.

Someone had drugged her friend, cut her life short... She couldn't walk away from that. "I'm doing this," she told Adam. "We're doing this—him and me—whether you think it's advisable."

"Laura—"

"This happened on our watch," she said, and the horror of that made her stomach lurch. "Someone killed her here. This is our home, Adam."

Adam planted a hand on her shoulder. "You are not responsible for Allison's death."

"Then help me catch who is," she insisted. "Don't get in the way. Please."

The last word splintered. He closed his eyes in reaction.

Voices down the hall echoed toward them. Adam's hand lifted from her shoulder. "We'll finish this discussion later," he concluded.

She raised her chin in response. Recognizing the voices as those of Joshua, Greg and Clive, she braced herself for what was to come. The family attorney stood as a buffer between father and son as he escorted them down the hall to the conference room. His Hawaiian-print shirt seemed loud and cheery, his smile in contrast with Joshua's scowl and Clive's expressionless face.

The only nondescript thing about Greg was the beige folder he was holding. He raised his free hand to wave at Adam and Laura. "We're not behind schedule, are we?" he asked them.

"We arrived early," Adam replied. He stepped aside, motioning for Clive to go ahead into the conference room. As his father moved beyond him and Laura, they both raised questioning looks at Greg.

He offered them a slight nod.

Laura's lips parted. She glanced between her brothers, noting Joshua's grim intent. She watched Adam button his suit jacket, the galvanized rods of his business mien snapping into place. He let Greg follow Clive into the room first. "Shall we?" he asked the others.

Laura wished she knew what was in that folder. As she

and Joshua entered the conference room, she leaned over and whispered, "Did Greg tell you what he found?"

"Nothing," Joshua answered.

She took her seat. They would each have a vote, she knew. It was how they handled anything that involved their mother's estate, resort capital or unnecessary risk. She folded her hands on the table, watching Clive settle in. He seemed relaxed. Expectant.

His statement about Quentin Randolph from yesterday came back. Had her own father sent a wolf to her door? She could hardly stand to look at him with that knowledge. Throughout lunch the day before, she'd wanted to ask if it was true. Had he known who Quentin was?

Would it influence her vote if she knew he had? She prided herself on separating business Laura from personal Laura. That was part of her success, just as it was Adam's.

That task was hard enough knowing how Clive had treated her mother through the years, and how he had neglected Adam, Joshua, her and their half sister, Dani. Adding the implications surrounding Quentin's place in her life would make being objective that much harder.

Clive adjusted his cuff links. He grinned. "Who calls the meeting to order?"

"It's nothing so formal as that," Adam informed him. "Though this time, I will ask Greg to start."

Greg took a pair of reading glasses from the neckline of his shirt. He put them on and opened the folder. "After yesterday's meeting, I placed a couple of calls to colleagues with a vested interest in Colton Textiles."

"Why?" Clive drawled. "This is a simple family matter. Nothing worth meddling in."

"I asked Greg to look into it," Adam told him.

Clive's serene smile dimmed on his eldest. "You don't trust me?"

Laura spoke up. "If we agree to your terms, we could risk as much as half a million dollars."

"Risk." Clive batted the word away. "Come now, Precious. I said it was a loan, and that I'd pay you back with interest."

"You wanted us going into this blind," Joshua surmised. "Look around you. We built this place because we were smart. You still think we're children you can easily bait and switch, don't you?"

"I'll ask you again to modulate your tone when you speak to me," Clive told him.

"Greg," Adam prompted again, "tell us what you found. Once the cards are on the table, the three of us will put it to a vote, yes or no, and that majority decision will be the one we go forward with."

Greg cleared his throat. "Right. The reality is that Colton Textiles is going under."

Palpable silence cast the room in a long shadow.

"I knew it," Joshua said under his breath.

Laura stared at her father in disbelief. "Going under? How?"

Adam frowned. "How long has it been in the red?"

"Two years," Greg revealed. "There are other investors, none of whom have seen a return on their investment."

"How could you let it get this far?" Laura asked. "If you were going to come to us, you should've done it from the moment there was trouble."

"Well, I'm here now," Clive said, dignified. He spread his hands. "You must want to save your birthright."

"If you cared about our birthright, you would have told us the truth," Joshua retorted.

"You owe me this."

Laura froze, feeling her brothers do the same. "What did you say?"

"You owe me," Clive stated again. "I paid for it all, didn't I? The house in LA. The private schools you attended."

"Let me stop you right there," Adam said. His hands slid onto the table, palms down. He leaned forward. "Because I sense this discussion going sideways. Our mother may have died when we were young, and you weren't exactly there to take her place. But I'm fairly confident when I say a proper parent doesn't talk like that."

"Now wait just a second—"

"No." Adam's voice invited zero rebuttal. "She paid for the house in LA. And she paid every dime of our tuition. And before you claim you put me, Laura or Josh through college, we paid our way through the trusts she left in each of our names, the remains of which we pooled to make Mariposa what it is. You have no fingerprint here. If you're going to come running to us to save the family company, I suggest you avoid leading with lies and grandiosity. That may have worked with your investors, but we know you. We know the real you."

"What good's a vote when you're all prejudiced against me?" Clive demanded.

"In this room, we're not your sons or your daughter," Adam pointed out. "In this room, we're owners and directors of Mariposa Resort & Spa, and we'll vote accordingly. All in favor of loaning Clive Colton half a million dollars to save Colton Textiles, say 'aye.'"

Neither Laura nor Joshua spoke up.

Adam raised a brow. "The nays have it."

Clive leaned back. In a jerky motion, he pulled down the front of his vest. "Very well." Climbing to his feet, he took turns frowning at each of them. "I should have expected as much. You chose your side years ago."

"Right around the time you made it clear you wanted nothing to do with us," Joshua returned. "How does that feel, by the way?"

Laura crossed to her father, keeping her voice low. "If you had come to us as soon as the trouble started, we would have helped you. We could have saved the company together."

"You can't dress betrayal up with excuses, Laura," Clive said. "Didn't your mother teach you that?"

She felt the breath go out of her. "No. But she did teach us common decency."

"Then why not throw the company a lifeline?"

Joshua stepped up behind Laura, supportive. "You can't save a man from drowning when history tells you he won't hesitate to hold you under water to save himself."

"Or bring down the entire ship," Adam chimed in as he stacked papers on his end of the table.

"*And* he insults your mother," Joshua added. He made a face. "I mean, come on. That's just wrong."

Laura couldn't look away from Clive's angry face. "I've been trying to forgive you for over a decade. She taught us to forgive. She forgave you—more times than any other woman would have had the grace to do so. And it didn't stop you. Still, I thought I could—one day—offer my forgiveness. And maybe I will. But not today."

"You know what I learned from your mother?" he asked. "Beauty can be all ice. She must've taught you that, too. Cold suits you."

Heat flooded her face. She felt it in the tips of her ears. "Please, leave."

Clive held her gaze for several seconds before his eyes

cut over her shoulder and locked on Joshua. He glanced to the head of the table at Adam. Without saying another word, Clive stepped toward the door.

Laura didn't breathe easily again until he was gone.

Joshua echoed her thoughts. "He'll be back."

"Maybe," Adam granted. "He's wrong, Laura. You're not cold, any more than Mom was."

"Of course not," Greg chimed in.

But the cold had seeped into every part of her, and she couldn't think how to comfort herself with Clive's accusations loud in her ears.

# Chapter 7

Laura woke the next day with her father's words still echoing. Would they bother her so much if they didn't correlate with Quentin Randolph's remarks when she had broken off their engagement a year ago?

She switched on the kitchen light and went straight to the coffeepot to wake it up, too. She left it running before bending down to scoop up the mass at her feet. Her long-haired tabby, Sebastian, cried out as she dropped kisses to the back of his head. She cradled him against her. His purring reverberated into her chest, easing the dregs of another terrible night of sleep.

She closed her eyes for a moment, pressing her cheek to his soft fur. "Good morning, handsome," she whispered.

Feeling generous, Sebastian let her cuddle him, only growing restless when the coffee maker hissed as it percolated. When he wiggled, she set him on his feet and followed him to his food bowl. "Breakfast," she agreed and set about preparing his morning noms.

Her mother had adored big hairballs like Sebastian. When it had come time to leave the house in LA, her brothers had agreed that Laura should take the cats. She had cared for her mother's felines for the rest of their natural lives.

Sebastian was the first cat she'd brought home after burying the last of her mother's. While shopping in Sedona one afternoon on her own, she'd stopped at the animal shelter. It hadn't been the plan, but two hours later, she'd returned home with Sebastian in her arms.

After the relationship with Quentin had blown up in her face, her failures regarding marriage and starting her own family had trapped themselves in an echo chamber in her mind. The humiliation of learning Quentin's true intentions had almost been too much. If not for Sebastian, work and her brothers…she'd still be living in that echo chamber.

Allison and Alexis, too, had helped. Their girls' nights had increased in frequency. As Laura slid aside the long glass door leading onto her patio, she thought of all the evenings she and the girls had spent talking, laughing and commiserating.

She closed the door so Sebastian would stay in. Unknotting her robe, she slid it off. The pool beyond the deck chairs and firepit was heated. She cast off a shiver at the cool kiss of winter's chill, setting the robe on the back of a chair. When she'd moved from her suite at L Building, she'd asked the bungalow's designer to include a starting block next to the pool. She stepped onto the platform and hooked her toes over the edge. Folding, she gripped the edge of the block with her fingers. She counted off, imagined the starting bell and sprang forward, streamlined from fingers to toes.

No sooner had she hit the water than she started swimming. She flutter kicked, rotating to one side as her arm swept over her head, digging into the water, before she repeated the motions on the other side. The freestyle strokes took her to the end of the pool and back before she flipped over and started backstroking. She did a lap down and back this way before she flipped again and crossed the pool by butterflying. Finally, she finished with the breaststroke.

She'd done the relay so many times, she knew how many repetitions of each stroke it took to get from one end of the pool to the other. She knew, down to the inch, how much space she needed between herself and the wall to flip and change direction. When she finished, she gripped the edge of the pool, catching her breath.

Her time was slower today. Hooking her arms over the lip, she tilted her head to one side to let the water drip from her ear. Maybe it was the sleepless nights. Maybe her thoughts were weighing her down. She wanted nothing more than to cast them off. She no longer wanted to dwell on her father or Quentin Randolph.

Boosting herself over the edge, she sat with her feet dangling in the water, letting the cold prickle across the wet skin around her one-piece bathing suit. She watched her legs circle under the surface and contemplated another relay to drown the voices in her head.

She heard Sebastian scratching at the glass door. Her coffee would be done, and she would need to eat, shower and complete her hair and makeup routine before her morning meeting.

She toweled off, then draped the robe over her shoulders as she went inside. The house felt warm. She sat before the glass door with Sebastian at her side, watching the colors of breaking day stain the sky over silhouettes of peaks, enjoying the ritual of her first cup of coffee.

As she washed and dried her mug, she heard the knock at her front door. She set it on the drying rack and sidestepped Sebastian so she wouldn't tread on his tail and upset him.

Joshua normally didn't show up for another hour. She snatched open the door regardless.

Dressed in a leather jacket and blue jeans that looked like a flawless fit, Noah Steele brooded behind a pair of dark sunglasses.

He stared at the parting of her robe and the black bathing suit with cutouts above each hip. His frown deepened. "You always answer the door like this?"

She drew the robe around her, belting it tight. "You're early."

"Yeah, well," he rumbled, removing the sunglasses. "I figured the sooner you and I figure out how to do...whatever the hell it is we're doing...the better."

"Come in," she said, stepping back to admit him. As he moved inside her bungalow, she dragged a hand through her wet hair. "I'm sorry I'm not dressed. If you give me a moment, I can—"

"No need for formality," he said. He stared at her in the low morning light from the windows. "Seeing the princess of Mariposa at the start of the day without makeup or any of the polish..." His mouth shifted into a side-cocked half smile. "It's a trip."

She looked away quickly. "There's coffee, if you'd like some."

Sebastian jumped onto the counter, eyeing the newcomer. Noah eyed him in return. "Who's this?"

"This is Sebastian," she said, dragging her fingers through the fur over his spine.

"You're a cat person."

"Yes," she said. "What about you?"

"I don't have pets."

"Oh," she said. She tried to contemplate coming home after a long day with no creature there to greet her.

He looked around, cataloging her everyday surroundings. "It's too neat."

She glanced around at her living space. There wasn't much out of place other than the throw blanket she had used the night before on the couch and the hardback she had left face down on the coffee table. "I have someone who cleans for me once a week."

"Must be nice."

She fought the inclination to sigh over his presumptive tone. "If you don't want coffee, we should get started."

"It's why I'm here."

She sat on the sofa. Because her legs were bare and the robe reached midthigh, she twitched the throw blanket into place over them as he sat on the other end. She curled her legs up on the sofa beside her to disguise the move. "I thought about it a lot last night. I think, if people ask, we should put our relationship at six months."

"Why six?" he asked.

Sebastian hopped up between them. When he sought the space next to her, she waited until he folded into a rest position to pet him. "Because that's enough time for us to get to know each other. Since we decided you're a musician and I'm here at Mariposa, we've been courting mostly over a long distance. Calls, texts, the occasional rendezvous."

"'Rendezvous,'" he repeated. "So the relationship's sexual."

She found she could blush. And he hadn't even smiled at the suggestion. "Do you know many rock stars who abstain from sex?"

"I don't know one rock star, period," he replied.

She eyed the leather jacket. It was soft from wear, scarred in places and sheepskin-lined. He hadn't bought it just for the cover story. And he wore it all too well. "Have you considered which place in the band you would like to be?" she asked, changing the subject. "Bass? Keyboards? Drums?"

"Rhythm guitar," he responded readily.

"Can you play the guitar?" she asked, curious.

"No," he admitted. "But, as you say, I'm not here to entertain. I'm here for a little R and R. And to see my girl."

She tried to ignore the sudden rush of feeling…the wave of sheer heat at hearing him refer to her as his girl. Tamping down on it, she turned her attention to Sebastian's belly when he rolled to expose it. "Six months will have given us plenty of time to grow loved up enough. There will be hand-holding involved. Hugging. Maybe kissing, to seal the illusion. Are you okay with that?"

"Are you?" he challenged.

"Yes." She hoped.

"I've done undercover work," he revealed. "It's all part of the act."

She opened her mouth to ask if he'd ever pretended to date another woman for the sake of work. The question washed away quickly. That wasn't what she needed to know about him. "How old are you?"

"Twenty-nine."

"So am I," she said, offering a stilted smile. "My birthday's May sixth. When's yours?"

"November seventeenth."

She nodded, filing the information away in case she needed it. "My middle name is Elizabeth."

"Why do I need to know that?"

"It's the sort of thing lovers would know about each other after a time," she commented.

He looked away. "My full name's Noah Nathaniel Steele. Nathaniel for my dad."

She felt a smile warm her lips. Nathaniel seemed awfully formal. Like a nice tie he kept tucked away in a drawer because he'd decided it didn't suit him. "Your real dad?"

"For this," he said carefully, "maybe I shouldn't be Noah Steele, former foster kid. Maybe the rhythm guitarist, Noah Steele, comes from a traditional home. A normal one. It's less complicated."

"Great artists rarely come from normal homes. But that's your decision. Where do you want the new Noah Steele to come from—California?"

"Washington," he decided. "I spent some time there with my mom before…"

As she trailed off, she willed him to say more. Was he speaking of his biological mother or his foster mom, the one he'd shared with Allison?

"Before…?"

He shook his head. "It doesn't matter. I'm from Washington State."

"I'm originally from LA," she pointed out. "Just for the record."

"I know."

She blinked. "Oh. You looked into me."

"Part of the job," he excused. "You want me to apologize?"

"No," she blurted. "There's nothing available that most people don't know. And it's good you know. For the sake of what we're doing."

"In that case," he said, "why don't you tell me what happened with Quentin Randolph a year ago? Why did you break off your Page Six engagement?"

She should have seen the question coming. It hit her like a wall. "He wasn't who I thought he was."

He lifted both brows when she said nothing more. "That's it?"

She felt her shoulders cave a bit. "Quentin loved the idea of my wealth more than he loved the idea of me. He wanted the connections that come with the Colton name more than he wanted me. And he fooled me into thinking otherwise for a little over a year before my brothers caught on to his schemes." She paused in the telling, then asked, "Is that enough or do you need more?"

Noah's tungsten eyes flickered. "Did you love the guy?"

"Would you agree to marry someone you weren't in love with?" At his marked silence, she rethought her answer. "I loved the version of Quentin he built for me—the one that turned out to be false. So, in a way, I suppose I didn't. Not really. And that makes it easier...until the humiliation sets in."

"He's a moron."

She blinked. "I beg your pardon?"

He spoke clearly, drawing each word out. "The guy's a stage-five moron. If someone like that had come sniffing around Allison, I would've taken care of him."

He would have, she realized. A shiver went through her. She blamed it on her wet hair and bathing suit, gathering the lapels of her bathrobe together. "When was your last long-term relationship?"

Rebuke painted his hard features.

She stopped his protest before it began. "These are things couples know about each other."

A disgruntled, growly noise lifted from his throat. "Six... seven years ago?"

"And how long did it last?"

"Five months."

"That's long-term?" she asked.

"I don't know." He cast off the admission. "What's your idea of a long-term relationship?"

"A year," she stated. "Or more."

"Women tend not to stick around that long," he revealed.

"Maybe you're dating the wrong type," she advised.

"What type should I be fishing for?" he demanded. "You know any trust-fund beauties who wouldn't mind slumming it with an Arizona cop?"

Laura chose not to answer.

"Before Randolph, did you date anybody else?" he asked.

"Yes," she said. She didn't want to talk about the other men. But she had probed him about the women in his life. It was only fair.

"Who?"

"Dominic Sinclaire."

"The diamond guy?"

"Why do you sound so derisive?" she asked.

"I don't know. Who ended things there?"

"I did," she said without thinking.

He narrowed his eyes. "I'm sensing a pattern."

"Should I have stayed with someone with a wandering eye?" she asked.

"The son of a bitch cheated?" he said, voice going low.

"Yes."

"He cheated. On Laura Colton."

Exasperated, she repeated, "Yes."

"What an ass."

"Charming," she commented.

"Sounds like he was charmless."

"Dominic has a great deal of charm," she explained. "The problem came when he employed it elsewhere. We're off topic." She tried to think of another question for him. The ink peeking out from underneath the collar of the jacket drew her gaze. "How many tattoos do you have?"

"I stopped counting." When her eyes widened, he asked, "Is that too many for you?"

"No," she said. She'd never known someone with too many tattoos to count. "Which one is your favorite?"

"I don't have a favorite," he claimed.

"I don't believe that for a second," she told him. "Even Francis Bacon had a favorite painting."

"Who?"

She redirected the conversation again. "It's your turn to ask a question."

"Okay," he said. "Morning or night?"

She frowned. "Really? You think that's relevant?"

"It would be," he weighed, "if we were really into each other."

"Ask something else," she demanded.

"Fine," he consented. "What's your drink of choice? No, let me guess. White wine spritzer."

"Martini," she corrected. "Dry. Yours?"

"A boilermaker."

"That's not a real thing," she assumed.

"Yes, it is. It's a glass of beer with a shot of whiskey."

"You can't have one, then the other?"

"I like to multitask."

Trying to plumb the depths of this man was more difficult than she had imagined. Noah didn't have quills. He had a hide like a crocodile.

Wanting to dig deeper, she asked, "What do you do for exercise?"

One corner of his mouth tipped into a grim smile. "I'm a morning guy."

She fought the urge to strangle him with her terry-cloth belt. "You wanted to do this, too. If you won't make something of an effort, what's the point of being here with me?"

The smirk fell away. A breath left him in a tumultuous

wash. Shifting on the sofa, he leaned over, planting his elbows on his knees.

"I'm sorry," he said after a while. "I'm not used to this."

"Answering personal questions?" she asked. "That makes sense. You're the investigator. You ask the questions. Don't you?"

"No. I mean I don't really get close...to people," he told her.

"Weren't you close to Allison?" she asked.

"We met when we were kids," he muttered. "She was my sister in all but blood. That may not make sense to you—"

"It does," she explained. "I have a half sister. Dani. She lives in London. We don't see each other much anymore. But it doesn't change the fact that she's my sister."

"Your father had an affair."

So he'd found that corner of the family history. She tried not to bristle. "He had many affairs. He paid off his main mistress. As a result, she gave up custody of Dani. She was mourning the loss of her mother as Adam, Josh and I were, too. The four of us... We were a mess." The house in LA had felt like a cavern of lost hopes. They had been four sad children, desperate for someone who wasn't there.

"I'll try harder," he said. "For Allison."

"Me, too," she promised. She nearly reached for his hand, then stopped, uncertain.

No, if they were going to do this, one of them had to break the intimacy barrier. Her heart flipped as she eyed the denim covering his thigh. She touched it in a gesture of support.

When his eyes swung to hers in surprise, she felt her face warm. A chain wrapped around her navel flashed to life, glowing orange, as if it had been living in hot coals.

He didn't move, didn't look away. His tungsten eyes

brought to mind electrical storms. The severe line of his mouth didn't ease as his gaze swept over her. She saw it land on her mouth.

She wasn't just playing with fire. This was a California brush fire with the wind at its back. Out of control. Destructive.

It would devastate her if she let it.

Her hand shied from his thigh. She gripped the edge of the cushion, wishing she knew what to say next. Wishing she knew what she was doing.

Would helping Allison's brother burn her to the ground?

He was still watching her. She felt his stare drilling into her profile. His voice was rough when he spoke again. "Do you want to keep going?"

Could she? Closing her eyes, she gathered herself, wishing the flush in her torso would cool. The robe felt stifling suddenly. She flicked the blanket off her legs, planting her feet on the cool tiles of the floor. "Where do you live?" she asked quietly.

"Sedona. I have a house there. And I row."

"What?"

"It's how I stay in shape," he revealed. "Rowing. There's a park near my house with a small lake. During the winter, I use a rowing machine at home."

Rowing. It made sense, she thought, judging by the muscles packed underneath his jacket. She tried not to think about muscles bunching along his back and stomach as he worked the oars. The flame inside her kicked up regardless. "Do you like to dine out or in?"

"Eating out is expensive."

"So you drink your boilermakers at home," she discerned.

"I'm more of a social drinker, I guess."

"You don't really strike me as a social guy," she admitted.

He made a satisfactory noise. "We *are* getting to know each other better," he murmured.

The rumble of his voice was appealing. She shrugged to release the knots of attraction digging in everywhere. "Is there anything else about you I should know?"

He was quiet for a moment. Then he said, "I was in the navy."

Her eyes went to his boots. They were the same ones he'd worn the first night. She'd thought some part of him was military—or militant. "For how long?"

"I enlisted out of high school. I left when I was twenty-three."

"That's when you became a cop," she realized.

"A rhythm guitarist for an Eagles cover band," he corrected.

She nodded swiftly. "Right." *Stick to the story, Laura.* She checked her smartwatch and stood up. "I really must get ready. Please, have a cup of coffee while you wait."

"So we're still on for breakfast?" he asked, getting to his feet, too.

"Of course." A romantic champagne breakfast for two at Annabeth with the entire resort watching. Nerves flared to life. "Give me forty-five minutes to make myself presentable," she insisted. "Then you can get started on your investigation."

"What should I call you?" he asked suddenly.

"I told you last night. Laura will be fine."

"Yeah, but don't most couples have sentimental names for each other?"

Distracted, she replied, "I believe I can trust you to come up with something."

"Are you sure about that?"

"Yes," she decided. Then she paused. Couldn't she?

\* \* \*

"Are you ready?"

Noah cataloged the faces milling beyond the open restaurant doors. Turning to Laura, he thought again of the way his tongue had practically lolled out of his mouth when she had emerged from her bedroom back at her bungalow perfectly coiffed and dressed to the nines in a black maxidress. This one had a transparent lace collar and sleeves, with a line of ruffles below her clavicle. The skirt was a mix of ruffles and lace. A buff-colored belt tied it together with a hat in the same color. The keyhole in the back of the dress had made his palms itch as much as the cutouts in her bathing suit.

He'd wanted to say something then.

*You look stunning.*

*You're too fine for the likes of me.*

Instead, he'd just stood there with his mouth hanging open like an idiot.

He took a steadying breath. "Let's get this over with."

"Take my hand."

Cursing inwardly, he snatched her fingers up in his and hoped to God his palms weren't sweaty.

"There's Tallulah," she murmured. "She's our head of housekeeping and has been with the resort as long as my family has. She lives on property like Adam, Josh and me, and she knows everything there is to know about her staff and the guests."

"Good to know," he said, sizing up the woman of average height and weight. When she saw Laura, her face lit up. "Last name?"

"Deschine. And she's not a mark," Laura warned under her breath. His steps had picked up pace and she hurried to catch up. "Everyone adores her. *I* adore her."

"Everyone's a mark," he informed her.

"Tallulah," Laura greeted her, going straight into the woman's arms.

Noah relinquished her hand as she hugged Tallulah. The woman placed both hands on Laura's shoulders and searched her face, speaking quietly. "How are you doing—with everything?"

Laura's smile dimmed slightly. "I'm okay. Are you?"

"I'm still in shock, I think," Tallulah murmured. "Poor Bella. She remains out."

Laura nodded. "Knox has taken some time off, too, but he's returning full-time today. We need him, but I hope it's not too soon."

Tallulah eyed Noah. "Who is this?"

Laura pivoted to him. She took his hand again, fixing that poised grin into place. "Tallulah, this is Noah. My boyfriend."

"Boyfriend?" Tallulah's focus flitted over the tattoos on his neck and hands, the leather jacket and rustic boots. She shook her head. "You didn't tell me you were seeing anyone."

"I've been keeping it quiet," Laura explained. She placed her hand low on Noah's back. "*We've* been keeping it quiet."

"We haven't had enough time together over the last few months," Noah said. "Have we, Pearl?"

Laura's gaze snapped to his. After a beat, she remembered herself. "No. But once Noah heard everything that's happened, he flew in to be with me."

"That's nice," Tallulah said, a smile warming her mouth. "She needs someone. It's good to meet you, Noah."

"It's nice to meet you, too, ma'am," he returned.

When Tallulah swept away, Laura took a moment to gawk at him.

"What?" he asked. "Have I done something wrong already?"

"No," she said with a slight shake of her head. "You called her 'ma'am.'"

"Shouldn't I have?" he asked.

"You absolutely should," she agreed. "It was just odd hearing something that polite come out of your mouth."

He rolled his eyes. "Right. Because I'm uncivilized."

She sighed at him. "Never mind."

As they ventured into the restaurant, heads swiveled in their direction. He tried not to squirm under the attention. Up front, he'd known that being Laura Colton's boyfriend would make people openly curious.

He had been right. The maître d' took his coat. Noah had put more thought into his appearance, for once. The black T-shirt with the Metallica logo exposed the web of tattoos down both arms. He placed his hand on Laura's waist as they were led to their table and could practically hear the buzz of speculation surrounding them.

"Thank you," she murmured when he pulled out her chair, aiming a high-wattage smile over her shoulder.

There was a flirtatious note in those baby blues. When they heated like that, they no longer reminded him of ice floes. They made him think of hot springs, and his body tightened. His hands hardened on the back of the chair. Leaning over her shoulder as she lowered to the seat, he whispered, "Don't lay it on too thick, Colton. Neanderthal like me might get the wrong idea."

He saw the tension weave through her posture again. She said nothing as he moved to the chair facing her and dropped to it. Without opening the menu, she told the server, "Billy, may we have the champagne breakfast?"

Billy looked back and forth between them, owl-eyed. "Just for the two of you?"

Laura smiled Noah's way. "Just us two."

Noah shook out his napkin. Billy skipped off to the kitchen, no doubt to spread the gossip. "We're an organized spectacle."

"You wanted in," she said, not losing the smile. "Too late to turn back now."

"You could make a scene," he pointed out. "Scream at me. Throw something at me. Demand that I sleep with the horses tonight and be on my way in the morning."

She shook her head. "I don't believe in making a scene."

He shot off a half laugh. "You enter a room and it's a scene, regardless of what you say."

She propped her chin on her hands. "I believe you're trying to give me a compliment."

"I'm telling you the truth, Pearl."

Her nose wrinkled. And even that looked pretty on her. "'Pearl'?"

"You said I could call you whatever I want."

"It makes me sound like a member of *Golden Girls*," she complained.

"What's wrong with *Golden Girls*?" he countered.

"Nothing," she said. "But I am still three months shy of thirty."

A woman passed their table. She did a double take and skidded to a halt. "Laura?"

Laura beamed. "Alexis! Noah, this is our amazing concierge, Alexis Reed."

He dipped his head to her. "Nice to meet you, Ms. Reed."

"And who're you?" she asked, skimming her gaze over his torso.

"This is Noah Steele," Laura said. "He's my…boyfriend."

Alexis slowly turned her stare on Laura, her shock plain. "Girl, you've been holding out on me."

"Noah's in a band called Fast Lane," Laura said. "We've been keeping things quiet because he's been touring."

Brows arched high, Alexis turned her stare back to Noah. She offered him her hand. "Is this your first time at Mariposa?"

"It is," he granted, taking her hand in his. He squeezed it lightly.

"How long are you staying for?"

"As long as it takes to make sure Laura's okay. The last week has been tough on her."

"I'll say it has," Alexis seconded. "Well, I'll let you two get back to it." She sent Laura a meaningful look. "You owe me a long talk over white wine."

"I do," Laura agreed. "Are there any problems I need to see to this morning?"

"Nothing I can't handle," Alexis answered smoothly. "Enjoy your champagne. I'll check in later."

Noah waited until Alexis walked away before speaking. "Fast Lane?"

"It's an actual band," she said. "If I'd given her a fake name, nothing would pop up if she googled it."

"Let's hope she doesn't google Fast Lane and Noah Steele together," he said. "That may blow my cover."

Laura shook her head. "I hate lying to the people I care about. This is going to be harder than I thought."

"Relax," Noah advised. "Once I find out who's responsible for Allison's overdose, you can tell everyone the truth."

Laura didn't appear to be consoled. Billy came back, setting a bottle of champagne and glasses on the table. He popped the cork, let the champagne breathe as he set a plate before each of them with a fruit medley and a croissant that smelled incredible. Then he poured the champagne into a pair of crystal flutes. "Can I get you anything else?" he asked.

"This is perfect," she complimented him. "Thank you, Billy."

As he walked away, Laura sipped her champagne. She lowered the flute, tapping her finger to the side. "I like your arms," she noted.

He glanced down at his forearms. The spider went up one wrist. Webbing chased it up his forearm. The primary feathers of the falcon on his upper arm peered out from underneath his sleeve. On the other arm, more bones. "Sure you do."

"I mean it," she said. "You're practically a work of art."

"Well, that was the idea," he drawled.

"You have to get better at this."

"At what?" he asked. Eating the croissant with his hands didn't seem right. Not with a grand piano snoozing nearby and crystal dripping from the ceiling. He picked up his knife and fork and sawed off a corner.

"Letting me be nice to you," she added.

"Hmm." The croissant practically melted on his tongue.

Carefully, Laura set the champagne flute down. "We've got Adam incoming."

Noah set his fork down. He lifted the napkin from his lap and wiped his mouth. "How did he take the news?"

"Not well," she warned. "Please, be good."

"Really? 'Be good'?"

She gave him a squelching look before greeting her brother. "Adam. Will you be joining Noah and me for breakfast?"

When Adam only turned a discerning eye on Noah, Noah lifted his hand. "Howdy."

Adam didn't respond. Noah noticed that both his hands

were balled at his sides. Amused, he asked Laura, "Is he going to call a duel or what?"

She frowned at him. "Noah."

"Will he accept pistols, or should I borrow someone's small sword?" Noah continued, undeterred.

"You're both being stupid. And everyone's watching."

Adam glanced around at the interested parties. His fists relaxed. But the sternness refused to leave his face. "Do you know what you're doing?"

"Of course we do," she said.

"I'm not asking you," Adam said.

Laura looked at Noah, pleading.

He stood up from the table and stepped into the aisle to face Adam squarely. "I'm here to see that Laura's okay," he told Adam, planting a hand on the man's shoulder. He had the satisfaction of seeing a nerve in Adam's temple vibrate. "She's lost a good friend, and she needs someone to lean on."

"And you're that person?" Adam asked skeptically.

"You're damn right I'm that person," Noah snapped. "The real question is whether her big brother is going to stand in the way of that."

Adam looked as if he'd rather swallow a handful of broken glass than allow Laura to continue this charade. He measured the hand on his shoulder with its skeletal ink. "All right," he said, his hard jaw thrown into sharp relief when the words came out through clenched teeth.

Laura stood, too. "I think Noah should stay in a bungalow."

Adam's eyes shuttered. "I think that's asking a bit much."

"There are a couple of empty ones," she stated. When he remained unmoved, she tilted her head. "I'll pay for it, if you're worried about that."

"Don't be ridiculous, Lou. This has nothing to do with money."

"Then say yes," she insisted. "The sooner Noah finds the perpetrator, the sooner everything can go back to normal."

Adam groaned. "He can stay in Bungalow Fifteen. It's better than him bunking with you at your place, which is where you'd put him if I refused."

"Thank you," Laura said. "You won't regret this."

Adam waited until she settled back at the table before turning fully to Noah. He leaned in, lowering his voice to a fine edge. "My sister just vouched for you. Don't let her down."

"And let you run me through with your princely sword?" Noah ventured. He shook his head. "I don't think so."

Adam shrugged his hand from his shoulder before he walked away.

Amused, Noah sat again. "I think he's starting to like me."

Laura gave him a discreet roll of her eyes, reaching for her champagne again. He didn't miss the way her lips moved around a whispered prayer before she tipped it back.

# *Chapter 8*

*"You're dating again?"*

Laura didn't think she could take another brother's disapproval. She swallowed, watching Joshua's expression as he took in the news.

"Why didn't you tell me?" he asked.

"I was being cautious," Laura tried to tell him. "Can you blame me?"

Joshua squinted off in Noah's direction. The pair had come to the stable so she could familiarize Noah with the grounds and introduce him to other members of staff. She hadn't expected Joshua to be there at this hour. His shock was palpable.

"Laura." Joshua's face broke out in a grin. "This is great!"

She blinked. "It is?"

"Of course it is," he said. "I didn't think after the Quentin situation you'd put yourself out there again. But look at you."

A relieved laugh tumbled out of her as Joshua gathered her in for a hug. "You're not upset?"

"Why would I be upset?"

"After everything with Quentin… You were so angry."

"He hurt you," Joshua told her. "He broke trust with all of us. Tell me you trust this guy, and I'm here for you."

"I do trust him," she breathed.

"That's fantastic," he said, pulling away. "Do I know him from somewhere? He looks familiar."

"You must've seen his band," she blurted. "Fast Lane."

"Maybe."

Before he could think more of it, she asked, "Did you speak with Erica?"

His smile tapered off. "Yeah, I did. She said nothing to make me think her and CJ Knight are more than they should be. Apparently, his manager—that Doug guy—isn't answering her calls."

Laura thought about that. "That's not good."

"Is there anything we can do about it?" Joshua asked. "What we should be worried about is Dad causing trouble for us."

"You think he will?" she asked.

Joshua nodded. "He's going to get that money somehow. And we know he plays dirty when he has to. Roland's been informed not to let him on the property without notifying one of us first."

"That's good, I suppose," Laura conceded. She watched Noah pet one filly who had come to the corral fence. The horse nickered as she nudged her muzzle against his chest. Noah's hands roamed into her mane before teasing her forelock and stroking her ears.

"Does he make you happy, ace?" Joshua asked.

Laura watched Noah and the horse, and something somewhere softened. It was difficult to associate the gentle horseman with the bullheaded one she knew. "Yes."

"Then I don't care who he is," Joshua explained. "I don't care where he comes from or what he does for a living. You deserve to be happy."

She looked back at her brother. "Thank you."

She would have hugged him again, but Knox hailed him. Joshua tossed her a wink and roamed back into the stable.

Laura crossed to the fence where Noah stood. "Penny has a taste for rebels."

"She's got spunk," he said, patting the horse's flank when she sidestepped for him to do so. "I like that in a filly."

She tried not to watch his hands. She couldn't miss how Penny nodded her head, as if agreeing with his every touch. "Do you ride?"

"I used to take Allison horseback riding on her birthday," he said.

"That's sweet," she said, trying to align him with Allison's indulgent brother. The pieces wouldn't have fit together so well if he wasn't giving Penny everything she wanted, including a treat he'd nabbed from the feed room.

Noah's head turned her way. "Do you ride?"

"I did," she replied. "My horse, Bingley, died last fall. I bought him when I moved to Arizona. He colicked overnight and…that was it."

"And you haven't ridden since?"

She shrugged. "I haven't had the heart to."

"You know what they say," he suggested.

"What?" she asked when he left the words hanging.

"To get back on the horse."

Her lips parted in surprise. "Allison said the same thing."

He stilled. "Did she?"

"Yes."

He looked away quickly. "If I'm going to stay on-site, I need to go back to my place to pack some clothes. I also need to go by Allison's."

"Why?"

"To look for anything that may point to her killer," he said. "She might have written something down. She could have received a note or a gift from someone. Since I don't have CCTV footage to fall back on, I thought that would be the best place to start."

"Let me come with you," she blurted.

He lifted his shoulders. "What good would that do?"

"Her killer is linked to the resort, and apart from my brothers, no one knows the resort like I do," she explained. "You could miss something I won't."

He shook his head. "I don't know…"

"I won't get in your way," she pledged. "If you need to take a minute when we get there, I can walk outside." She wrapped her hand around the spider etched on his forearm. "Please, Noah. This is something I need to do as much as you do."

He rocked back on his heels, pulling a breath in through his teeth. "You talked Adam into letting me stay and investigate," he said. "I owe you one."

"Is that a yes?"

"It is," he admitted.

"We can take my car."

"At what time does it turn into a pumpkin?"

"Ha." She gave his shoulder a light pinch. There was no give in the tight-roped muscle underneath his sleeve. He didn't even flinch.

*Rowing*, she thought in wonder. Turning away from him and Penny, she looked across the corral. "Oh," she said as Knox and Joshua looked away quickly. She dropped her voice. "Maybe you should kiss me."

"Now?"

"We have an audience," she whispered.

He stopped himself from looking around. Just barely, she sensed, as the muscles of his throat and jaw jumped warily. Somewhere far away, she thought she heard her heart pounding. Or was that his? She didn't see his chest rise. Was he even breathing?

The chain around her navel heated again. She still held his arm. Of its own accord, her thumb stroked the spider's spinnerets, soothing the cords of sinew underneath.

He took a half step closer.

Her pulse skittered. Every inch of her was aware of him, tuned to him.

He seemed to hesitate, uncertain. Then his head lowered, angled slowly.

He dropped a kiss onto the corner of her mouth. His hand skimmed the outside of her lace sleeve, and he lingered, head low over hers.

She wished he'd take off his sunglasses. Would the storms reach for her as they had on the sofa this morning? Would his eyes be tender? Were they capable of that?

She wondered what that would look like.

"We should go," he said.

The words skimmed across her cheek. Then he moved away, and she drew in a stuttering breath.


"This isn't a car."

Laura kept her eyes on the road and her hands at ten and two. "What are you talking about? Of course it's a car. It's got an engine and tires—"

Noah held up a hand to stop her. "This is a Mercedes G63 AMG. Calling this bad boy a car is like calling Cinderella's glass slipper a flip-flop."

Her lips curved. "You should see how she handles off-roading."

"You off-road?" When she lifted a coy shoulder, he tipped his head back to the headrest. "Don't take this the wrong way, Colton. But that is *sexy*."

"I've opened her up a couple of times on the interstate." She bit her bottom lip. "She goes really, really fast."

Reaching up, he gripped the distress bar. He shifted in his seat. Was she *trying* to turn him on? "You're killing me."

She snuck a glance at him over the lowered, fur-trimmed hood of her puffer jacket, her smile climbing. She wore large sunglasses that hid her eyes, but the smile may have been the first full, genuine one he'd seen from her. "Maybe we should take this time to keep getting to know each other."

"We're only a few minutes from my condo," he claimed. Their morning session of Twenty Questions had nearly been his undoing. It had exposed more than he'd intended.

His walls were already down, he reminded himself. He may not have completely come to terms with Allison's death. But he was an open wound, one Laura's questions had gone poking at without mercy.

"One quick question, then."

He tried not to squirm. "Fine. One question." Damn it, he could handle *one question*.

She took a minute to consider. Then she asked, "Tell me a secret."

"A secret?"

"Something about you no one else knows," she added.

He shook his head. "I don't have any."

"None?"

"No," he said.

She looked pointedly at his tattoos. "Do you really expect me to believe that?"

"Sure." He glanced at her. "How about you? What're your secrets?"

"I'll tell you mine if you tell me yours," she offered.

"This match is a draw," he concluded. He pointed to the end of the street. "Turn left there. My condo's on the right."

She made the turn, then swung into the inclined drive. She leaned over the wheel to get a look at the white two-story. "This is you?"

He popped the handle and pushed the passenger door open. Dropping to the ground, he dug his keys from his pocket. "You don't have to come in."

Laura was already out of the vehicle. She walked around the hood, zipping the silver puffer to ward off the dropping temperature. "You don't want me to come in?"

He'd been in her place, he thought. What did it matter if she saw the inside of his? "It won't take but a moment."

"I think I can handle that," she said, on his heels as he followed the path to the front door. He'd dumped rocks into the garden beds so that only the heartiest of desert plants jutted up through them.

There were two dead bolts on the door. He unlocked them both and the knob before pushing it open. After scooping up the mail on the welcome mat, he tossed the keys on the entry table. "Make yourself comfortable," he said, eyeing the return addresses. He set aside the bills for later and tossed the junk mail into the kitchen trash on the way to the bedroom.

He took down his old duffel from the top of the closet. Then he opened and closed the dresser drawers, selecting what he would need for a few days at the resort. He tossed his toothbrush, toothpaste, shampoo and beard trimmer into a toiletry bag. It fit inside the duffel.

On his bedside table, he exchanged his everyday watch for his good one, flipping his wrist to fasten it. In a small ceramic dish, he saw the leather bracelet Allison had given him when he'd left for the navy to match her own.

The evil eye in the center of the braided cord stared at him, wide-eyed. It was blue—like Laura's eyes.

He frowned as he scooped it up. Shoving it in his pocket, he knelt on the floor and opened the door on the front of the nightstand. His gun safe was built in. He spun the lock once to the left, then the right, left again. It released and he turned the handle to open the lead-lined door.

Inside, he palmed his off-duty pistol. It was smaller than his service weapon. Since his work at Mariposa was off the books, he couldn't carry his city-issue.

He tucked the pistol in its holster before strapping it in place underneath his leather jacket. He picked the duffel up by the handle. Through the open closet door, he could see the black bag that held his suit.

Steinbeck hadn't released Allison's body. But that time would come. There would be a funeral.

Noah had to bury her. He drew his shoulders up tight, already hating the moment he would have to unzip that bag, don the godforsaken suit she'd helped him pick out for a fellow cop's funeral years ago and stand over her coffin.

He pushed his fist against the closet door, closing it with a hard rap. Then he switched off the overhead light and walked out of the bedroom.

Laura stood in the center of the living room.

He followed her gaze to the large painting above the couch. Looking back at her, he raised his brow. "You look like you've seen a ghost."

She lifted her hand to the painting. "It's Georgia O'Keeffe."

"Is it?"

She squinted at him. "You didn't know?"

"Allison bought it shortly after I moved in," he said. "She said it was a replica. But she thought it'd look good in the space. She teased me for never putting anything on the walls.

I waited a long time to own a home, and I didn't want to put holes in the plaster. I put the damn thing up to make her happy." And it had, he thought, remembering how she'd beamed and clapped her hands when she'd seen it on the wall for the first time. His chest ached at the memory. "What about it?" he asked, wanting to be away from it. There was nothing of his sister here. And yet there was too much.

"The painting's called *Mariposa Lilies and Indian Paintbrush, 1941,*" Laura stated. "It…was a favorite of my mother's."

Noah made himself study the painting again. This time he shifted so they stood shoulder to shoulder. "Yeah?"

"Mariposas were her favorite flower," Laura breathed.

"Hence the name of the resort," he guessed.

She nodded silently. Abruptly, she turned away from him. "I need some air."

He veered around her quickly. If she cried…here, of all places…he didn't know how he'd handle that. Opening the door to the back patio, he held it wide.

She didn't thank him. Head low, she stalked out on long legs.

He gritted his teeth, wondering whether to follow or hang back. Watching, he tried to gauge how unsteady her emotions were.

She crossed the terra-cotta tiles to the railing. Clutching it with both hands, she viewed the sheer drop to the crevasse below. In the distance, the sun slanted low over white-tipped mountains. The clouds feathered overhead, wild with color. Her shoulders didn't slope. Her posture didn't cave. She stood tall, another exquisite fixture on the canvas he saw outside his back door.

After a while, she said in a voice that wasn't at all brittle, "I can see why you picked the place."

Noah tried to choose a point on the horizon just as fas-

cinating as she was. His attention veered back to her, mag-
netized. "It was this," he admitted. "And the quiet. It's far
enough outside the city, I don't hear the traffic."

She folded her arms on the railing and didn't speak. It
was as if she was measuring the quiet. Absorbing it.

*Quiet strength*, he thought. It came off her in waves. He
opened himself to it, wishing he could make room in his
grief for it. How had she learned to do that—move past it?
Or was he supposed to move *through* it?

Was that why he felt like he was losing this race? He
had to stop trying to go *over* the grief and go through it?

Somehow, that seemed harder.

He jangled the keys he'd picked up from the counter.
"We should get to Allison's."

She waited a beat. Then she turned and crossed the tiles
to him, placing one boot in front of the other. She gathered
her jacket close around her, her breath clouding the air.

As she breezed past, her scent overcame him. He felt
his eyes close. Even as he wondered what he was doing,
he caught it, pulled it in deep and held it.

It was a classy fragrance, something no doubt with a
designer price tag.

He swore it was made to chase his demons.

That was his secret. And he'd take it to his grave.

He shut the door and locked it, promising himself he'd
come back to the view when Laura no longer needed him.
When she was gone. When he'd found Allison's killer, put
him or her in a cell…if he didn't kill the person first.

He'd come back here and learn, somehow, to wade through
the fallout.

Allison's one-story house was a little Spanish-style residence across town. Noah had a key to the door on the same

ring as his. Silently, he worked it into the lock before pushing the door open.

The lights were out. He switched them on as the door squeaked, echoing across hard floors.

It was the opposite of his place, Laura observed. It smelled faintly of incense. The walls were bright yellow and cluttered with artwork. There were little eight-by-ten paintings, woven dream catchers, and a whole quilt draped on the wall of the dining room. The plush rugs sank under Laura's boots. As Noah flipped on more lights, Laura caught herself clasping her elbows. There was a hammock hanging in the dining room where a table should have been.

A pair of UGGs sat by the back door.

Noah bent over a table where books were stacked. He went through them one by one.

She circled the space once before she saw the little notebook on the edge of the bar. She opened it and was confronted with Allison's pretty, sprawling handwriting. "I might have something," she whispered.

Noah looked up. He saw the notebook splayed across her palms and rose.

As he crossed to her, she turned so he could see what Allison had written. "It's not really a journal. It's mostly Zen proverbs." She flipped a few pages and shook her head fondly. "She dotted her *i*'s with hearts."

He said nothing as he pried the notebook gently from her hands. Lowering to a stool at the bar, he journeyed through the pages, one after the other.

She turned away. His expression might be inscrutable, but she could feel the sadness coming off him.

The photo on the fridge caught her attention. It was a stunning snapshot of Allison in dancer's pose on top of Merry Go Round Rock. Underneath, a flyer was pinned with Allison's yoga class and guided meditation schedule for the New Year. She'd made small notes next to each time to help keep track of repeat students with their initials and Vinyāsa sequences.

Laura took down the flyer and folded it in two, wondering if Noah would find something useful on it.

The photograph behind it slipped to the floor. Laura crouched to pick it up and was shocked to recognize a young Allison next to a fresh-faced Noah.

In the photograph, Noah was clean-shaven. The wide, uninhibited smile underneath squinty green eyes and the brim of a navy dress-blue cap struck Laura dumb. His smile made him ridiculously handsome, not altogether innocent, but happy.

She stood to pin the photo back to the fridge with a Buddha magnet. A glass of water had been left on the counter. There was an empty breakfast bowl in the sink, unwashed. Alstroemerias in a vase next to the sink drooped.

She couldn't stand to think of them being left to die. Laura picked the vase up by the base and lowered it to the bottom of the sink. She turned on the tap and filled it halfway.

Noah stood. He tucked the notebook into the back of his jeans under his jacket before wandering toward what could only be Allison's bedroom.

Laura didn't want to follow. But she couldn't imagine him facing everything in there, in his sister's most private space, on his own. She tailed him.

The bed was half-made. Dirty clothes were still in the hamper. Noah had switched on the bedside lamp and was dragging the tip of a pen through the little ring bowl on her dresser. He opened a drawer, then another.

"What are you looking for?" she asked.

"Bracelet," he said, riffling through a jewelry box.

"I can help," she told him. "What does it look like?"

He shut the box, then thrust his hand deep into his pocket. He opened his fist to reveal an evil-eye pendant on braided leather strings.

"That's Allison's," she realized.

"This one's mine," he argued. "I picked it up at the condo just now. She wore hers, always."

Laura frowned. She couldn't remember Allison without the bracelet either. "Wasn't it on her when she…?"

He shook his head. "I viewed the personal items found on her person. The bracelet wasn't among them."

Laura looked around. "If it's not here…"

"Then it's lost," Noah finished, "or her killer has it."

"I'll look over here," she said, pointing to the bathroom.

They searched for another twenty minutes, combing each drawer, cabinet and closet space. The bracelet was nowhere to be found. Laura gathered the scarf she'd bought Allison for Christmas. She'd seen the warm, cozy wrap with its bright rainbow pattern and fun fringe at a local arts and crafts festival and had instantly thought of her friend.

She ran her hands over it and felt tears burn behind her eyes.

"Did you find it?" Noah asked from the door.

She lifted her gaze to his.

He froze, wary, and turned his stare elsewhere. "You need to come out of there."

Relinquishing the scarf, she stepped to the door. He let her pass under his arm before he closed it. Once more, she hadn't let tears fall, but she rubbed her hands over her cheeks anyway, to be sure. "I didn't find the bracelet," she told him. "I take it you didn't either."

"No dice," he replied.

There was violence in him, she saw in his taut jaw, his electrode eyes. He barely had it restrained. She saw him as she had the first night. Only this time, the readiness and anger weren't gunning for her.

She wasn't sure why she did it or what compelled her. She simply thought of the way he'd kissed her at the paddock. Just that brush of his mouth at the corner of hers and the softening she felt inside herself...

Fitting her hand to the bulge of his shoulder under the jacket, she held him.

His brows came together. "What are you doing, Colton?" he asked, hoarse.

She didn't answer. She didn't have to lift herself all the way to her tiptoes to stand chin to chin with him.

*Just enough*, she thought, touching the hard line of his jaw. She brushed her thumb over the center of his chin. The hair there was thick and soft. Up close, he didn't smell nearly as dangerous as he looked. He smelled like worn leather and clean sweat.

She leaned in. Even as he tensed, she closed her eyes and touched her mouth to the corner of his.

She felt his hands gather in the material of her jacket over her ribs, but he didn't wrest her away. Nor did his body soften, even as she pulled away, lowering to her heels.

His eyes searched hers, scrambling from one to the other and back in escalating questions. "What was that for?" he asked.

She considered what was inside her—what he was fighting. "You're not alone."

His brows bunched closer. The skin between them wrinkled in confusion.

She licked her lips, tasting him there. "I have something to tell you."

"What?" he asked, the line of his mouth forbidding.

"Adam's setting up a fund in Allison's name," she informed him. "It's to help pay for funeral costs."

He shook his head automatically. "I don't need your money."

"Noah, please. We just want to help. Let us. You must be overwhelmed by all this—"

"I'm fine." He moved away.

"She told me once that for the longest time you were the only person she had in this life," she blurted. "It's the same for you, isn't it? She was the only person you had. And now she's gone and a big part of you is lost. Even if you don't want anyone to see it."

"I think we're done here," he said.

She rolled her eyes heavenward. She might as well bang her head against the wall.

In the living room, he'd switched off all the lights. As he went to the front door to leave, she caught sight of the alstroemerias. The petals were so delicate, she could see the light from the window through them.

She'd take them home. She'd care for them, as Allison would have. Then she'd return the pretty crystal vase to Noah when they wilted.

As he locked up, she cradled the vase against her chest and frowned at the stiff line of his back. "What was Allison's favorite flower?"

"How should I know?" he grumbled, checking the handle to make sure it was locked. Shoving his keys in his pocket, he stalked back to her Mercedes.

"You can't expect me to believe that you never bought your sister flowers," she retorted.

It wasn't until she'd fit the base of the vase in the cup

holder between the driver and passenger seats that he spoke again.

"Orchids."

She fastened her seat belt and paused, then started the car. "What?"

"Allison liked orchids," he said again, his expression flat as he stared out the windshield. "Not that I know why. They're fussy. She was the opposite of fussy. I got her these blue and purple ones once. She cried when she had to throw them out."

Laura was happy she'd taken the flowers from Allison's. She couldn't think about them falling to the countertop one petal at a time. Methodically, she shifted the Mercedes into Reverse. "Let me know when you decide the funeral should be."

"Why?" he asked.

She set her jaw, watching the backup camera and turning the wheel as the Mercedes reversed onto the street. She could be stubborn, too. "If you won't accept my family's help with the service, you can expect several dozen orchids to grace the proceedings."

Noah thought about it. Then he bit off a laugh. "Before this is all over," he contemplated as she pointed the vehicle toward Mariposa, "you're going to drive me crazy."

She mashed the accelerator to the floor and watched the needle on the speedometer climb. "The feeling's mutual."

## Chapter 9

Bungalow Fifteen had every amenity Noah didn't need. The decor was tasteful and minimal. He could have eaten off the bamboo floors. Fresh flowers populated surfaces and there were no paintings here either. Just lots and lots of windows framing more showstopping views of Arizona. The bathroom off the bedroom had given him a moment of pause with its plush, all-white linens, marble tub and glass walk-in shower. On the back deck, there was a hot tub.

What Bungalow Fifteen lacked was a murder board.

So the coffee table in the living room had become Noah's work area. There, he'd arranged maps of the resort, lists of names, including staff and guests from the time of Allison's murder, pictures of the discovery scene at the pool cabana, Allison's notebook, and the schedule Laura had pulled from her fridge.

On the couch, folders were open to the Coltons' history. The section on the patriarch, Clive Colton, was doubly thick.

One manila folder lay closed. Inside lurked pictures of Allison's body at the pool cabana and others from the morgue, close-ups of the entry wound from a needle and abrasion marks on the backs of her legs.

She hadn't died in the pool cabana. The killer had drugged

her at an unknown location and then transported her to a public place that would appear less incriminating.

Was Allison aware when the needle had gone in? Was she afraid? Or had she simply floated away like the dandelion tufts she often picked from the cracks in the sidewalk and blew into the wind?

Noah locked down that train of thought as the ache inside him let out a train-whistle scream. He avoided looking at the photos unless absolutely necessary.

He picked up the list of names, culling members of staff, crossing off those he'd been able to pin down alibis for with a few well-placed phone calls. Most people had been at home in Sedona. The exceptions were, of course, those who lived on property—Tallulah Deschine and the Coltons.

The tip of Noah's pen hovered over Laura's name. He wanted to strike her from the list of possibles. He knew on a primal level she had been precisely where she had told Fulton she was during the interview process—alone at home in bed.

But the cop in him wouldn't allow it. Not because he doubted her innocence. Because striking anyone from a list of suspects was impossible without corroboration. The only witness to Laura's activities during the time frame of Allison's murder was the tabby cat, Sebastian.

Noah would have sat the feline down and questioned him if he could have.

Tallulah, Adam and Joshua were still on the list, too. All claimed to have been in bed, sleeping, according to Fulton's notes. Knox Burnett, the horseback adventure guide who had tried to revive Allison the morning her body was discovered in the pool cabana, hadn't been able to confirm his whereabouts in the wee hours of the morning. He had also taken several days off from his work at Mariposa, claiming emotional distress.

Noah had cleared the concierge, Alexis Reed, whose neighbors had seen her arrive home around dinnertime that evening and whose car hadn't left her driveway until sunrise. But he hadn't crossed off Erica Pike, the executive assistant whose whereabouts hadn't been as easy to establish.

Between security, housekeeping, maintenance, transportation, the spa, gym, restaurant, bar, stable and front desk, there were one hundred staff members at Mariposa. There could also be one hundred guests if the bungalows were booked solid.

They hadn't been, he noted, the day the murder took place. February was supposedly the calm before the storm of the long hospitality season that stretched from March to October. Still, the chill and intermittent snow flurries hadn't deterred everyone. Seventy-two guests had been booked at Mariposa for the week the crime had taken place. With some legwork, Noah had obtained some alibis there as well.

This left less than two dozen possibles on his short list.

Noah rubbed his chin, reading the four names he had circled. There were more questions around these names than others—like actor CJ Knight. Knight had checked out ahead of schedule the morning Allison was discovered in the pool cabana. Noah's calls to his manager, Doug DeGraw, had been pointedly ignored.

He eyed his notes where he'd cross-checked possible suspects with those who had attended Allison's meditation or yoga classes. There were fewer names on the list he'd cross-referenced with the late-night stargazing excursions she had tagged along on.

The bracelet she had given him lay among the maps,

photos and notes. The evil eye stared at him baldly. He'd searched the pool cabana. It had been swept already by crime scene technicians, and the police tape had come down, clearing it for use. Noah had found nothing in or around the area they had missed.

He lamented the absence of security cameras. The pool area was along a major thoroughfare. CCTV could have easily picked something up if the Coltons weren't so concerned with the discretion of their overclassed clientele.

A knock made him drop the sheet of paper in his hand. He felt the weight of his off-duty gun on his belt. Rising, he grabbed the leather jacket from the back of a chair and swung it on as he approached the door.

Peering through the peephole, he scanned the two people on his doormat. His teeth gritted. Trying to relax his shoulders, he did his best to cast off the pall of tension that shadowed him everywhere. He snatched open the door and fixed what he hoped was a devil-may-care grin on his face—something befitting a rock-and-roll guitarist.

Adam and Joshua Colton may have shared similar heights, builds and coloring. But they couldn't be more different. Adam stood as high and straight as a redwood. No trace of a smile touched his mouth.

On the flip side, Joshua grinned widely, a sly twist teasing one corner of his mouth higher than the other. His hair was longer than his brother's and carelessly wind-tossed. While Adam's eyes injured, Joshua's practically twinkled. "Hey, Fender Bender!" he greeted Noah, earning a groan from Lurch at his side.

Whether it was because Joshua's enthusiasm reminded him of Allison's or because his ready familiarity with Noah made Adam uncomfortable, Noah felt a strong chord of amusement. "Fender Bender?"

Joshua lifted a shoulder. "Adam told me not to lead with 'Motherplucker.'"

A choked laugh hit Noah's throat. He covered it with a cough as Adam cast a disparaging look over at his brother. The elder Colton shifted his weight and attempted to start over. "We're going for a morning run."

"Okay," Noah said uncertainly.

"You should come with us," Joshua suggested.

"Or not," Adam dropped in. "I'm sure you're booked."

Joshua nodding knowingly. "With Laura."

Adam shifted gears fast. "You're coming with us, Steele. No ifs, ands or buts about it."

"Pretty please," Joshua added, posthaste.

Noah lifted a brow. He glanced at his jeans. "You know, I'm not really dressed for—"

"We'll wait," Adam inserted.

When Joshua moved forward, Noah stiffened. He wouldn't have time to hide the mess on the coffee table. "Ah… It won't take long for me to get changed."

Joshua's smile turned stilted. "What're you hiding in there, Keith Richards?" He craned his neck to get a look. "Burned spoons? Coke? Heroin? Women?"

On the last word, the younger Colton's voice dropped to a dangerous bass. Noah would've been offended if he wasn't so impressed by the hard gleam in his eyes. He tried to laugh it off. "None of the above," he said. "I just don't want it to get back to Laura that I'm a slob."

Joshua lifted his chin slightly. "Sure. We'll wait."

"Just a minute." He shut the door and shrugged off the jacket, cursing viciously. Throwing it over the back of the chair, he then unlaced his boots. In the bedroom, he removed the gun holster and tucked it safely under the mattress.

Quickly, he exchanged the jeans he wore for an old pair of sweatpants. He left on the 1969 Johnny Cash San Quentin State Prison T-shirt and grabbed the sneakers he'd stuffed in his duffel as an afterthought. Happy for the foresight, he scrubbed the back of his hand over his bearded jaw, left his jacket on the chair and opened the door to find the Coltons waiting with varied levels of patience.

Stuffing his bungalow key card into the pocket of his sweats, he injected a hint of nerves into his voice as he asked, "You two are going to go easy on me, right? Being on the road doesn't leave a lot of time for exercise."

Joshua and Adam traded a glance as they led the way up the path. "Sure thing," Joshua replied before he broke into a jog, getting a head start.

Noah caught up with Adam and muttered, "Thanks for your help back there."

"You want Josh's trust," Adam retorted, "earn it yourself."

Adam pulled ahead, trailing behind his brother. Noah was forced to kick it into gear. A cloud of warm air plumed from his mouth as the cold slapped his face.

He kept up with them just fine, even as the path turned rough around the edges and the bungalows fell behind. They passed signs for a trailhead. The path declined, forked, inclined, forked, declined and inclined again. Caution signs zipped past, as well as guardrails looking out over long drops.

They reached a high point and Adam and Joshua let up finally. Adam doubled over, holding his hamstring while Joshua paced, panting.

Noah tried not to grope for the trunk of a nearby shrub tree. He liked to think he was in good shape, but he sipped air that felt thin. They'd pushed him, either to test his mettle or as some kind of Colton initiation rite.

They would need to work harder to throw him off the scent, he thought with a lick of triumph as he caught Adam's wince. "Is this the halfway point?" he called out.

Joshua spared him a look over his shoulder. "This is as far as we go, Steele."

No more "Fender Bender." Not even a "motherplucker." Noah circled, swept up in the panorama. "Hell," he whispered, impressed. He could understand why people paid thousands of dollars to stay at Mariposa. The state parks were littered with people. To find a solitary hike these days, a person had to wander off the map.

Here, there didn't seem to be anyone around for miles. The quiet struck him. He raised his face to the sun. No wonder Allison had been in love with this place.

*I get it now*, he told that part of his mind that still felt connected to her somehow.

Another thought struck him. He'd been lured away from other guests with only Laura's brothers for company. He eyed the long tumble of rocks down to the bottom of the hill. "Is this where you kill me?"

A laugh left Adam. It sounded grim. "I wish."

*At least big brother's honest*, Noah mused.

Joshua turned on him, hands pressed into his hips. "What do you want with Laura?"

The question shouldn't have caught him off guard. He'd have done this, too, had Allison brought a man around to meet him. He searched his mind.

And found that some part of him could answer the question. Something inside his chest that had cracked like an oyster.

What did he want with Laura?

*Everything.*

No, he schooled himself. That wasn't the right answer. That couldn't be the answer at all. He didn't want anything from Laura.

Except her mouth. Her smile—the real one he found so elusive. Laughter he'd never heard. Her banter. Hell, even her rebuttals.

He wanted her hands, he thought, unbidden. Soft, clean, manicured fingers tangled up in his, spreading through his hair...

He shifted when that image alone turned him on. Shifting away from the Colton men, he put some distance between them and him. He didn't think they would be amused if they saw what the simple thought of their sister did to him.

Joshua didn't let up. "Answer the question."

Noah thought about it, vying for an appropriate response that would appease them both. What came out was "I want her to know she's safe."

"Of course she's safe," Adam snapped at his back. "Mariposa's safer than anywhere else."

Noah whirled on him. "Is that right?"

The light of challenge died in Adam's eyes.

"Would I be here if she felt safe?" Noah pressed.

Joshua shook his head. "I'm not sure how you could make her feel any safer than Adam and I can."

"Someone was murdered under your noses," Noah pointed out. "Someone she cared about."

"She blames herself," Adam mumbled.

"Allison's death had nothing to do with Laura," Joshua said.

"How do you know?" Noah asked. "How do you know she's not the next target?"

Both men froze. Noah struggled against the need to press further, to question them more about Allison. But Laura had warned him not to give himself away to Joshua if he could help it.

If Joshua did have loose lips, then Noah's cover would be blown before he could avenge Allison. "She needs me," he said and wondered if it was true, because he knew all too well that the next part was. "I can't let her do this alone."

Adam and Joshua remained studiously silent. After a few minutes, Joshua stretched for the return run.

It wasn't until Joshua had started back for the trailhead that Adam spoke up again. "Allison gave private lessons to some guests."

Noah nearly skidded on a patch of ice. "Why didn't you mention it before?"

Adam chose not to answer that. Instead he told him, "She'd go to them."

"Their bungalows," Noah muttered.

"Yes," Adam replied. "When she came to me with the idea, I advised against it. Our goal is to keep the staff presence to an absolute minimum, in and around the bungalows. Maintenance crews and Housekeeping don't go there unless a guest has a spa treatment or excursion scheduled. All requests are seen to personally by the concierge."

"You asked her not to do it?"

"Allison has a way of talking you into things." Adam grimaced. "Sorry—she *had* a way. I told her she could start taking on a handful of private lessons at a time, as a trial run. If everything went well, she could take on more in the spring."

"Do you know which guests signed up?" Noah asked. "Do you know which ones had private lessons scheduled during the week she was murdered?"

"I don't know their names," Adam explained. "I just know she had three signed up during that time, two she taught that same day. She was excited. She enjoyed helping people, whether it was in a group setting or one-to-one." Adam cursed under his breath. "Did she die because I gave in—because I let her go into people's bungalows against my better judgment?"

If the private lessons had led to Allison's undoing, what were the three names on her exclusive list?

# Chapter 10

Laura hurried toward the front desk. A raised voice had brought the lobby to a standstill and one of the front desk clerks seemed to shrink before a painfully thin platinum blonde whose designer handbag swung in a threatening motion. "I don't want Bungalow Eighteen! My husband and I always stay in Bungalow Three! My last name is Colton, too, you know!"

At Laura's side, Roland spoke briskly. "I'm sorry, Ms. Colton. The guard at the gate didn't realize who she was until she was past the checkpoint."

"It's all right, Roland," Laura assured him. Someone needed to rescue poor Clarissa from her stepmother's rant. She picked up the pace to intercept.

"I can escort her out."

"No, that will just make things worse." Laura had never known her stepmother to visit without Clive or to make a scene. But she knew the indicators of escalation. She could feel the open curiosity and horror from people gathered around. "I can handle this."

Alexis breezed in, planting herself behind the desk in front of Clarissa. "Ms. Colton," she greeted Glenna smoothly. "How very nice to see you again."

"Don't patronize me," Glenna snapped. "I've been on a plane for two hours. I want my bungalow!"

"Clarissa has informed you that Bungalow Three is currently occupied," Alexis informed her. "If you had called ahead, we could have told you it wasn't available."

"I don't care that it's not available—"

"Ms. Colton, reservations are required for Mariposa's bungalows," Alexis went on. "We need at least six weeks to see to personal requests. This is a five-star resort. Not a fly-by-night motel. Because you showed up without prior notice, you will enjoy all the amenities Mariposa offers with a complimentary spa package from the comfort of Bungalow Eighteen or I can call Sedona's Hampton Inn. I'm sure they'll be happy to give you their best room."

Glenna bristled. She hissed. But Laura saw the handbag droop as her arm dropped. "I see I've been painted into a corner."

"No, ma'am," Alexis said, her incisive gaze not leaving Glenna as Clarissa handed her the welcome package, complete with key card and spa vouchers. "Our policy is bungalow by reservation only. Anyone who behaves as you have is normally showed the door. And yet *you* are getting a key card and a free massage from Arizona's very best masseur." She thrust the envelope at Glenna. "We hope you enjoy your stay at Mariposa, Ms. Colton. If you need anything further, my name is Alexis Reed. I'll be your concierge. My number's in the packet. Please, *do* call me."

Glenna took the envelope slowly, as if afraid the thing contained anthrax. She tossed her hair over her shoulder and strutted out the entry doors, no doubt to hail one of the golf cart operators to take her to her assigned bungalow.

People roamed the lobby freely again, and Laura approached

the front desk. She caught Alexis's eye and mouthed, *You are my hero.*

Alexis lifted both hands in a prayer pose and tipped her chin down.

"Drinks on me at L Bar tonight," Laura told her.

Prayer pose turned into a discreet fist pump. Alexis stopped when the next check-in appointment came forward. Brushing Clarissa out of the way, she said, "Take five. I'll handle this."

"Thank you," Clarissa breathed and practically fled. She looked at Laura. "I'm sorry, Ms. Colton. She just started yelling. I didn't know what to do."

"It's all right," Laura assured her. "Go to the break room. Brew a cup of tea. I believe Tallulah left a dish of brownies for everyone there. Come back in half an hour. I'll help Alexis and Sasha cover the front desk."

Clarissa lit up. "Thank you so much! I was doing the meditation classes with Allison. Since something happened to her, I've been out of sorts…"

"I know exactly what you mean," Laura said. "This has been a difficult time for everyone."

"People keep asking for yoga classes. I just keep handing them spa vouchers."

"That's the best we can do for now," Laura reminded her.

"Any idea when a new yoga teacher is coming?"

Distress trickled down Laura's spine. She hadn't given a thought to hiring anyone else. It would be her responsibility to do so. "Not at this time."

Clarissa nodded solemnly. "I'll be back in thirty minutes, on the dot."

As Clarissa speed-walked out of L Building, Laura pressed her hand to her stomach. The idea of putting out the call for a new yoga instructor, conducting interviews and placing genuine effort into finding a replacement for Allison made her feel sick.

Roland took her elbow. "Are you all right, Ms. Colton?"

She gave him a tight nod. "Sure. Please let me know if Glenna makes any more waves."

"Will do," he agreed. "I'm going into a briefing with Adam. Should I tell him she's arrived?"

"Yes," she said. "The snow's melted off, so Josh is directing Jeep tours. He'll be off property for the better part of the day. I'll text him and warn him before he returns."

Roland walked toward the offices but snapped his fingers and backtracked. "I've got something for you."

"Oh?" Intrigued, she watched him dig a folded piece of paper out of his pocket. "What's this?"

"I ran into your friend Mr. Steele out by the stable earlier," he revealed. "He said he was looking for you."

Laura thought quickly, her fingers tightening reflexively around the note. "I did tell him to meet me there. I suppose I forgot."

"I wouldn't worry about it," Roland returned consolingly. "He was friendly enough."

Laura tried not to laugh at Noah being referred to as "friendly."

"He gave you this?"

"Yeah. He said he knows how busy you are. He knew I'd be seeing you, so he wanted me to pass along a message."

"Thank you, Roland," Laura said. When he nodded and walked away, Laura unfolded the small slip of paper and stared at the tidy, slightly slanted handwriting.

*Pearl,*
*I missed you. There's a new gelding here you need to check out. He's calm and sweet, like you. His name's*

*Hero if you're still interested in getting back on the horse. If you're not busy later, meet me at L Bar at six. I'll have a martini waiting.*
*Yours,*
*Noah*

Laura lingered on the closing. *Yours.* She felt herself soften again.

The note hadn't been sealed, which meant Roland could have easily read it. Noah would have guessed that. That was why he'd used the nickname he'd picked for her. Was that why he had invited her to drinks this evening? Or why he'd said such sweet things about the new gelding's nature and her own?

She folded the note again, trying to shove the questions into a drawer. What she couldn't ignore was how the written words had made the waves of sickness she'd felt moments before ease.

She made a mental note to drop by both Glenna's bungalow for a chat and L Bar for a date.

L Bar hummed with activity. Still, the atmosphere felt comfortably intimate. Patrons hovered around high-topped tables or the long bar where the personable bartender, Valerie, built drafts and mixed cocktails.

"You're Laura Colton's man," she guessed when he introduced himself.

"I am," he said.

"How'd you manage that?"

He chuckled because she meant it more as a ribbing than an insult. And she had a point. "Beats the hell out of me."

"Is she joining you tonight?" Valerie asked.

"I hope so," he said, looking at the doors—as if he couldn't wait for Laura's arrival.

Who was he kidding? He'd glanced toward the doors half a dozen times already. "She'll have a martini, dry. I'll have a Corona and lime."

"Coming right up," she said as she built his beer. "You arrived just in time, if you ask me. The boss doesn't burn the candle at both ends. She's too smart for that. But word is, she's broken up about what happened."

"You're right." He tried to think how to broach the subject without drawing eavesdroppers into the conversation. "You never forget the shock when something happens like that. I lost a friend of mine a few years back. It's tough."

Valerie passed the beer to him. She grabbed a cocktail shaker for Laura's martini. "I don't think anyone who knew Allison will get over it."

Noah folded his arms on the bar. He allowed his shoulders to droop over them. "I don't think anyone ever really gets over it. I'll never forget what I was doing when I heard the news about my buddy."

"I won't forget either," Valerie replied. "I closed the bar that night same as always. It was close to the weekend, so it was open later than it is on weekdays. My roommate woke me up the next morning with a phone call from Laura. That's who hired me and everybody else. If there's a staff bulletin, she makes sure everyone knows about it. Even those of us who aren't scheduled to come in until later. That must've made things harder for her—having to call around and deliver the news to all the staff."

Noah nodded. He made a mental note to track down Valerie's roommate and confirm that she had been home around the time of Allison's death.

"I'm glad she has someone," Valerie mentioned as she

poured the cocktail into a martini glass. She topped it with an olive. "You're a real sweetheart for being there for her."

He flashed a smile. "Wouldn't have it any other way."

"Is your band coming to Arizona soon?" Valerie asked. "I'd like to check it out."

"I'll have to check our schedule," he said. "We're taking a break right now. We've been touring for a while."

"Enjoy it while you can," she advised. "Nobody knows more about burning the candle at both ends like a genuine rock-and-roll superstar."

"I'm no superstar," he said.

Valerie leaned toward him over the bar, lowering her voice. "Her stepmother showed up this afternoon."

He searched his memory files for a name. "Glenna?"

"That's the one. Made quite a scene at the front desk. I hear there's trouble with her father, too. She and her brothers turned down his request for a loan. Now he may be out for blood."

Lifting the beer to his mouth, he made a noncommittal sound.

"That's how the old man operates, from what I understand," Valerie said, easing back with a shrug. "He never gave a hoot for his kids. But when the chips are down…"

"How else do you expect an eel to operate?" Noah groaned.

Valerie laughed. "Hey, it was nice to meet you."

He dipped his head. "Nice to meet you, too." Backing away with the drinks, he let her move on to the next customer. He saw the empty table in the back corner and made a beeline for it.

Laura arrived moments later in another fur-trimmed jacket—this one camel-colored. It looked as soft as he knew her skin to be. The hem floated around her knees. She stopped to speak to Valerie for a moment, then let a guest snag her attention. She passed around smiles and assurances in a manner any PR representative would have admired.

The smile didn't dim when she found him lurking at the back table. "I'm behind schedule," she said when she reached him. "I apologize."

"No need," he said, standing to take her coat as she slipped it from her shoulders.

Her bare shoulders. *Christ*, he thought, seeing the delicate ledge of her clavicle on display above the off-the-shoulder blouse. Every lover-like thing he could have said seemed too real. Too sincere.

*You're a knockout...*

*I am the envy of every man in this room...*

*What the hell are you doing with me, Pearl?*

He held out her chair for her. When she settled, smoothing the pleat of the sunshine-yellow linen slacks she wore, he draped her jacket on the chair behind her. And, because this was L Bar—because he could feel every Tom, Dick, Harry and Valerie watching—he took her shoulders.

She turned her head slightly, and he felt her spine straighten.

He told himself it was all for show as he dropped his mouth to her ear. "I'd've waited," he murmured for her. "I'd've waited all goddamn night for you, Colton." Even as he chastised himself for being a moonstruck moron, he closed his lips over the perfumed place beneath her lobe.

She tilted her head. Not to shy away. He knew it when she released an infinitesimal sigh, when her pulse fluttered against the brush of his mouth as he lingered, sipping her skin like a hummingbird. He cupped the other side of her face as she presented him with the regal column of her throat.

Her shiver pulled him back. It roped him to the present,

to what was real and what wasn't. He wrenched himself away, watching his hands slide from her skin. "You're better at this game than I am," he muttered before slinking off to his chair where he belonged.

She watched him as he set the martini in front of her and tipped the beer up. It took her several minutes to taste her drink, sipping in a ladylike fashion that drove him to distraction.

"What kept you?" he wondered aloud.

She set the glass down without a sound. "My stepmother arrived unexpectedly this afternoon and was disgruntled when she didn't receive the VIP treatment she thought she deserved."

"It fell to you to unruffle her feathers?" he asked. "Don't you have enough to handle?"

"Glenna's family," she said cautiously. "At first, I thought their marriage was more business than anything. Her and Clive's courtship happened swiftly. Before we knew it, they were married. But I know Glenna takes care of him. He's getting older. When they married, I won't lie and say I wasn't relieved."

"Because that meant he was no longer your responsibility."

She winced. "Does that make me callous?"

"Not if the rumors about Clive Colton are true," he said. "Not if he only comes to you and your brothers for money."

Her gaze riveted to his. "How do you know about that?"

"I've spoken to over half your staff over the last few days," he reminded her. "While they respect you, Adam and Joshua, they talk."

She looked away, noting those at the surrounding tables. In a self-conscious move, she ran her fingers through her straight-line bob.

He wanted to tell her how surprised he'd been by the loyalty of her employees—how the ones who knew about Clive's recent visit to Mariposa had sided with the siblings, bar none. Not one disparaging word had been spoken about Adam, Laura or Joshua. Noah knew that had nothing to do with the nondisclosure documents everyone had signed and everything to do with how Mariposa was run, how staff were treated, and how devoted the Coltons were to the resort and the people who worked for them.

She wasn't the princess of Mariposa; she was the queen, and her subjects loved her dearly.

She sighed. "I just want to know why she showed up without warning. Why she came alone. Her behavior is outside the realm of anything I've seen."

"Breaks in patterns of behavior are tells," he advised. "Dig deeper and you'll find a motive."

"Have you made any headway in the investigation?"

"I have a short list of people with no alibis."

"Who?"

He tried dousing the question with a warning look.

She braced one elbow on the table's edge, rested her chin on her hand and leaned in. From the outside, it looked intimate. Especially when her eyes roved the seam of his mouth. "Are we still in this together, Noah?" she murmured.

He, too, leaned in, setting both arms on the table. He hunched his shoulders toward the point of hers. Wanting to rattle her chain as much as she was rattling him tonight, he dipped his gaze first over her smooth throat. Then lower to the straight line of her bodice. For a split second, he wondered what was keeping it in place. The curves of her breasts were visible, and she wore no necklaces to detract from the display. The effect made him lightheaded, slightly giddy. Did L Bar have an antigravity switch?

His gaze roamed back to hers and latched on. He was half-wild with need. The effort to steer his mind back to the investigation and Allison felt arduous.

Frustration flooded him, anger nipping at its heels. *Damn it.* It shouldn't be this easy to make him forget why he was there. "Why didn't you tell me Allison was giving private lessons to guests in their bungalows?"

Her eyes widened. "She…what?"

"I thought you were her friend," he hissed. "You say you knew her. How could you not have known what she was doing?"

Laura's lips parted. "She didn't tell me."

"I'm supposed to believe that?"

Her eyes heated. "Do you really think so little of me?"

"Adam knew."

She gripped the stem of the martini glass. "Why did neither of them think to involve me?"

"You'll have to take that up with your brother. He said she had three clients the week of her death, two the day she died. I need to know who they were."

"I don't have that information," she said coolly, pulling away from him. "You didn't answer my question."

She'd asked about his list of suspects. "You won't like it."

"It's a little late to spare my feelings," she informed him.

Remorse chased off his anger. He fell prey to so many mixed emotions around her, and it floored him. He'd never known anyone who could make him *feel* like this.

"Tallulah," he said.

She laughed shortly, without humor. "If she's at the top of your list, you're reaching."

"Erica Pike," he continued. "Knox Burnett. Adam. Joshua. You."

Laura stiffened. "Me?"

"You don't have an alibi for the time in question," he said. "Not one anyone can corroborate. I can't cross you or the others off my list until you give me one."

"I'm a suspect." On the outside, she was all ice. "This may be the worst date I've ever had."

"It's not personal, Laura."

"No," she agreed. "You've made that very clear. Haven't you? And it's surprising."

"What is?"

"That a guy like you can be so by the book."

He felt a muscle in his jaw flex. "A guy like me?" he repeated.

"You don't really think I hurt her," she said.

"No, I don't thi—" Fumbling, he course-corrected quickly. "That's not the—"

"You don't really think my brothers killed Allison either," she surmised.

He caught his teeth gnashing together and stopped them before he ground his molars down to the roots. "It doesn't matter what I think. I go where the facts are."

"Speculation figures into detective work," she said. "I've read enough true crime to know that. What would be Adam or Josh's reason for drugging our yoga instructor? For that matter, why would Tallulah or Erica do such a thing?"

"I don't have motive," he said. "Just a list of people who claim to be sleeping at the time of her death."

"You've ruled guests out?"

"No," he said. He tossed a look toward a man in an open-collared shirt who was lifting a glass of whiskey in a toast to Valerie. "Roger Ferraday doesn't seem to know where he was or what he was doing during the night in question. As it sits, he's Fulton's chief suspect."

"Ferraday," Laura said numbly. "He's staying here with his teenage son, Dayton."

"Who has a list of hushed-up misdemeanors back home in Hartford," Noah revealed, tipping his beer to his mouth to drain the glass.

"He's fifteen," she said.

"Doesn't make him or Daddy innocent," Noah told her. "I'm also taking a look at CJ Knight."

Her gaze pinged to his, alarmed.

He narrowed his eyes. "Does that name ring a bell?"

"Yes," she said. "He left the morning Allison's body was discovered. We haven't been able to reach his manager to find out why."

"DeGraw won't return my calls either."

"CJ Knight was one of Allison's repeat students," she whispered. "And I understand he has Bungalow One booked again after Valentine's Day."

"Think he'll show up?"

"I can't say at this point."

"If he keeps his booking, I want to know the second he checks in."

She rubbed her hand over her arm, discomfited. "I don't know how you do this—look at everyone…every person without an alibi and peel back the layers to see which one of them has murder written on their heart."

"With some people, it doesn't leave a mark," he said. "For some people, killing is in their nature."

"God," she said with a shiver.

"There are those, too, who don't seek to harm others," he said. "They start small and escalate. Or they claim it was an accident. Throw in the occasional plea of insanity."

"It must do something to you," she said, "to do this every day. To look at the dead."

"You get used to it."

"Do you ever have trouble sleeping?"

*All the time*, he thought. He didn't grimace, but it was a near thing. "Somebody's got to speak for them. The victims. Somebody's got to fight for them."

Her expression softened at long last. "My brothers took you running this morning."

He rolled his eyes. "If that's how they treat all your suitors, I'm starting to understand how so many dickheads slipped through the cracks."

"Meaning?"

"Meaning if they wanted to warn someone off, they wouldn't do it at first light. They'd do it at night. They'd rustle them out of bed, blindfold them and drop them off in the middle of the desert. See if they can make it back on their own before daybreak."

"Why does it sound like you've done this before?"

"I plead the Fifth."

"Is this why none of Allison's boyfriends ever lasted all that long?" she asked.

Before he could answer, he spotted Alexis cutting through the crowd. "I think your friend's looking for you."

Laura turned and waved. "I wasn't sure if you'd join us," she said. "I'll fetch a glass of white for you."

"Not just yet," Alexis said. She placed her hand on Laura's. "We have a situation."

Laura's smile dropped like a stone. "What kind of situation?"

"There's been a leak," Alexis answered. "There's a van from the local news station at the gate and the front desk is getting calls. It's about Allison."

Laura rose quickly. "Does Adam know?"

"Yes," Alexis said. "He's waiting in his office."

"Tell Roland to delay the news crew at the gate as long as possible while Adam and I reassess," she said. "We'll need at least ten minutes to shift into damage-control mode."

"I'm on it," Alexis assured her. "Who could have done this? Who would have talked to the press?"

Laura shifted her eyes to Noah.

He understood the question she was asking. "Leave it with me."

She nodded shortly. "I have to go."

"Go," he urged. When she leaned in, he did the unthinkable. She'd meant her pursed lips to skim his bearded cheek. He turned his head automatically and caught the kiss on the mouth.

Her hand gripped his arm. Her fingers dug through his sleeve.

Again, he didn't think. If he had, he wouldn't have opened his mouth. Her eyes watched his. He didn't close his either as he grazed his teeth lightly over her round bottom lip.

A noise escaped her. He pulled back. The heat refused to bank. His heart racked his ribs.

She stared at him, as shocked as he was.

Did she feel the heat, too?

Alexis said her name. Laura blinked. She backed away from him, turned, and followed Alexis to the doors and out.

He caught the curious looks he'd earned from those around him. Turning away, he saw the jacket Laura had left on the back of her chair.

Noah dug the cash out of his pocket, dropped it on the table, gathered the coat and left to fade into the night.

# Chapter 11

"Why are you here?"

Noah ignored Fulton as he escorted his guest into the station. She'd fought the cuffs like a wet cat. As she bristled against his lead, he warned, "People get tossed into lockup for fighting custody, sweetheart. I'd calm down if I were you."

Glenna Colton twitched in indignation. "You're hurting me!"

"I'm not," he said firmly, guiding her toward the back of the Sedona station, where the interrogation rooms were located.

"I want my lawyer!"

"You're entitled to a representative during questioning," he acknowledged. "You'll need one when this is all over."

"I still don't understand what I'm being charged with," she said.

"Assaulting a police officer, for one," Noah said, knocking on the door of Interview Room 1. When no one answered, he opened it and poked his head in. The room was clear. He maneuvered her inside. "Sit down, be a good girl, and we'll see about getting the cuffs off."

She sneered at him. "I get a phone call. I *want* my phone call."

"In a minute, Veruca," he said.

No sooner had he shut the door behind him than he heard, "Steele!"

Noah stopped, gritted his teeth, then turned to face his superior office. "Sir."

Captain Jim Crabtree, a weathered barrel of a man with twenty-plus years on the force, bore down on him. "Aren't you supposed to be on personal leave?" he asked. "Who is this woman?"

Fulton peered through the blinds of the interview room and cursed a stream. "That's Glenna Bennett Colton. Wife to Clive Colton. His children own Mariposa Resort & Spa."

Crabtree spoke in a steely, quiet manner that wasn't any less threatening than the sound of his yelling. "We went over this. You asked if you could approach Mariposa. You asked me for my permission to investigate your sister's death and I told you it's against departmental procedure."

"Yes, sir," Noah said.

"You are *not* about to tell me you picked this woman up on the streets of Sedona," Crabtree warned.

"No, sir."

A knowing gleam entered Crabtree's dark eyes. "How long have you been poking around the resort?"

Noah pressed his lips together. He respected the hell out of Crabtree and couldn't lie. "Several days."

Fulton let out a disgruntled noise. It was cut off by Crabtree. "You went against orders. That makes you eligible for administrative leave. I could send you before the review board."

*Hell.* He couldn't lose his badge. Not with Allison's killer on the loose.

Not when being a homicide detective was the only job that had ever made sense to him. It was the only box he'd ever fit in. "Respectfully, sir, I'm asking you not to do that."

"Give me one reason I shouldn't."

Noah caught Fulton's fulminating stare and wasn't cowed in the least. "I've been operating at Mariposa on and off for the last week without the primary investigator any the wiser."

"Jesus, Steele," Fulton tossed out. "You're a son of a bitch. You know that?"

"Also," Noah said, moving on, "with the help and permission of the Colton family, I've been operating undercover. People don't see a cop walking around. They see the man staying in Bungalow Fifteen. Laura Colton's boyfriend."

"How the hell did he pull that off?" another detective, Ratliff, muttered behind him. General assent went up through the ranks of watching cops.

"I have a short list of suspects and inside access to guest quarters and staff buildings," Noah continued. "I've built a rapport with regulars and employees alike, and I'm looking at a handful of people who were close to Allison while Fulton fights for crumbs from the table. If you pull me out now, we lose our best chance of tying up this case."

"You expect me to believe you can think clearly— objectively—when your sister's the victim?" Crabtree challenged.

"I know how to do my job," Noah said. "I've got the best closure rate in my division."

"Yes," Crabtree granted. "But she was your family."

"I'm going to close this case," Noah informed him, "just as I've closed dozens of cases before hers."

"I don't need a loose cannon on my hands," Crabtree warned. "If you find her killer, how do I know you won't take matters into your own hands?"

It was a fair question, one Noah had asked himself a

dozen times. When he found the man or woman who'd killed Allison…when he looked them in the eye at last… would he be able to follow procedure? Was his belief in due process strong enough when confronted with the person who'd squashed what was most precious to him?

Noah took a breath. "I won't let you down, Captain."

Crabtree stared him down. "When you're ready to make an arrest, bring Fulton in and let him handle it. Do not approach the suspect. If you so much as touch them, Steele—"

A muscle in Noah's jaw twitched in protest, but he made himself answer. "Yes, sir."

"Now explain to me why the Coltons' stepmother is in interrogation," Crabtree demanded.

"I believe she's responsible for the news leak at Mariposa," Noah said. "When I approached her with evidence, she swung at me. I cuffed her and brought her in for booking."

"Did anyone see you do this?"

"No. My cover's still in place."

Crabtree nodded in Fulton's direction. "Fulton will take care of it. Either go home and clear your head or go back to Mariposa and find me an actual suspect."

"Yes, sir." Noah subsided and let Fulton pass into Interview Room 1 to finish his job.

"It was Glenna?" Laura asked. "She leaked Allison's homicide?"

Noah nodded. "The timing was right. From there, it was just a matter of pressing the right buttons. Once cornered, she didn't hold back."

"She always seemed so even-tempered," Laura said, struggling to understand. "Why would she do this?"

"You can't think of any reason?" Adam asked from behind his desk. "We had Security watching the gates for Clive."

Her lips parted in surprise. "So he snuck Glenna in here under our noses to cause trouble on his behalf?"

"She said something as I was hauling her in," Noah added. "She said her husband would get what he wants, and Mariposa only exists because he allows it to."

"That's inaccurate," Adam said mildly.

Laura's brow furrowed. "Roland asked me if he should escort her out when she made a scene in the lobby. I should've let him. Valentine's Day is this weekend. I should've thought about the wedding party coming in. Once the families hear about the murder…"

"They signed a contract," Adam assured her. "If they cancel, they'll pay the cancellation fee."

"If that wedding falls through, then who's saying the next one won't?"

"How long will Glenna be detained at the SPD?" Adam asked Noah.

"She wasn't just booked on assaulting an officer," Noah said. "You and Fulton had an understanding that the investigation would be kept quiet to aid in the search for the killer. By leaking it to the press, Glenna interfered in a police investigation. Her lawyer's there now, doing his song and dance. She'll likely be released on bail tomorrow morning. But she won't get away scot-free. She's facing charges."

"And she's going to be angry," Laura pointed out.

Adam rolled his pen between his fingers. "We might as well have poked a beehive."

Laura felt tired just thinking about it. "You have to finish this," she told Noah. "You have to find who did this and get them away from the resort."

"I will."

For once, he didn't argue. The little ship in a bottle she carried inside her anchored up to his strength. It was a port in this storm. "We're running out of time."

"So am I," he said. "My CO found out what I'm doing. He's not wild about it."

"You're not leaving."

His eyes didn't stray from her. "I'm not going anywhere."

The assertion made her feel lighter, if only for a moment. She thought things over, picking through the cluttered mess in her mind. She sought something…anything they'd overlooked. "The schedule from Allison's fridge. Do you still have it?"

"It's at my bungalow. Why?"

She faced Adam. "You said Allison had taken on three people for private lessons?"

"As a test run," he said, "yes."

Laura remembered the letters on the piece of paper. "There were three sets of initials written on the schedule. I thought they were repeat students. But what if they're the names of the guests who requested private lessons?"

Noah's eyes cleared. "*CJK.* Those initials were on there."

"CJ Knight," she clarified. "Is that enough evidence to issue a warrant for him?"

Noah shook his head. "I need him to come back to Mariposa. I need him to keep his reservation."

Laura thought about it. Then, injecting as much promise into her voice as he had at L Bar, she said, "Leave it with me."

# Chapter 12

Laura couldn't cast off the tension. Since she'd learned Noah had taken Glenna into custody, she felt as if she was waiting for the other shoe to drop.

Sebastian was in no mood for a cuddle. Alexis had gone home for the night, so an impromptu girls' night was out of the question. She couldn't call Joshua to confide in him because she was still lying to him about Noah's part in all this.

She winced at that, hating that she and Noah continued to keep him in the dark. What would he think when he discovered her subterfuge?

Laura told herself not to think about that now. She told herself not to think about anything, but her mind was so full, she couldn't relax.

A hard rap on the front door of her bungalow made her jerk. Sebastian hissed. She dropped the book she had been trying to read to the coffee table and rose from the sofa. Tiptoeing to the door, she peered out through the peephole.

At the sight of Noah, she felt a stir. Snatching open the door, she asked, "What are you doing here so late?"

He held up Allison's schedule. "I thought we'd go over this."

"Oh," she said and stepped aside. "Come in." Before Sebastian could dart out between her legs, she scooped him up. "Naughty," she muttered and waited until Noah shut the door before setting him down again.

"If he wants to be an escape artist," Noah stated, "he should lay off the Fancy Feast."

"He's not fat," Laura said. "He's fluffy."

Noah smiled the knowing, self-satisfied smile that never failed to get her dander up. "Whatever you say, mommy dearest."

"That's my coat," she said, pointing to the camel-colored jacket draped across his arm.

"You left it," he explained, handing it over, "at L Bar the other night."

"You didn't have to bring it to me."

"If you don't leave your things around for others to steal, I wouldn't have to."

Laura tucked her tongue into her cheek. As she led him into the kitchen and den, she indulged herself by asking, "Did my stepmother really hit you today?"

"She grazed one off me," he replied. "What about it?"

"At the moment, I'm having trouble blaming her. You have a very slappable face."

He threw his head back and laughed. A full-bodied laugh, straight from the gut.

It went straight to hers. She sucked in a breath as the corners of his eyes crinkled and his teeth gleamed. For a split second, she saw the man as he had been in the navy uniform in the photograph at Allison's, and her heart stuttered.

He caught her staring at him, aghast, and the laughter melted in a flash. "What? Why are you looking at me like that?"

It took her a moment to speak. "I didn't think you knew how to smile—really smile...much less laugh."

His frown returned, all too at home among his set features. "You sound like Allison. 'You don't smile enough, relax enough. You don't put yourself first enough.'"

The words echoed in her head. Allison had said something similar to her. She shook off the odd feeling it gave her. "What about the piece of paper?"

Paper crinkled as he straightened out the creases and handed it to her. "*CJK* is obviously CJ Knight. But what about these initials? *DG*."

She studied them. "You couldn't find someone on your short list to match them?"

"No," he admitted. "Is it possible you missed someone when you gave me the names of staff and guests?"

She shook her head. "No. There's another set of initials. *KB*."

"That's Kim Blankenship, your guest in Bungalow Seven," he proposed, "or your horseback adventure guide."

"Kim Blankenship is in her late sixties. She's here with her husband, Granger. She built a cream cosmetics empire and is here taking a well-deserved break. And Knox?" Laura instantly rejected that idea. "The private lessons were for guests."

"Maybe Allison made an exception," Noah pressed. "Didn't you say he was flirtatious with her?"

"Yes," Laura granted. "But Knox is flirtatious with every woman. Even me."

"Don't like that," he muttered.

"Why not?" she challenged. "It's not like you and I are really…"

As she trailed off, his gaze became snared on her. "Really what? Kissing? We've done that. Touching? We've checked that box. The only thing you and I aren't doing right now, Pearl, is sleeping together."

Her mouth went dry. She forced herself to swallow. "It's not real."

His eyes tracked to her mouth before bouncing back to hers. Her body reacted vividly. Her heart rammed into her throat.

She wanted his mouth on hers. She wanted to know what it would be like, she realized, for Noah to kiss her and mean it. Not for show—for himself and her.

She demurred. They wouldn't be able to uncross that bridge. Once they went to the other side, she wasn't sure she could swim back to safety. She feared what she would find with him. Fire and brimstone, perhaps? Too much, too hard, too fast?

It sounded wonderful. She reached for it even as she turned away. "Knox Burnett didn't kill Allison," she said clearly, walking into the kitchen.

Noah's voice dripped with sarcasm. "The queen of Mariposa has spoken."

She reached for a wineglass. "Quentin called me 'queen.' Or 'queenie.' Sometimes, he just called me Q. Except when he left. Then he just called me a cold hard bitch who would get what was coming to her." She pulled the cork out of the bottle next to the coffeepot and poured a liberal dose. "Dominic thought I was cold, too—in bed and out of it. Do you want some?"

He didn't spare the wine a glance. "You never should've given those assholes the time of day."

"But I did," she said, raising the wine to her lips. She tasted, let it sit on her tongue, then swallowed, swirling the liquid in the glass. "Which makes me either stupid or desperate."

"It's simple," he stated. "Stop dating pretty playboys."

"Who should I date instead?" She gestured with her wine. "You?"

He cracked a smile that wasn't at all friendly. "You'd run screaming in a week."

She lowered her brow. "Why is that, exactly? Do you have pentagrams drawn anywhere on your person?"

"No."

"Are you mangled?"

"No."

"Do you keep tarantulas or dance with cobras?"

The lines in his brow steepled and she sensed he was trying not to give in to amusement. "I told you. I don't have pets."

"Do you have some sort of fetish most women find offensive?"

"No."

She shrugged. "Then why would I run from you, exactly?"

"I'm not Prince Charming."

She clicked her tongue. "I've looked for Prince Charming. No luck there."

"Doesn't mean you and me are meant to be," he asserted.

Some part of her wanted to challenge that. Even the part of her that knew better wanted to know what it would be like…the hot mess they would be together. When heat fired in her again, she drowned the images with more wine.

"And, for the record," he said, "you're not hard or cold. You're calm and together, and you have a strong sense of what's right for you and what isn't. You know how to take out the trash. That's why the playboys have come and gone. And so has your father."

She looked away. "My father has nothing to do with this."

"Your daddy's got everything to do with it," he said. "It was him who taught you what toxic people look like."

She thought it over. "If I'm together or strong, I learned it from my mother. She kept my brothers and me together through the upheaval. Even when she was sick, she had spine. She was incredible. I can't fathom why she never kicked my father to the curb. They lived separate lives by the time she bought this place, but she never divorced him."

"Maybe he made it impossible for her to do so," he intoned.

She felt the color drain from her face. "You're having a glass," she decided, handpicking another piece of stemware. She poured him one and passed it to him over the countertop. "I don't believe in drinking alone."

He lifted the drink, tipped it to her in a silent toast, before testing it.

She watched his throat move around a swallow. Her own tightened. She was growing tired of the tug-of-war between her better judgment and the side of her that wanted to dance in the flames. She was having difficulty quantifying both. "What was your mother like?"

His glass touched down on the counter with a decisive *clink*. "I don't talk about my mother."

She culled a knowing noise from the back of her throat. "That's what's wrong with you."

A laugh shot out of him, unbidden.

*Another one*, she thought, satisfied.

He shook his head. "God, you're a pest."

Even as he smiled, she recognized the pain webbing underneath the surface. "She died, didn't she?" she asked quietly.

The smile vanished. He masked the hurt skillfully with his hard brand of intensity. "So what if she did?"

She took a moment to consider. "That would mean we have something in common."

He stared at her...through her.

There was a lost boy in there somewhere. The foster kid who'd been dumped into the system while he was still coming to terms with losing the woman who'd raised him. She ached for that child, just as she ached for that part of her that had listened to Joshua cry himself to sleep every night and had been helpless against the tide of grief.

The line of his shoulders eased. He lifted the glass and downed half the wine in one swift gulp. Frowning at the rest, he cursed. "She'd just kicked my stepdad to the curb. He was a user with a tendency for violence. We moved around some to throw him off the scent. I didn't mind. Stability's fine and all, but I had her, and she had me, and that was...everything."

He chewed over the rest for a time before he spoke again. "There was this STEM camp I wanted to go to. I didn't think I'd get to go. It cost money, and she was working two jobs to keep the building's super off our backs. She put me in the car one afternoon, said we were going out for groceries. She drove out of town and pulled up in front of the camp cabins. She'd packed me enough clothes for a week. I was so happy. I don't remember hugging her goodbye. I just remember running off to join roll call."

She waited for him to go on. When he didn't, she asked, "Is that the last time you saw her?"

"Alive?" He jerked a nod. "The son of a bitch found her. Bashed her skull in with a hammer. Next time I saw her, she was lying in a casket."

"I'm sorry." She breathed the words. "I'm so sorry, Noah."

"He got off," he added grimly. "Broke down on the stand

and got sent to a psych ward instead of doing his time up-state."

The wine on her tongue lost its taste. She winced as she swallowed. "No closure for you, then."

"Hell, no. All things considered, it's better than what Allison went through before she got shuffled into foster care."

"What happened?"

"The truth's too ugly to speak here," he grumbled.

"Where else could you speak it?" she asked.

Turning up the glass, he swooped down the rest of the wine and reached across the counter to place it in her deep-basined sink. He gripped the edge of the counter, bracing his feet apart. "Her mother was killed, too. Her father did it, right in front of her, before he shot himself."

"Oh," Laura uttered. She closed her eyes. "She never... She never told me."

"And you'd never know." He gave a shake of his head. "Even as a kid, she was all sunshine and rainbows. She had this raggedy stuffed bunny she carried around by the ear. There was nothing anyone could say to convince her it wasn't alive or that it should be washed or thrown away. She called it Mr. Binky."

Laura found she could smile after all. "You wound up in the same home she did."

"I'm not sure what would have happened to her if I hadn't."

"Why?"

He hesitated again. "She didn't have anyone else."

"Your foster parents—"

"—didn't give a damn. I was fourteen when I went out and got my first job. I had to. Otherwise, Allison and I wouldn't have eaten. I had to teach myself to cook. There's nothing more motivating than that pit in your stomach—that one that's been there for days because someone drank away the grocery budget for the week. I was scared the reason Allison's cheekbones stood out was because she'd gotten used to that feeling. She was so used to it, it wasn't remarkable to her anymore. She'd just come to accept it. So I worked, and I cooked so she'd never have to know what hunger was again."

"I had no idea it was like that for her," Laura said.

"In that home, nobody hit us," he explained. "Nobody snuck into our rooms at night. Nobody screamed at us. But there's a different kind of abuse and that's straight-up neglect."

Laura had felt neglected, too, but not like that. It wasn't the same. Her father's indifference didn't compare to being left to starve or fend for herself.

She had starved, she realized. For his approval. For affection. After her mother died, she'd had to learn to stop. Men had disappointed her, even those before Quentin and Dominic—because she'd half expected their approval and affection to die off, too. She'd taken the safe route out every time.

"Allison told me the same thing she used to tell you," Laura mused. "That I don't live enough. Smile enough. Put myself first enough." Suddenly, what she'd told Joshua the day after Allison's body was found rushed back to her...

*I think you two could have made each other happy, at least for a time, and... I don't know. All this reminds me not to waste time if you know what's right for you...*

Behind him, she saw the blue glow of the pool through the glass door to the patio. Air filled her lungs, inflating her with possibilities. She set aside her glass and rounded the counter. "Let's go for a swim."

"What?"

"Let's swim, Noah," she said, grabbing his hand. She tugged him toward the door. "Just you, me and the moon."

"Wait a second," he said, trying to put on the brakes. "I didn't exactly bring a bathing suit."

*Be brave for once, Laura*, she thought desperately. Buoyed by wine and a spirit she'd ignored too long, she told him, "Then I won't wear one either."

Noah's eyes lost their edge. His resistance slipped and he turned quiet.

She slid the door open and stepped out into the cold. "Don't worry," she said when he hissed. "The water's heated."

He stared at the steam coming off the surface, then at her as she took off her socks and untied the drawstring of her loungewear pants. "So we're doing this," he said.

She frowned at his jacket and boots. "Are we?"

When she shimmied out of her pants, his brows shot straight up. He shrugged off the jacket one shoulder at a time. "I can't let you swim alone."

"And you say you're not a hero," she said, pulling her shirt up by the hem so that she was standing in the cold in her gray sports bra and matching panties. She shivered, dropped the shirt and crossed her arms over her chest. "Hurry up, Steele, before I lose my nerve."

The jacket hit the ground. He grabbed his T-shirt by the back collar and pried it loose.

Muscle and sinew rippled and bunched under a tapestry of black-and-white pictures. The wings she'd gleaned under the sleeve of his shirt took the shape of a large falcon. It spread across his upper arm and shoulder, finishing with another wing that reached as far as his left pectoral. The designs boasted more bones mixed with clockwork, as if he had tried to convince the world that he was half human, half machine. They were vivid and detailed. Although some lines and shapes had faded more to blue than black with time, none of them bled into others.

The effect was…breathtaking, she found. She was stunned by her own reaction.

Laura tried not to stare at him—at all he was—as he unzipped his fly and pushed the denim down. He fought with his boots before discarding them and the jeans completely, leaving him standing in his boxer briefs.

She reached for him, happy when he let her lace her fingers through his. Drawing him up to the top of the starting block, she grinned. "On three."

"One," he began.

"Two…"

"Three," he said and pushed her.

She flailed for a second before breaking the surface. She opened her mouth to shout at him but shrieked when he cannonballed in after her. The residual splash was impressive. She swept the water from her eyes as he surfaced, grinning. "Prick!" she shouted, tossing water in his face.

"You look good wet, Colton."

She felt more than stirrings of heat. The tendrils of steam off the water's surface could've been from her. Unsure what to do with herself, she floated on her back. The moon was directly overhead. She drifted for a moment, watching it and the stars before flipping onto her stomach for a lazy freestyle lap.

She'd drowned parts of herself in this pool. The pool hadn't been installed for fun or leisure. She'd needed it to stay fit and sane. Water purified. It cleansed. It took away her doubts and reinforced what she needed.

*Usually.* Still unsure of herself, she did another lap.

"Hey, Flipper," he tossed out when she came up for air.

She swept the water from her face. "What?"

He nodded toward the starting block. "Want to race?"

She laughed at the idea. "Sure. But, fair warning—I won the California state championship two years in a row."

"Do you still have the trophies?"

"Maybe."

"Of course you do," he said knowingly. He gripped the edge of the pool and pulled himself out.

She tried not to groan. He wasn't just ripped and inked. He was wet, his boxer briefs clinging. Peeling her eyes away from him, she climbed the ladder to join him. She slicked her hair back from her face. "Ready to lose?"

He didn't answer. Glancing over, she caught the wicked gleam in his eye as he gave her a thorough once-over. She felt her nipples draw up tight under her sports bra. "Would you like to frisk me, Detective?"

His gaze pinged back to hers. He blinked. His mouth fumbled.

Without warning, she threw her weight into him so that he tumbled into the pool.

Before he could come up for air, she executed a dive. Without looking back, she pumped her arms and legs into motion.

She felt the water churning to her right. As she raised her arm in a freestyle stroke and tilted her face out of the water, she saw him gaining, cutting through the water like a porpoise. She quickened her strokes.

They were coming up to the wall. She reached out blindly, groping for it.

Fingers circled her ankle, bringing her up short. She spluttered, arms flailing, as he held on.

Then she heard laughter—deep, uninhibited. She stopped fighting. As he drew her back against his chest, she abandoned the competition for lightheartedness. Delighted, she dropped her head back to his shoulder and belted a laugh to the sky.

His arms had hers pinned, and he tightened them. She could feel the reverberations of joy from his chest along her back and listened to the colonnades of his laughter. She closed her eyes, absorbing them.

The laughter wound down slowly and his body stilled, an inch at a time. He said nothing, holding her as steam curled around their joined forms.

She felt his breath on her ear. Then the bite of his teeth on the lobe, light and quick. "Laura?"

She shuddered at the sound of her name. "Yes?"

"In our game of Twenty Questions, I never asked you the most important one."

She tilted her cheek against his as he drew her closer still, his lips grazing her jaw. "What's that?"

"How do you like to be touched?"

The breath left her. It bolted. She felt the flush sink into her cheeks. It sank lower, deeper. And it turned darker, more shocking and satisfying.

*Take what you want, Laura*, she told herself.

She touched the back of his hand. Raising it to her breast, she brought it up to the ache, snug beneath the heavy curve. Spreading her fingers over his so that he mirrored the motion, she let her fingertips dig into his knuckles and encouraged him to grasp, take.

He obeyed. Her mouth opened on a silent cry as he molded her, kneading her through her sports bra.

"Don't be a lady," he told her. "Don't be quiet."

She swallowed, the sounds clawing up her throat. "You... you want to know my secret?"

"All of them," he said, brushing his thumb over the unmistakable outline of her nipple. "I want to know every last one of your secrets, Pearl."

A bowstring drew taut between her legs. Urgency quivered there. "I hate when you call me that," she said. "And I think about you even when I shouldn't."

"When?"

*He is so good at this*, she thought, arching back as the kneading quickened. "All the time."

"When?" he said again, the note dropping into his chest as his hold tightened.

"I think about you when I work," she rattled off. "I think about you when I'm with others, when I'm alone. In bed. In the shower."

He groaned. Turning, face-to-face, she saw the answering heat and need behind it. "I think about you kissing me... touching me..."

"Is that what you want?" He was close, but he pulled her closer, so his mouth brushed her own. "You want my hands on you? My mouth?"

She heard herself beg, "Please."

His eyes closed but not before she saw his relief. "As you wish," he whispered before taking her mouth in a decisive kiss.

He didn't kiss softly. He took, and she clung. She wrapped her arms around his neck and held on for dear life.

His hands spanned her waist. They cruised, flattening against her ribs, as he licked the seam of her lips, encouraging. She parted for him. One hand rose to the back of her head as he plumbed, touching his tongue to hers.

Her body bowed against his. Every inch of him was hard and fine. She spanned her fingers through the short hair at the nape of his neck, looking for purchase.

There was none. With him, there was nothing but that slippery slope of want and need, and she was going under.

She felt the pool tiles on the wall at her back. Pinned, she felt her excitement focus, sharpen. It arrowed toward her center.

With a harsh noise that sounded almost angry, he snatched his mouth from hers. He cursed, placing his hands safely on either side of her head.

She sucked her lower lip into her mouth. It stung. The tip of her tongue tingled.

His jaw muscle flexed. It was rigid. His eyes were alive, knife-edged, electrifyingly tungsten. The hands planted against the wall clenched in on themselves. She felt him go back on his heels and grabbed him by the arms. "Where do you think you're going?" she demanded.

He shook his head. "I'm no good for you."

"I don't care," she blurted. When he opened his mouth to protest, she reached up to cover it. "You're not Prince Charming? Fine. But I want this, and you want this." She replaced her hand with her mouth, skimming softly in a gliding tease.

His hands dropped to her shoulders and latched as she lingered. He drew a quick breath in through the nose.

She broke away and saw the ardor on his face. "I won't run from you tomorrow or the next day. I'm here." She kissed him again, deeper. "Take what you want," she invited.

He winced. "There's nothing you could ask me that I wouldn't give. That scares the hell out of me. I don't care what those other fools told you. You're not ice. You're a four-alarm fire. And I'm burning, damn it. I can't afford this. I can't afford you or what you do to me."

"I'm not going to run," she whispered. She thought of Allison, his mother... "I won't be gone tomorrow."

His hands still clutched her shoulders, firm, but they were no longer keeping her at arm's length. They pulled her into his circle of danger and heat. His muscles were still rigid, his grimace unbroken. But she felt him give... With her hands sliding from his waist to the backs of his hips, she angled her mouth to accept his.

It wasn't an onslaught this time. His tongue flicked across hers and he nibbled her lip, but the clash took on a different hue. She ached with it, the ball of need inside her roughening. It grew diamond bright.

"Tell me again," he instructed. "Tell me what you want me to do to you."

Fitting her palms to the backs of his, she used them to sweep her body from throat to thighs. She slowed the motion down as they followed up the seam of her legs where her thighs came together, up her belly, over her breasts, cheeks, hair...

He raked his fingers through the damp strands, then did it all again on his own. His hands slid firmly down her torso, teased her inner thighs before putting on the brakes, slowing the motions, skimming the folds of her sex so that her hips circled and she sought. She clamped her hand over the back of his, encouraging.

He didn't whisper so much as breathe the words again. "Show me. Show me exactly how to make you come alive."

Her touch worked urgently against his, demonstrating.

He caught on. "Like this?"

She nodded, then stopped when he increased the rhythm. She gulped air.

His hand slipped beneath her underwear. She moaned and churned.

This would break her, she decided. That was his endgame. He wanted to watch her come apart one molecule at a time. The flames inside her raced and leaped as she climbed the ladder fast.

She came, biting the inside of her lip.

"Let it go, Pearl," he bade. "For Christ's sake."

She couldn't leash it. A cry wrenched from her, unpolished and visceral. Everything he made her feel.

"Yes," he encouraged, his mouth on her throat.

She shuddered as she came down off the high, messy and resplendent. Something bubbled up her throat. It crested, escaped. A sob, she heard, distressed. "Oh, God," she uttered. She felt rearranged and so sparkly and sated, she thought she could taste stars.

"Hold on," he said, tossing one of her loose arms around his neck, then the other. Grabbing her around the waist, he hoisted her out of the water.

She fumbled over the ledge of the pool, coming to rest on her hands and knees. Every limb felt like a noodle. "Oh, sweet Lord," she said, then snorted a laugh. Quickly, she covered her mouth, wondering where it had come from. When he didn't follow, she asked, "Coming?"

He swiped his face from brow to chin, gave a half laugh and glanced down at his waist.

Understanding gleaned. He may have slaked her need, but not his own. Looking toward the wicker cabinet where she kept towels and a robe, she dragged herself to her feet.

She retrieved two towels, the long ones that wrapped around her twice. She folded herself into one, knotting it beneath her collarbone.

Behind her, she heard a splash and turned to see him emerging from the water. He passed a hand over his head as he turned from her, slicking the hair back away from his face.

She went to him. "Here."

"Thanks," he said and reached for the towel.

She pulled it away, trying to compress the sly impulse to smile.

He saw it form on her lips anyway. "You think this is funny?" he asked.

"I do," she admitted, holding the towel high.

He cursed and rearranged his feet so that he was facing her.

She saw what he'd been trying to hide from her. His erection was at full mast, the soaked boxer briefs straining to contain it. "I think it wants you to let it out."

"You're right." He snatched the towel.

She watched him scrub the terry cloth roughly over his face and hair. He toweled off his chest and arms before wrapping the towel around his waist. "What's stopping you?"

"What if you don't like what happens when I do? What then?"

She considered him. "What wouldn't I like?" When he didn't answer, she gripped the towel on either side of his waist and yanked him toward her. She stole a kiss while she had him on the back foot, hardening her mouth over his to prove a point.

He hummed in unconscious agreement.

She pushed him away abruptly and watched him fumble for a second in protest. "You want to know another secret?" she asked when he opened his eyes.

"I told you," he said after a moment. "I want all your secrets."

"There's nothing I don't like about you, Noah Steele," she revealed.

His chest lifted in a rushing breath.

"Why not show me the rest?" she suggested.

"You don't do this," he ventured. "You don't just take a man to bed. Not without flowers, dinner. Hell, candles. Silk sheets. Some ridiculous dress meant to tie your man's tongue in a knot."

"Maybe."

"We didn't have dinner," he noted. "I didn't bring you flowers."

"No," she admitted.

"I don't see any candles."

The candles were all inside her, she thought desperately. They stood tall under columns of flame. The wax melted away and puddled, refusing to cool. She wanted his hands all over her again, and it was driving her wild.

She wouldn't beg this time. She wanted him to beg.

She would make him.

"I'm not wearing a dress," she pointed out.

"You're not wearing much of anything and damned if that helps."

She smiled. "But I do have a bed with silk sheets."

"And you want me to mess them up?"

"Don't you get it?" she challenged. "You can shred my sheets, for all I care."

A slow grin worked its way across the forbidding line of his mouth. "You are, far and away, the most bewitching woman I know."

She closed her hands over the knot of her towel, untying it. Letting it fall to her feet, she grabbed him by the hand. "You know what's better than flowers?"

"What?"

"That."

# Chapter 13

The room was dark. The sheets were blue. Their skin was damp and bare. She clung to him. Afraid she'd see all the dark and treacherous ridges of his desire, he touched her gently, feathering his hands in and out of her curves.

She rained kisses over him as she braced her hands on either side of him. "It's your turn to tell me."

"What?" Indulgent, he blindly traced the raised surface of a mole on her navel.

"How you like to be touched."

He chuckled, then stopped swiftly when she closed her mouth over his nipple. It tautened and grew pebbly. The skin at the small of his back drew up tight and goose bumps took over. She would drive him over the edge.

He rolled over her, pinning her to the sheet. Taking her hand, he moved it between them.

Her gaze didn't stray from his in the dark as he showed her how to stroke him. How to drive him over the edge— a firm-handed hold, a deep-seated stroke, slow to start, then quickening.

She kissed him as he let her take control, curling his hand into the sheet. He breathed hot against her mouth.

"More," she told him.

Something like a growl leaped from his throat as he took

her wrist. Taking her hand away, he turned it up against the pillow over her head. "Not yet." He thought about his wallet on the pool deck. Out in the cold. "Damn it."

She pointed to the nightstand. "Top drawer."

Turning her loose for a second, he pulled out the drawer. Relief whistled out of him. "Were you a Boy Scout, Pearl? Because you prepare like one." He tore the corner off the wrapper with his teeth.

She snatched it from him, then shoved his hands away when he tried to fight her for it. "Lay still, hard-ass," she said none-too-gently.

Not only did he obey. He laughed deeply and fully. Then choked when she took her time rolling the condom into place, drawing out his needs. Her eyes glowed at him in the dark, watchful.

"I'm not sorry you're not a hero," she told him. "Or a prince."

"That's good," he said helplessly. He tugged her back to him when she was done. Then he flipped their positions, so she was beneath him. He turned her knee outward with his. "Because I'd hate to disappoint you, like all those other bastards."

He slid home. Her nails dug into the bed of his shoulder blades. They scraped as he took her through the first glide.

It wasn't soft. When she bit her lip, he wondered if he should be.

*She has silk sheets, you meatball*, he thought. *Of course she wants it soft.*

She sighed, tracing the line of his vertebrae with her fingertips. "Then don't stop."

He lost himself and didn't look back.

She was perfect. The way she held on. The way she met him stroke for stroke. The way she pressed her heels to the bed and said his name. He forgot why they shouldn't be together as she pulsed around him and her fingers found his, clinging.

Raising them above both their heads, he wove them together like a basket. He took her mouth as he tripped toward the edge and flung himself over like a man on fire.

He fell hard, tumbled end over end and face-planted.

*Had that coming*, he thought. The landing wasn't any softer or safer than their lovemaking. He lay panting, wreathed in sweat, tuning in slowly to the brush of her fingers through his hair.

"Noah?" she said, muted.

"Hmm?" he managed.

"Are you all right?"

He opened his eyes, saw the afterglow shining off her so brightly it made his eyes water.

She was so beautiful it made his eyes hurt.

He swallowed, still unable to catch his breath. "Why wouldn't I be?"

"You're shaking a little."

He took stock and felt the fine tremors in his joints. "I'll be all right. Just give me…"

He trailed off because she was caressing his face in soft, loving strokes that made him still.

Her eyes were all too blue in the dark.

His heart stuttered, banged, fired and drummed. And it hit him.

He'd never loved a woman. Naturally, it took him a minute.

It hit him like a Sherman tank going max speed, artillery firing.

He released her hands, sliding his away. Careful not to hurt her, he pulled out of the nest of her thighs before rolling to his back beside her.

She turned onto her side, skimming a kiss across the ridge of his shoulder. Laying her hand on his chest, she placed her head on the pillow and closed her eyes. "Stay."

It wasn't a question. Still, the answer was there before he could make himself think. "Yeah," he said.

"Your heart's still racing. Are you sure you're all right?"

He gathered her hand from its warm spot on his chest and pulled it away, up to his mouth. He kissed her knuckles to distract the both of them from what was happening inside him. "Pearl?"

"Yes?"

"Go to sleep."

She gave a little sigh. Her fingers played lightly through his beard until she dozed off and he lay awake—wide the hell awake—trying to fathom how far and fast he'd fallen.


Laura bolted upright in bed, alarmed at the sight of sunlight peeping at her from between the curtains and the sound of knocking from far away. "Oh, no," she said to Sebastian, who peered sleepily at her over his mustache of orange fur.

She slid out of bed, groping for the robe over the back of the purple wingback chair in the corner. She fumbled it on, tied the belt, then combed her fingers through her hair.

Scenting coffee like a bloodhound, she spotted the mug, still steaming, on the nightstand next to the framed portrait of her mother. There was a small scrap of paper next to it with Noah's handwriting.

*L.,*
*Fulton called. I have to run. We'll talk later.*
    *Made you something. It's in the oven.*
*N.*

The knock clattered again, louder this time, followed by Joshua's voice. Laura stuffed her feet into her slippers and padded quickly from the bedroom to the entry corridor.

When she snatched open the door, Joshua looked immensely relieved. "Ah, jeez, Laura. You had me worried."

"I'm fine," she blurted. "Sorry. I slept through my alarm."

Joshua gave her a puzzled once-over. "You never sleep in."

"I know," she said, frazzled. "I was up late and must have crashed hard."

"Noah spent the night here."

She shook her head automatically. "I don't know what—"

"Come on, ace." Joshua rolled his eyes. "I saw him head out just a few minutes ago."

"Oh." She cleared her throat and reached for it awkwardly. "It's not what it looks like."

His brows came together. "Why not? Haven't you two been together for six months?"

"I…" She caught back up and nodded, clutching the lapels of her robe together over her collarbone. "Yes. Yes, we have."

He lifted his hands. "Hey, I'm not judging. You say he makes you happy. I believe you."

"You took him running," she recalled.

Caught, he lifted both shoulders in a sheepish shrug. "Adam's idea."

"Oh, give me a break, Josh," she snapped. "I heard you were the pace car. I also heard you took him up the advanced hiking trail. Even Adam thought his legs were going to fall off."

Joshua pursed his lips. "It's not my fault I'm in better shape than everybody else."

She gave a half laugh. "If you'd believed me when I told

you he makes me happy, would you have put Noah through his paces?"

"He kept up just fine."

He didn't sound pleased about the fact. "You like him."

"Maybe," Joshua said. "And he said something that scared the hell out of me."

"What?" she asked.

Joshua took a breath, rolled his shoulders back as if trying to dislodge tension and said, "He said he was here to keep you safe. He said you could be the next target of whoever killed Allison."

She shook her head. "Nothing's going to happen to me."

"That's what she thought, too," Joshua said. "I may be your brother, but I like that he's staying the night with you. I like that you have someone watching over you when Adam and I can't. Until the police find out who killed Allison, I'm willing to look the other way when Noah's around. Bonus points that he looks like he could scare off a grizzly."

She smiled. It wobbled around the edges. "You don't have to worry about me so much."

"That's the thing," he drawled. "As long as Steele's around, I worry less. Where'd he go, anyway?"

"Sedona," she said. "He had something to do there."

Joshua lifted his chin. "Right. Valentine's Day's tomorrow."

"Valentine's…" She shrieked and ran back into the house, leaving the door open for him. In the bedroom, she dressed quickly, did her hair and applied makeup faster than she ever had before.

How could she sleep in the day before the wedding?

She snatched the coffee off the nightstand and downed half of it as she eyed the cat still curled up at the foot of the bed. Normally, Sebastian woke her if she even thought about sleeping past her alarm. He required a prompt meal at the break of every day.

As she ventured into the kitchen, where she found Joshua pouring coffee from the pot into a mug of his own, she peered into the cat food bowl. The remnants of a feast were scattered across the bottom of the porcelain dish.

Noah had fed her cat? Stunned, she took the bowl to the sink to rinse it. Then she remembered the note. Turning to the oven, she pulled open the door.

One of her china plates sat in the center of the upper rack. She pulled it out and found a still-warm western omelet.

Joshua peered over her shoulder as she set it on the range. "That looks incredible."

"It smells incredible," she said in wonder.

Joshua was quiet for a moment. "You used to make us breakfast—Adam and me. After Mom died."

"Yes." She remembered.

Regret tinged his voice. "Nobody's ever made breakfast for you in return, have they?"

She didn't reply. The note had said Noah had had to run. But he'd made her coffee, fed Sebastian and thrown together a whole omelet?

The walls of her heart gave a mighty shake.

A fork clattered onto the range next to the plate. She turned to see Joshua grin. "Eat your heart out, ace."

The morning meeting wasn't quick, but it was concise. Laura let Adam lead, still reeling from her naughty night with Noah.

Alexis lingered after Adam called the meeting to an end and the other members of staff bustled out to prepare for the next day's event. "I did what you asked," she told

Laura. "I called the number you tracked down. It was CJ Knight's cell phone."

"Did he answer?" Laura asked hopefully.

"I left a message." She took her phone from the pocket of her blazer. "He texted me a reply."

Laura tilted her head to read the phone's display.

Ms. Reed, I apologize for leaving Mariposa on short notice. Yes, I will keep my reservation for 2/16.

"He's coming," Laura said to Adam.

"That's good," he said with a nod. "Thank you, Alexis."

"Yes," Laura chimed in. And because she was so sick of withholding information from Alexis, Laura added, "Mr. Knight may have information."

"What kind of information?" Alexis asked, narrowing her eyes.

Adam cleared his throat, warning Laura to tread lightly.

"About Allison," Laura answered.

Alexis assessed them both. "You think he had something to do with what happened to her?"

"No," Laura said quickly. "But he departed Mariposa the next day. Police couldn't question him. It's possible he saw something or heard something that could lead police to the person responsible."

"That makes sense," Alexis allowed after a moment's contemplation.

"If you could avoid mentioning this to him when he arrives, that would be great," Adam added. "We need to let the police handle their investigation."

"Right," Alexis said.

Laura walked with her to the door of the conference

room. "You'll see that the other concierges have their assignments as the wedding party filters in today?"

"I will," Alexis replied.

"I appreciate it," Laura told her.

"That was clever of you," Adam noted after Alexis had departed. "You didn't lead her to believe the police are considering Knight as a suspect."

"I want this to be over," she blurted. "I hate hiding things from the people I care about. Alexis. Josh. Tallulah."

"This was your idea, Lou."

"I know," she said with a wince. "I didn't think it through."

"You were thinking about Allison," he discerned.

She nodded, silently knitting her arms over her stomach. It twisted with guilt.

Adam changed the subject quickly. "I just got a call from a friend of mine, Max Powell."

"Yes," she said, remembering. "The celebrity chef. You went to college together."

"Your attention to detail is one of your many strengths," he said fondly. "Max is taking a break from his TV show's filming schedule and wants to spend a few weeks at Mariposa."

"Let me know the date of his arrival," she replied. "I'll make sure he receives the best treatment."

"Thank you." A smile climbed over the planes of his face. It was a relief for her to see it and the light in his eyes. "The bride and groom check in at eleven?"

"Yes," she said. "Alexis and I will escort them to their bungalows. From there, she'll take them to their first spa treatment, and I'll check in with the parents and wedding party at Annabeth. They're surprising the happy couple with a prewedding margarita lunch. I've enlisted Valerie and her bar staff to help the kitchen staff with the drink rotation. I expect the celebration will go on for some time. I also expect every member of the wedding party to be tipsy when the minister arrives for the rehearsal on the golf course at five."

Adam thought about it. "Talk to the transportation staff. See if they can't have shuttles ready to drive them there. We don't want tequila behind the wheel of the golf carts."

"Good idea," she said.

"How's it going with Steele?"

Her smile froze. Joshua knew Noah had spent the night with her. How long would it take for Adam to find out? "It's going."

"When's he coming back from Sedona?"

"I'm unsure," she realized. "He didn't say, exactly."

"He may be keeping his distance."

"Why?"

He paused, planting his hand on the jamb. "Valentine's Day comes with certain expectations."

She lowered her chin. "Are you speaking from experience?"

He evaded the question. "Let me know of any problems between arrival and luncheon. I'm crunching numbers again with the father of the bride."

"Have fun with that," she muttered.

She felt like she was walking on eggshells for the rest of the day. Weddings and talk of murder mixed like oil and water. She felt she and Alexis handled the wedding party's questions about the investigation well, though.

Laura spotted Fulton lurking around the bungalows before the intendeds' surprise luncheon. His badge and gun were in full view. She wrung her hands and wondered what he was up to and if Noah had returned to Mariposa with him.

Thinking about Noah was doing her no favors. Vivid, distracting memories of the night before followed her everywhere. The things he had done to her...the things she had done to him... The heat in her cheeks refused to leave.

Her body carried its own memories, its own markers. She couldn't cross her legs without the tender ache of coupling causing her nerve endings to remember. She'd worn a high-necked blouse to ensure that the marks from Noah's beard on her neck and chest were tucked away from prying eyes.

Wishing he were feeling the aches as he went about his day, she hoped it was distracting him from his work as much as it was distracting her, if not more. And she wondered if she'd left any guilty marks on him to remind him of their exploits.

By the luncheon, her thoughts turned to speculation. Had he really had to return to Sedona—or was he just avoiding her? She had no missed calls from him, no texts. Just the note he'd left with Sebastian and the empty omelet plate at home.

Was Adam right? Was Noah steering clear of Mariposa because he was allergic to Valentine's Day? Would she even see him tomorrow? She'd thought about calling him again to tell him what she'd learned about CJ Knight. To ask if he knew what Fulton was up to, but her doubts had given her other ideas.

"You look ready to tear the heads off those shrimp."

Laura glanced up from where she'd been hovering next to the buffet. Alexis had finished her to-do list in time to witness the end of the luncheon. Laura stepped away from the shrimp bowl. "Sorry."

"Don't apologize," Alexis said, turning to angle herself

toward the festivities. "I just thought you'd like to know your face says, 'Approach me and die.'"

Laura smiled a bit. "I'm in a weird headspace today," she admitted.

"Want to talk about it?" Alexis asked.

Did she ever. She wished she could confide everything to Alexis—the whole confusing fake relationship that didn't feel fake but might still be. She felt terrible for making her friend believe that she and Noah were actually... Wait, but weren't they? What did last night mean? Would Allison approve? Or would she hate what Laura was doing with the brother she'd adored?

Laura tried to think about what to say exactly. Something—anything—to make sense of her actions and his. "Noah spent the night last night."

Alexis arched a brow. "Did he?"

"Mmm."

She frowned. "Haven't you two done that before?"

Laura wanted to curse. "Yes." Fighting for an explanation, she continued. "But last night... Last night was..."

"Oh," Alexis said significantly. "What you're trying to say is last night, you and Noah had *the* night."

"Precisely," Laura replied.

"All right." Alexis grinned. "Now that you mention it, I do detect a strong afterglow."

"I'm...*glowing*?"

"Like a menorah."

Laura snorted a laugh and covered her mouth as Alexis folded her lips around a muted chuckle. It took them both a moment to contain themselves.

Laura sighed. "Allison lived for conversations like this."

"She did," Alexis said reminiscently. "She'd say these are the talks that keep us young."

Laura sobered. "Taco Tuesdays won't be the same."

"No," Alexis granted. "She would want us to keep doing it, though."

"Then we will," Laura determined. "After the memorial."

"When is the memorial? Have you spoken with her family?"

"A little." Every time she'd brought it up with Noah, he'd shut her out. She wasn't looking forward to having the same conversation again. "The coroner's office hasn't released her, so I don't think they've put burial plans into motion yet."

"Adam's coming," Alexis said swiftly. "And…good Lord. What is it with you Coltons and your collective wrath today?"

Laura glanced up and found Adam pushing toward her on fast-moving legs. His face wasn't friendly. Her stomach knotted.

"May we speak in private?" he asked.

"Of course," Laura said. She nodded to Alexis, who moved off to give them a moment to themselves.

Adam's eyelid twitched. "Josh tells me Steele was at your place this morning."

"He was," Laura replied.

"Alone. With you."

"Yes, Adam," she said, feeling weary.

"What are you doing?" he demanded.

"It wasn't supposed to happen like this," she began.

"Jesus, Laura." He pressed his fingers into his eyes before remembering himself. He glanced around and lowered his voice. "Are you buying into your own cover story? Is this all some fantasy you had to indulge?"

"No," she said, offended. "Of course not."

"He's not a rock star," he told her. "He's a cop."

"I know that!"

"And he's not actually in love with you!"

*Ouch*, she thought. Shaking off the strange pulse of hurt, she straightened her posture. "I know."

"Every bit of this with him is pretend," he went on, undeterred. "And you're setting yourself up to get hurt all over again."

"Stop it, Adam."

"I'm not going to let you get hurt again!"

"Please," she begged, eyes brimming with a sudden wave of hot tears. "I said stop."

He saw the tears and his expression darkened. "I'm not a violent man, Laura. You know this. But if he's making you do this, I swear—"

"It was me," she said. "I was the one who told him to stay. He didn't make me do anything. I wanted him."

His jaw loosened.

She shook her head. "Don't act so shocked. I'm a grown woman. I choose who I go to bed with, just like Josh. I'm responsible for my own actions, just like you. If I get hurt, then that's my problem. Not yours."

"I have to watch," he said from the pit of his stomach. "I have to watch you pick up the pieces and move on. And it guts me every time."

She touched his arm. "It's going to be okay. I…I know what I'm doing."

"Are you sure about that?" he asked.

She wasn't, but she nodded. "I do."

He shook his head in disagreement. "You're always so careful. You're not considering the consequences from every angle."

"Maybe not." She could grant him that. "But ask me if I have any regrets."

"I think it's a little early for that," he considered.

"Do not talk to Noah about this," she said, knowing him. "I don't need you chasing him off like a coyote before—"

"Before what?" he challenged. "Before he shows you what kind of man he really is?"

"Don't pretend to know who he really is," she advised.

"Fine," he returned. "Then you shouldn't either." He turned and left her with the shrimp.

She looked around the tables, making sure no one had caught wind of the argument. She caught Alexis's sympathetic gaze from across the room and tried to erect a reassuring smile.

It slipped as she glanced toward the exit and saw Noah standing just outside the doors of the restaurant.

# Chapter 14

"Your stepmother made bail."

Laura nodded slowly. "We knew she would."

"You should prepare for whatever else she's planning," Noah cautioned. "I know her type. She's a schemer—a wrench in the system. She'll make trouble for Mariposa and your family again. I guarantee it."

Laura's brow furrowed. "I think you might be right."

"Fulton believes he has enough to close Allison's case by the end of the week."

Laura frowned. "How can he? There's not enough evidence to convict anyone. Is there?"

"No," he said.

"Then why the urgency?" she asked.

Noah shifted uncomfortably as the laughter from the open doors of Annabeth spilled out into the afternoon air. "I told you he was looking hard at Roger Ferraday. While I was at the station, I looked closer at his background and his son's." He showed her the folder in his hand. "Roger Ferraday has one DWI on his record. There were others that've been expunged because he's got money and power and he's got a high-priced lawyer who plays racquetball with judges and prosecutors alike." He opened the folder and angled it toward her. "This is his son's rap sheet."

Her hand touched her mouth as she read the felonies and misdemeanors. "How is he free to come and go as he pleases with a record like this?"

"Papa Ferraday flew his bouncing baby boy to Arizona on their private jet because whispers of date rape and drug abuse are getting the attention of people who don't care who he or his lawyer are," Noah revealed. "There's talk of locking Dayton Ferraday up for good."

"How does this tie back to Allison?" she asked.

Noah didn't want to spell it out for her. "Dayton has used fentanyl at least once in a case of date rape. The victim was a minor and charges were dropped, thanks to Roger's influence. But the connection's there."

She stared at him, distress painting her. "You think Allison's death had something to do with…rape?"

"Fentanyl is a date rape drug," he confirmed. "Come on, Laura. Think. For what other reason would her killer inject her?"

This time, both hands rose to cover her face. She stood still for a moment. Then her shoulders shuddered.

Noah wanted to take it all away. The likeliest truth was too ugly for him to process. He didn't want her to have to do so as well. "Hey," he said, sliding his palm over her shoulder. When she didn't raise her head, he rubbed circles over her back. "Hey, it's okay."

He didn't know why he said it. Nothing about this was okay. But he needed her to be. If she broke down, he didn't know what he would do. The confluence of rage and violence he felt for whoever had hurt his sister didn't mix well with a lack of self-control.

Laura had to know, he reminded himself. If there was a rapist at Mariposa, no one was safe. Not the maids. Not the concierges, front desk clerks, masseuses… Most especially not its queen bee, who drew playboys like flies and slept alone a heartbeat away from where Allison was killed.

The need to protect her whistled in his ears. He wanted to get her out of there, away from the resort. The danger was too close to her.

Sweeping the soft strands of her hair aside, he lowered his lips to the nape of her neck. His anger and torment over Allison lived shoulder to shoulder with his panic over what he felt for Laura, his need for her. He felt too small to contain everything inside him. Something was going to have to give soon or he would explode.

"I can't believe..." She took several shallow breaths, trying to get the words out. "...someone would do that to her...take advantage of her like that... Did he mean to kill her or did he just...want to have his way with her?"

"Either way, the son of a bitch is going to spend a long time behind bars. Unless Fulton rushes it, screws it up, and the guy gets off on a technicality. I have to make this right."

Even as her eyes flashed with tears, her voice was firm. "We both do."

He'd denied it for the better part of the day. He'd held himself back from the truth of what he felt. But he felt himself fumbling over that blind, terrifying cliff again. He felt himself go over the edge. Fear chased him, but he couldn't not see her. He couldn't stop feeling what he felt. In what he hoped was a perfunctory motion, he lifted his hand to her face to wipe the tears with his thumb.

Her eyes went soft, and he knew he'd failed. "Thank you for the coffee and omelet this morning."

"It was nothing," he lied.

"You fed my cat."

He had. "I didn't want him to wake you."

"You were trying to sneak out?"

"I told you. I got called into the station."

"Adam knows about us. About last night."

"You told him?" he asked incredulously.

"Josh did. He saw you leaving my bungalow this morning."

He rocked back on his heels. "I'm surprised I made it through the gate."

"Do you still want to talk to CJ Knight?"

He nodded. "Someone needs to."

"He's returning to Mariposa on the sixteenth," she told him. "Looks like you're going to get your shot."

"What's he booked for—spa, golf, excursions?"

"I'll have to check with the front desk," she replied.

"Find me an in," he told her, "and I'll find out if he's Allison's killer."

"I will," she promised. She looked across the grounds, past the pool to the tumble of rocks on the far horizon. The sun was low. It fanned across her lashes, and he saw they were still wet. Something inside him constricted. "Do you want me to keep Bungalow Fifteen available for you?" she asked.

She could smell the distance he was trying to erect between them. "Yes," he said, hating that he was too spineless to spend the night in her bed…too terror-struck to put himself at her mercy again.

He'd be a fool to let her play with his heart again.

"Very well," she said stiffly.

Before she could veer back through the doors to the restaurant, he took her by the elbow. Without thinking, he pulled her in.

As always, he went a step further. He kissed her. Her arms linked underneath his. They fanned across his back, and she made a noise that flipped his restraint like a wrestler's hold.

He opened his mouth to hers, recapturing the heat from last night. He let it coil around him. It was as if he'd never left.

He tipped his head up and away from hers. Her nails scraped across his scalp, making his mind go dangerously blank.

"Last night, you left a path of little reminders across my skin," she told him. "I've spent the whole day hating you for it."

Last night, she'd drawn little maps across his soul in carbon black. He'd spent the better part of the day trying to come up with enough elbow grease to erase them. He'd failed miserably.

"Hate me, Laura," he invited. "It's better for both of us." He touched her shoulders and held her away from him. "I'll see you."

Her expression folded, but her eyes glinted with promise. "Yes, you will."


Between the wedding and resort operations, Laura stayed busy. Too busy to think about the man in Bungalow Fifteen or the path between his bungalow and hers that, as promised, remained scant on foot traffic over the next few days. No one questioned why they didn't spend Valentine's Day together. The wedding was an all-day spectacle that had her limping back to her house well after hours on Saturday. She found Sebastian waiting for her there alone, demanding Fancy Feast and cuddles on his terms. *Just like a man*, she thought as she juggled a martini and Sebastian's large, round form in her favorite corner on the couch.

She ran into Roger Ferraday a handful of times on Sunday and struggled to maintain her demeanor. She skirted Adam, his warnings and assumptions.

Most of which she had to admit were true. She had gotten carried away by the illusion of her and Noah. But not rock star Noah. The real Noah—the one she'd thought she knew. And maybe she *was* setting herself up to get hurt.

Maybe she was her mother's daughter. Maybe she sought the one person she knew would never let her stand beside him without pretense.

When Tallulah tapped on the open door of Laura's office in L Building on Monday morning, Laura couldn't have been more relieved to see her. She closed the proposal Adam had prepared for her about a new line of more efficient bulk washing machines he wanted to splurge on for housekeeping. "Right on time, as always," she greeted her.

Tallulah stepped into the office and closed the door. "Were you expecting me?"

"No," Laura said, propping her chin on her hands as she watched Tallulah settle into one of the faux cowhide chairs across the desk. "But your visits are always welcome."

"You look tired, Laura," Tallulah murmured, studying her.

"Things have been busy," Laura said by way of excuse.

"Yes, they have," Tallulah agreed.

"Do you want to have coffee with me?" Laura asked, already reaching for the Keurig she'd tucked lovingly into the corner with mugs with the Mariposa logo.

"I would," Tallulah admitted, "but I have something I need to speak with you about."

"I'm all ears," Laura said, easing back into her chair.

Tallulah folded her hands carefully in her lap. "It's about Bella."

"The maid?"

"Yes," Tallulah said. "She came to me this morning in tears and handed in her resignation."

Laura blinked in surprise. "I'm sorry to hear that."

"So was I," Tallulah stated. "She's wonderful at her job, and she's a good girl."

"Did she give you a reason for leaving?" Laura asked.

"Not at first," Tallulah said. Her dark eyes flickered. "But when pressed, the story came out."

"'Story'?" That didn't sound good.

"She says she was assaulted," Tallulah said quickly, as if in a hurry to get the words out. "By a guest."

Laura stiffened. "Assaulted?"

"Yes," Tallulah replied. "It happened Friday, and she didn't tell anyone. She didn't tell me."

Laura wrapped her hand over the edge of the desk. "Tallulah, what kind of assault was it? Did she say?"

Tallulah's eyes grew wide. "Oh, Laura. She said she was manhandled, sexually. She was cleaning Bungalow Three because she thought the guests there were out for the day and she was attacked."

"Bungalow Three." Laura bit down on the urge to scream. "That's where—"

"The Ferradays," Tallulah confirmed with a nod.

"Which one?" Laura asked and heard her voice drop low where anger coiled.

"The younger," Tallulah answered. "And after what she told me, I'm in a mind to march down there and pour boiling water over his head."

Laura pushed back from the desk. She stood. "We need to report this."

"She doesn't want to involve police," Tallulah said. "I could hardly get her to talk to me."

"You don't understand," Laura said as she picked up her phone and dialed Noah's number. "This has happened before."

"With the maids?" Tallulah asked, shocked.

"No," Laura said. "Back in Connecticut, where the Ferradays live when they're not here."

"You knew this?" Tallulah stared at her, aghast.

Laura hated herself for it. "He's already under investigation. That's why his father brought him here. Probably in hopes that things would quiet in his absence." She swallowed hard. "Tallulah. I didn't think he'd do something like this. I'm so sorry."

Tallulah nodded in a vague, distracted motion.

Laura wrestled with her guilt. The call went to voicemail and she redialed. "Come on, Noah. Pick up."

"Why are you calling him?" Tallulah queried.

Laura knew she couldn't explain. She waited through a second procession of rings, then all but growled when it went to voicemail. "Noah. It's Laura. I need you to call me back as soon as you get this. It's urgent." She dropped the phone back to the cradle. "Where is Bella now?"

"I had Mato drive her home," Tallulah admitted. "She was too upset to drive herself."

"We'll need her to make a statement," Laura said. "She's already told her story to you. Do you think she'll do so again if you're there with her?"

"Maybe," Tallulah offered after a moment's thought. "But she was adamant, Laura. No police."

"She may not have a choice." Laura headed toward the door. "Can you call Roland and have him meet me at Bungalow Three? I'm going to have a word with Roger Ferraday."

\* \* \*

"Ms. Colton." Roger Ferraday grinned winningly when he found Laura on his doorstep. "This is a surprise."

"Mr. Ferraday," she greeted him. Roland hadn't arrived yet, but she'd knocked on the door of Bungalow Three regardless. "Is your son here?"

"Dayton?" Roger gave her a puzzled look. "Why?"

"There's been a security breach. We're just checking to make sure all guests are present and accounted for."

"Security breach?" Roger's smile tapered. "Should I be concerned?"

"We don't believe so," she blurted. "If you could assure me your son is in residence, please…"

"He is," Roger assured her. "I think he's still in bed."

"When was the last time you saw him?" Laura asked.

"You're scaring me, Ms. Colton," Roger said, visibly paling.

"Have you checked on him this morning?" she asked. "Are you sure he's in his bedroom?"

"I'll go check," Roger said, and he left the door open as he fumbled away. He called his son's name, rushing.

Laura took the open door as an invitation and stepped inside the bungalow. She smelled men's cologne and takeout. The table was crowded with to-go containers, and she spied a pile of wet towels through the door to the pool deck. Housekeeping hadn't come through yet.

*Thank goodness*, she thought.

"Here he is," Roger announced with obvious relief as he returned to the living area with his son. "He was sleeping in, just as I told you."

Laura eyed the slouch-framed boy with a messy lid of black curls. He peered at her, unhappy to have been roused from sleep.

"What's the big deal?" he asked in a baritone. He was of medium height, skinny, but she saw deceptive strength in the long arms that hung from the sleeves of his oversized Ed Hardy T-shirt.

If she searched his room, would she find fentanyl?

Had he killed Allison?

She unscrewed her jaw so that she could speak. Fury tried to bite down on the words. "I'm going to have to ask you to stay here."

"Me? What did I do?"

She glared at him. "You know exactly what you did."

His eyes narrowed, and he took a step forward. "Are you accusing me of something?"

Betrayal and disbelief worked across Roger's features. "You...tricked me?"

"Our security team will be here any moment," she stated. "They'll take your son into their custody and await police."

"Dayton didn't do anything," Roger said with an expansive gesture. "Listen, Ms. Colton. I'm sure there's something I can do, some arrangement we can come to—"

"I'm afraid not, Mr. Ferraday," she said with a shake of her head. Where was Roland?

"In that case, I'd like to speak with your brother," Roger requested. She could see sweat forming on his upper lip. She noted how he'd planted himself between her and Dayton. "Adam, isn't it?"

"You're lucky I'm the one handling this matter," she informed him. "Neither of my brothers would wait for Security to haul your son out."

"You know." Dayton spoke up, inspecting Laura. His pupils were as black as water beetle wings. "You're a smart-mouthed bitch."

"Shut up, Dayton!" Roger snapped. "I'm handling this!"

"No," Laura said, staring back at Dayton. "Go ahead."

"Okay," Dayton said, and his shoulders squared. "You're a big, loud, smart-mouthed bitch and you're going to eat your words. Just like the rest of them."

She took a step forward, drawing herself up to her full height. "You're right about one thing, Dayton. I'm a really big, really loud, really smart bitch. And I'm going to make sure you never hurt another woman again."

Roger held his hands up. "Ms. Colton, please. I'm sure we can solve this unfortunate matter together. There's no need to involve Security or the police. Dayton and I will leave your resort quietly. Just name your price."

"Bribery won't work here," she told him.

He had the nerve to smile. "Only because I haven't named the right price."

"Maybe I haven't made myself clear," Laura said, raising her voice. "Your son is a rapist and, possibly, a murderer, and he's leaving Mariposa in handcuffs."

"A murderer?" Roger repeated, smile fleeing. His face reddened, and he advanced on her. "That's a lie!"

"Yeah," Dayton spit. "What the hell?"

"Get out!" Roger shouted at her.

She heard the knock on the door. "Ms. Colton?" Roland called as he stepped into the open entryway. "Are you all right?"

Roger Ferraday's arm snaked out, hooking her around the throat. The other pinned her arms to her sides.

"What are you doing?" she cried out.

"Back off!" Roger warned Roland. "Back the hell off or I'll hurt her!"

Roland's Taser was already in hand. He didn't back away. "Mr. Ferraday," he said, focused on the face next to Laura's. "You're making a big mistake here. The police are right behind me. If they see you've taken Ms. Colton hostage, you'll be charged with holding her against her will. And the accommodations at the state penitentiary lack the luxury you're accustomed to."

Laura could smell the fear and sweat pouring off Roger. It dampened his shirt and hers as he pressed his front to her back. It slicked across her ear as his cheek buffered against it. Holding herself still, she kept calm, knowing her fright might encourage him to carry this through.

The tension shattered when the glass sliding door exploded. Glass rained, skidding across the floor, and a dark figure darted through the opening, gun between his hands. "Hands in the air!" he yelled.

Laura barely had time to register the lethal focus on Noah's face before Roger shoved her aside. Her boot heel slid across a loose piece of glass, and she went flying. She reached out to grab the table's edge, but she was going too fast. Her head arced down to meet it and she was helpless to stop her momentum.

Little white lights broke across her vision. Then the world came rushing back to her as she met the floor, little glass shards poking through her blouse. She reached for her head as pain split her temples.

When she pulled her hand away, blood smeared her fingers.

# Chapter 15

It was well after dark when Noah returned to Mariposa. He wasn't able to go back to Bungalow Fifteen. Not after going several rounds with Roger and Dayton Ferraday at the police station.

He hadn't accepted Captain Crabtree's orders that Fulton be the one to question them. He'd gone about the task himself with grim determination.

Roger Ferraday would do time. The Coltons' lawyer, Greg Sumpter, had shown up with Adam on Laura's behalf to demand that he be brought up on assault charges while Joshua had escorted Laura to the hospital to get checked out.

The younger Ferraday wouldn't get away from rape accusations this time. Bella, the maid, had changed her mind about not testifying after Adam and Tallulah had spoken to her personally. She was traumatized and scared but had seemed determined to put Dayton away once she found out about the other girls he had assaulted in Connecticut.

Fulton, certain Dayton was Allison's killer, had Bungalow Three searched, confident fentanyl would be recovered from the scene.

Instead, small quantities of Ecstasy were found in Dayton's mattress.

When Noah had leaned harder on Roger, the man cracked

under the pressure and admitted the reason he had no alibi for the night of Allison's homicide was he had found the bulk of his son's drug stash and the two of them had snuck out under the cover of night to dump it on the hiking trails.

By the end of the interview, Noah had wanted to lock Roger up on more than assault. He'd expressed no regret about holding Laura against her will or harming her, and he'd blamed Bella and the other girls for his son's criminal behavior.

Noah had thought of little more than punching the bastard in the face. But he'd known Crabtree was watching through the two-way glass, anticipating the moment Noah lost his cool.

He'd kept it—but only just.

Now he trudged up the walk to Laura's place. The door opened before he could get to it and Joshua, Adam, Tallulah and Alexis stepped out together. They stopped talking collectively when they spotted him.

Tallulah reached for his hand. "Laura's okay. It's good you're here. She doesn't need to be alone tonight."

The feeling of her hand in his felt foreign, but it was pleasantly warm. "You had dinner with her?"

"You weren't exactly here to keep her company," Joshua said in accusation.

Adam surprised Noah when he argued, "Go easy on the man, Josh. I'm sure he has his reasons."

When the four of them looked at him expectantly, Noah said, "I had to go up to Flagstaff. I got delayed there and didn't get Laura's message until she'd left the hospital."

"That was hours ago," Joshua pointed out. "Flagstaff's half an hour away."

Noah swallowed. "I'm sorry."

Alexis eyed the bag in his hand. "Do you come bearing gifts?"

He thought of what was in the bag. A blip of panic made him itch for something more—a better offering. "Yes."

"Good," Alexis noted. "There's no concussion, but doctors advised her not to imbibe for the next twenty-four hours."

"Noted," he said.

"Good night to you, Noah," Tallulah murmured before walking away. Alexis followed her. Joshua said nothing as he moved off.

That left Adam. "Anything you have to say to my sister can wait until the morning."

Noah searched for the right words. "I'd like to see her."

Adam studied him. "You were good with Bella. You made giving her statement easier."

"So did you," Noah said, "and Tallulah."

"Roland told me what happened at Bungalow Three," Adam explained. "He told me how Roger had her in a choke hold and how you apprehended him."

"She got hurt," Noah noted dully. The scene was on a loop in his mind. Ferraday shoving Laura away to save his own ass, her skidding into the table, knocking her head against it and falling to the floor, bleeding.

"I've asked Roland not to reveal your real identity," Adam pointed out. "Not until your investigation comes to a close."

"Thank you," Noah said.

"Laura says Dayton Ferraday may have killed Allison."

Noah shook his head. "He and his father confirmed each other's real alibis for the night in question."

"So you're back to square one?"

"Not if you tell me CJ Knight checked in this morning," Noah told him.

"He did," Adam confirmed.

Noah breathed a small sigh of relief. "That's something."

Adam gave him a tight nod. He started to go, then stopped. "Go easy on Laura. She puts up a good front for all of us, but she's raw tonight."

"I will." He waited until Adam had gone before knocking.

He lingered for two minutes. When she didn't answer, he tried the door and muttered something foul when he found she hadn't locked it behind the others.

"Laura?" he called through the house as he stepped inside.

The door closed behind him. Everything was quiet, eerily so.

"Laura!" he shouted.

He checked the bedroom. Her sheets hadn't been turned down. The door to the connected bathroom was open, and the light was off. He moved to the kitchen. Five plates and cups were stacked in the dish drain next to the sink. The couch in the living room was empty except for the unimpressed tabby who flicked his bushy tail at him. "Where is she?" he asked.

Sebastian lifted a paw and started to clean it.

"You're no help," Noah groaned. Then a movement on the other side of the glass caught his eye. He peered out. The steam of the heated pool rose to meet the cool night. In the blue glow of the pool lights, he could see arms cutting across the water like sharks.

He slid open the door, similar to the one he'd thrown a brick through earlier. Walking out on the patio, he watched her lap the pool four times without stopping, hardly coming up for air in between.

She cycled through freestyle, then backstroke, butterfly, then breaststroke. By the time she stopped, finally, he was ready to go in after her.

She gripped the edge of the pool, gasping. He saw the shaking in her limbs.

"Are you trying to hurt yourself?" he asked.

She jerked in surprise. "What are you doing here?"

He stared at the goose egg on her forehead. She'd taken off the bandage. There were no stitches, but bruises webbed across her brow.

As he surveyed the damage to her face, the fury came sweeping back in stark detail, and it crushed him.

She looked away. Using her arms, she pulled herself from the water.

He gripped her underneath the shoulder, helping her to her feet.

"I've got it," she said, taking a step back.

He dropped his arm. "Sure you do."

She reached for the towel she'd set on the nearby lounge chair. She patted her hair dry, then her face, hissing when she pressed the towel to the bump on her head.

He reached for her even as she turned away to dry her arms and legs. Then she wrapped the towel around her middle and knotted it as he'd seen her do before. Finished, she bypassed him for the door.

He tailed her, feeling foolhardy. "I should've punched him," he grumbled.

"That would have been counterproductive," she muttered. "Isn't your CO scrutinizing you?"

"Why did you go into that bungalow?" he asked. He'd needed to ask from the moment he'd found out she'd gone. "You thought Dayton Ferraday killed Allison, and you went to confront him and his father? Why?"

"It's my fault," she said. "He could only assault Bella

because I didn't warn Housekeeping or others that he was a predator. I should've told them to steer clear of Bungalow Three. I went because I wanted to be the one to tell Dayton Ferraday that he will spend the rest of his life paying for what he's done."

"Ferraday didn't kill Allison," Noah told her.

She stopped. "What?"

"Father and son gave their real alibis," Noah explained weightily. "They check out."

"But the date rape…the fentanyl…his attack on Bella… It all fits."

"Small traces of Ecstasy were recovered from Bungalow Three," Noah went on. "There's no sign of fentanyl."

"What does that mean?"

"It means CJ Knight is now the chief suspect in this investigation. But that's for me to worry about. You can't do this to me again. You can't go charging into a suspect's bungalow and try to take matters into your own hands. Whoever killed Allison will most likely kill you."

"I am not Allison!" she said, raising her voice.

"The man had you in a choke hold."

"I was doing my job."

"So was my sister," he reminded her. Unable to stop himself, he reached out to feather his touch across the first stain of bruising. "It's starting to hurt. Isn't it? And he scared you. That's the reason you were doing laps out there. Because you were alone long enough to feel the fear again." He pressed his cheek to hers, felt the shaking in her limbs and pulled her close, not caring that she was wet and he wasn't.

When he lifted her into his arms, she protested. He quieted her by touching his mouth to the rim of her jaw. "It's a soak in the tub for you. Then bed."

"You sound like Tallulah."

"Do you listen to her?"

"Sometimes." She pillowed her head on his shoulder, giving in as he sidestepped through the door to the bedroom so she wouldn't catch her toes on the jamb. There, he set her on the wingback chair.

"Take off your suit."

"Do you want me to dance for you when I'm done?" she drawled.

He ignored that and went into the bathroom to draw her a bath, throwing in some Epsom salts. When he came back for her, she was naked and shivering still. He bundled her up again, took her into the bathroom and lowered her into the water.

She let out a sharp breath as she sank in.

"Too hot?" he asked.

"No." She tipped her head back against the lip. "No. It's perfect." She flicked a glance at him when he lingered. "I'm not going to drown."

Reaching into his back pocket, he took out the little bag he'd brought to her door. "I bought this while I was in town."

She eyed the box he held with mixed levels of curiosity. "For me?"

When she didn't reach out, he opened it himself. "I found it while I was in Sedona." On a small cushion, a delicate strand of gold held a single pearl teardrop.

Her eyes rushed up to meet his. "You bought this—for me?"

He bit his tongue, trying to come up with the right thing to say. "It's not flowers."

"No," she said.

"Or dinner. But it looked…right."

She only stared.

He groaned at her reticence. "If you don't want it, I can take it back. I've got the receipt right here—"

"Shut up," she said without heat. "Just…shut up and put it on me."

She straightened, her shoulders rising above the water. Lifting her hair, she turned.

He took the necklace out of the box, unclasped it and lowered it over her head. Securing it at the base of her neck, he eased back as she turned to him again. The pearl rested just above her sternum in the dip between her breasts. She touched it. "How does it look?" she asked.

He shook his head. "It looks like I brought feldspar to an empress."

She leaned over the tub wall, meeting his mouth with her own, silencing him and his doubts.

He brought his hand up to her face. *Easy*, he told himself, feeling the quaking in his bones again. Not fury this time. The fear was there and the need, too. Always.

She pulled away. Her eyes flashed blue. "Stay with me?"

It was impossible to argue. "That's a hard yes."

Her smile was a tender curve meant for him alone as she reclined again against the tub wall and gripped his fingers on the ledge.

He watched over her until the water cooled. Then he helped her dry and dress for bed.

Back in her sheets, he held her until he felt her soften into repose. It took a long time to follow, but when he did, he had his nose buried in her hair and his arm tight around her middle, unwilling to let her go in the silent, anonymous hours between night and day.

# *Chapter 16*

Noah was relieved when Laura took Tuesday off after waking with a fierce headache. It took everything he had not to stay and take care of her. He made her coffee and breakfast and fed Sebastian again. As he ate over her sink so he wouldn't get crumbs on her spotless countertops, the cat bumped his cheek against Noah's ankle, then, purring, started weaving figure eights around his boots.

Noah watched, puzzled. When his plate was clean, he scooped the feline up in one hand. "It's your turn to watch her," he informed him as he carried the tabby back to the bedroom where Laura dozed. "Don't screw it up."

His phone rang. Sebastian twisted, unhappy as Noah juggled him to dig the device out of his pocket. Setting Sebastian down, he swiped at the long strands of cat hair clinging to the front of his shirt before answering.

"Steele," Adam greeted him.

"Colton," Noah replied just as flatly.

"I have a proposition."

Noah braced himself. "I'm listening."

"I don't expect Laura to come to work today."

"Damn right," Noah said.

"I'll be stepping in for her," Adam told him, "to help with the investigation."

"Thanks," Noah mused, "but I'm good."

"Meet me near the paddock in an hour," Adam said, ignoring Noah's refusal. "Dress for a riding excursion."

The line clicked. Noah looked at his phone and saw that Adam had ended the call. "Sure, cupcake," he muttered, sliding the phone back into his pocket.

An hour later, Noah said, "You know, I don't think me and you kissing is going to have the same effect on people as Laura and I do."

"Just once," Adam said mildly, "I'd like to see you go an entire day without vexing me."

"Not likely," Noah responded. He adjusted the Stetson he wore low over his brow as they walked to the paddock together. "You're sure Knight signed on for this thing today?"

"Yes." The corner of Adam's mouth curled. "But if he backs out at the last minute, I won't lose sleep knowing you're Josh's problem. Not mine."

"You realize I know how the internet works, right?" Noah said. "If baby brother abandons me like a lost calf on the trail, I'm dropping a one-star review for Mariposa on Tripadvisor."

Adam's smile morphed. "You wouldn't."

"How do you figure?"

"Because what you've done for your sister these last few weeks tells me you're a man of honor," Adam admitted. "If you have as much regard for Laura as she has for you, you'll leave Mariposa alone when this is all over."

Noah scowled, eating up the ground with long strides. He could smell the horses, the saddle leather... He could hear the chink of cinches and stirrups and the nickers and snorts of the animals as the guides and riders readied them for the long drive ahead.

All he'd wanted to do over the last few weeks was find

Allison's killer. He hadn't considered what would come after. Once the perpetrator was caught and Noah's actual reasons for being at the resort were revealed, would he be welcome there?

He couldn't think about Laura and what he wanted with her when this was all over. He couldn't think about losing her. Leaving her.

"I know you spent the night with her again last night," Adam revealed.

Noah felt a muscle in his jaw tic. "She was in pain."

"So you didn't sleep with her?"

He chose his next words carefully. "I slept next to her." At the sight of Adam's grimace, Noah nearly gave in to his own frustration. "I know the hospital said she didn't have a concussion. I wanted to make sure." He'd *needed* to make sure. "She didn't need to be left on her own. Ferraday didn't just hurt her. He scared her." And for that, Noah wanted to drive back to Sedona and toss the man across his holding cell.

"She shouldn't have been there to begin with."

Finally, something the two of them could agree on. Noah saw the knot of people in the horse paddock and scanned for his mark. "Where is he?"

"There," Adam said with a jerk of his chin to the left.

Noah had memorized the file on CJ Knight. He knew the man was twenty-seven, approximately five-eleven, one hundred and eighty pounds, with brown hair and blue eyes. Noah also knew he was unmarried and that he resided primarily in Los Angeles as an up-and-coming film actor.

CJ removed his cowboy hat, so the wind tousled his wavy locks. Under his plaid button-down shirt and jeans, he had the trim body of a gym rat.

Like a true actor, he'd dressed the part for the day's trail-riding adventure, led by Knox and Joshua. Noah's goal was to ride next to CJ and get to know him and hope Joshua didn't have other ideas—throwing Noah into a gorge, for example.

Among the others assembled, Noah recognized Kim Blankenship and her husband, Granger. He remembered the initials on Allison's refrigerator schedule: *CJK*, *DG* and *KB*.

Maybe today Noah could knock out two birds with one stone. Was Kim Blankenship *KB* or did Noah need to look harder at Mariposa's cowboy, Knox Burnett?

He needed to find the identity, too, of the mysterious *DG*.

Joshua spotted Noah and Adam on the approach and he nodded in their direction. "The gang's all here. Where's your riding gear, Adam?"

"I'm not staying," Adam stated. Everyone fell quiet as he brought his hands together. "I'd just like everyone to know that Joshua and Knox are the two best guides in Red Rock Country. You're in expert hands today." He patted Noah on the shoulder, either in assurance or warning. "Come on. I'll introduce you."

Noah walked with him to CJ Knight and the mare that had been chosen for him from the stable. "It's good to have you back, Mr. Knight," Adam said.

CJ shook Adam's offered hand. "It's good to be back. I'm sorry I left with so little notice before. I got called back to LA without warning."

"Is everything all right there?"

"It was a callback on an audition," CJ said. "And it wound up getting canceled, anyway. I wish I'd never left."

"Let us know if we can do anything to make your stay with us better this time," Adam replied. He turned to Noah. "I don't believe you've met Noah Steele. His band Fast Lane's making a splash. He'll be riding out today, too."

"Nice to meet you," CJ said, reaching out to grip Noah's extended hand.

Noah pasted on a smile. "Likewise. Have you done this before?"

"A few times," CJ said. "I love Red Rock Country. Are you new to trail riding?"

"It's been a long time," Noah admitted. "I hope I can keep up."

"Knox normally rides behind with the stragglers," CJ informed him. "Josh keeps pace, but most of the time it's leisurely, so we can enjoy the view."

A man flanked CJ. He had light hair and dark eyes and an unrelaxed posture that looked almost unnaturally upright. "Doug DeGraw," he introduced, shaking Noah's hand. "I'm CJ's manager."

"Noah Steele," Noah returned. He glanced down at the man's feet. "I believe you're wearing the wrong shoes for this."

CJ chuckled as Doug looked down at the business-like brogues he had donned. He patted Doug on the back. "Doug's not used to riding." He lowered his voice and said to his manager, "I told you I'd loan you a pair of boots. And you didn't have to come. You hate horses."

"I'll be fine," Doug said with a slight wince, looking around at the bay he had been assigned. "I'm told fresh country air does the body good."

"I can vouch for that," Adam agreed. "I'd better be getting back to L Building. Enjoy yourselves." He exchanged a significant look with Noah before departing.

Knox brought around a familiar horse that had been saddled. "Mr. Steele. You remember Penny?"

Noah couldn't help but smile as he raised his hand to the filly's mouth for a nuzzle. "I do. Is she mine for the day?"

"She is," Knox said. "She's new to the trails, but she's done well in practice. Want to give her a shot?"

"Absolutely," Noah said as Penny blew her whiskered breath across his palm. He took the reins. "Thanks. Hey, by any chance, do you know when a new yoga instructor will be hired? I've got this pain between my shoulders blades, and I really need a stretch."

Sadness lay heavy on Knox's face. "I don't, no. I'm not sure management's even thought about it. You could ask Laura."

"I will," Noah returned. "Sorry I brought it up."

"It's okay," Knox replied. "Allison hasn't even been buried yet. It's hard thinking about a replacement for her."

"It's a shame she died," CJ added. "I liked Allison. I'd just started private lessons with her."

"Oh?" Noah said, feigning surprise. "I didn't know she offered that sort of thing."

"We got one session in before I had to leave," CJ explained. "I didn't hear of her passing until it hit the news. She was so full of life. I don't understand how anyone could hurt her."

"Are you talking about the yoga instructor?" a voice said from the right. Noah looked over and saw that they'd drawn Kim Blankenship into the conversation. "Allison?"

"Yeah," Knox said, his voice lost in his throat somewhere.

"I knew her!" Kim said with wide gray eyes in a heavily made-up face. Under her hat, her bottle-blond hair was perfectly curled. She mixed a down-home, don't-mess-with-Texas attitude with vintage movie star glamour. "She came to my bungalow the morning before she was killed and led me through a personalized yoga routine. I'd overdone myself hiking a few days before, and she knew exactly what to do to help me work out the kinks. She was so sweet and personable." Kim planted a gloved hand on her hip. "Why, if I knew who did such a thing to her, I'd tie them behind my horse and drag 'em across the desert."

"I'm with you, sweetheart," her husband, Granger, agreed.

This struck up talk among most other members of the excursion. Noah watched CJ nod and concur as others voiced their opinions about Allison and the person who had brought her life to an untimely end. Noah wondered how good an actor the guy really was.

"You ride well, Steele."

Noah looked around as Joshua pulled his big, spirited stallion, Maverick, alongside Penny. "I detect disappointment."

Joshua laughed. "Did Adam tell you I'd leave you for the coyotes?"

"Something like that," Noah drawled.

"You can stop looking over your shoulder, Fender Bender. Accidents on the trail are bad for business."

"That's reassuring," Noah grumbled.

"You've been talking to CJ Knight."

"And you've been keeping tabs on me," Noah acknowledged.

"Part of my job," Joshua explained. "Did he mention Erica Pike?"

"Your brother's secretary?"

"Executive assistant."

"He didn't. Why?"

"No reason," Joshua said quickly.

"Why?" Noah pressed.

Joshua nickered to the stallion when the animal bobbed his head impatiently. "Laura thinks something may have happened between her and Knight. I asked Erica. She said it didn't."

"You don't think she's being truthful?" Noah asked.

Joshua shrugged, obviously uncomfortable with the subject. "It's no good—relationships between staff and guests. Or management and staff, for that matter."

"No wonder you think so little of Laura and me," Noah noted.

"That's another matter," Joshua told him. "You met her before you came here. And you're hiding something." He spotted Noah's look of surprise and snorted. "I'm the second son of Clive Colton. I know when a man isn't being truthful. I don't expect you to tell me what you're lying about, but I will ask you not to lie to Laura. Come clean with her or coyotes will be the least of your worries."

Noah knew what it was to be a brother. It was a shame Joshua would never know that he and Noah had something so crucial in common. "Laura knows who I am."

"I hope so," Joshua said sincerely.

Noah glanced back at CJ Knight. He was lifting his canteen to his mouth and taking a long drink. His manager, Doug DeGraw, unsettled on his mount, struggled to keep up. "That guy's a nuisance."

"Who?" Joshua turned in the saddle. "CJ's manager? We rarely get inexperienced riders on challenging drives like this one. But he insisted."

"Doesn't look like he's having much fun," Noah said.

"The man's sweating bullets," Joshua observed.

"I'm surprised he hasn't turned back."

"Knox offered to take him. He seems determined to stay by Knight's side."

Noah frowned. "Seems more like a nanny than a manager."

"I'm surprised you and Knight are getting on so swimmingly."

"Why's that?"

"Unlike you," Joshua said, "he's a Boy Scout."

"You think so?"

"Yeah. Like any celebrity, he values his privacy. But he's personable with other guests and staff. He's uncomplaining. He tips well and not because it's expected of him—because he's grateful."

"You like him," Noah stated.

"I do," Joshua said.

This coming from the guy who claimed he could spot a liar at fifty paces. If Joshua had guessed that Noah wasn't being entirely truthful, wouldn't he have been able to do the same with Knight if he was the killer?

Joshua tapped Maverick with his heels and rode ahead. He turned the horse to face the riders. "Congratulations! You've all reached the south point. We'll rest our mounts for a while before the return journey. Dismount. There's a creek down at the bottom of the hill where you can lead your horse to water."

A resounding thump brought Noah's head around.

Doug DeGraw sprawled beneath his horse.

CJ shook his head as his boots hit the ground. Gathering Doug's horse's reins, CJ extended a hand to him. "Something tells me you're going to need a masseuse."

"Forget that," Doug said, brushing himself off. He struggled to his feet with CJ's help. "Get me a stiff drink and an hour with a nimble woman."

Kim Blankenship rolled her eyes. "That one's a winner," she muttered as she led her horse down the hill past Noah and Joshua.

Noah took Penny to the creek. "Good girl," he said as she bent her head to the water that burbled busily over its smooth rock bed. He took a moment to admire where they were. There was no fence to mark the boundary of Mariposa, just an old petrified tree trunk with a butterfly carved into its flank. He could see familiar formations from the state park in the distance.

He'd always been drawn to that perfect marriage between the cornflower blue sky and the red-stained mountains, buttes and cliffs that jutted toward it. The wind teased his hair as he took off his hat and opened his canteen for a long drink.

Someone stumbled over the rocks, making Penny sidestep. Noah patted her on the neck until she settled. Then he watched Doug pry off one dirt-smudged brogue. "I told you those were the wrong shoes."

Doug groaned as he rubbed the bottom of his socked foot. "I miss LA. I can't understand why CJ keeps getting drawn back to this place."

Noah lifted his eyes to the panorama. "Can't you?"

"No." Doug stilled as a woman from their party brought her horse to drink. He lifted his chin to her in greeting. "Ariana, right?"

"Yes," she said. "And you're Doug, CJ's guy."

"Just Doug," he said. "You're the host of that new game show—*Sing It or Lose It.*"

"I am," she said, beaming. She was young, a redhead with large green eyes and long legs encased in jodhpurs. "Well, I don't exactly host. I'm the DJ."

"You should host," Doug asserted. He slid a long look over her form. "The network would draw far more viewers if they made you more visible."

She favored Allison. The resemblance jolted Noah, and he fought a sudden overwhelming urge to put himself between her and Doug.

Ariana stepped back a little, as if she didn't care for the

way Doug was coming on to her either. Politely, she fixed a smile into place. "Thanks."

Noah cleared his throat, doing his best to draw Doug's attention away from her. "Your shoe's making a break for it."

"Huh?" Doug did a double take when Noah pointed out the brogue racing across the surface of the creek. He swore viciously and ran after it while Ariana giggled.

With Doug out of earshot, Noah moved toward her. "Here," he said, taking her horse's bridle. "They're building a fire. You go get warm. I'll make sure your horse is taken care of."

"Oh, thank you," she said, surprised. "Her name's Autumn. She's a sweetie. But I will join the others. That guy's vibes are way off."

"I'm starting to get that," Noah said.

"Hey." She touched his wrist. "That's an evil eye."

He looked down at the bracelet peeking out from under the cuff of his shirt. "Yeah. My, uh…" Licking his lips, he absorbed the pang above his sternum. "My sister gave it to me," he finished quietly.

"Did you know the evil eye dates back to 5000 BC?" she asked. "It's also used in symbolism across various cultures— Hindi, Christian, Jewish, Buddhist, Muslim…not to mention Indigenous, pagan and folk societies."

"I didn't know that," he said truthfully.

She rolled her eyes at herself. "I sound like a geek. But I love that sort of thing. You've got a light blue eye. It's supposed to encourage you to open your eyes to self-acceptance and the world around you."

"Interesting," he said.

"Is it?" Doug snarled as he returned with one dripping shoe.

Ariana stiffened. "I'll go get a seat by the fire."

"Sure," Noah said. He blinked when she was gone. For a moment, it had felt like he was talking to his sister again.

"Look at that ass work."

Noah sent Doug a long scowl. "A little young for someone like you, wouldn't you say?"

"I like them young," Doug said as he worked his foot into his shoe. "Things tend to be more high and tight, if you know what I'm saying." He chuckled nastily, cheered by his own imagery.

If the man didn't shut up, Noah was going to shove both brogues down his throat.

Doug stood finally and grabbed the reins of his mare roughly. She rebuked him with a jerk of her head. "I knew someone with one of those."

On the verge of telling him to can it, Noah looked warily to where Doug pointed.

To Noah's wrist. He was pointing at Noah's wrist and the evil-eye bracelet.

Noah felt his jaw clamp and his stomach tighten. "Yeah?" he managed to drawl.

"Yeah." Doug lifted a brow. "That one… Ah, man. She was a real peach."

*Was?*

Under the watchful gaze of a high-noon sun, Doug led his mount up the hill, limping a little as he went.

"Son of a bitch," Noah muttered, clutching Penny's reins. He fit his hat to his head and led her and Autumn to the cluster of riders, wishing hard for his badge.


"You're supposed to be resting."

Laura looked up from her desk and spied the dusty man framed in the open door to her office. She noted the Stetson and the wide silver buckle on his belt. Noah looked dirty and dangerous, and her heart caterwauled as he propped the heel of his hand on the jamb above him.

The man was the human equivalent of devil's food cake.

Setting the papers in her hands flat against the desktop, she studied his comfortable scowl and smiled broadly despite the ache in her head that had persisted throughout the day. "You're probably going to take what I say and run with it, but…you look good enough to eat, cowboy."

The scowl wobbled, and warmth chased the moody slant of his eyes. Pushing off the jamb, he closed the door.

As he came around the desk, she turned the swivel chair to face him. Angling her chin up, she tilted her head. "I'm happy to see Josh didn't bring you back to me in splints."

Noah leaned over, pressing his hands to the arms of her chair, caging her in. He scanned the mark on her brow and its ring of dark bruises. Then he searched each of her eyes in a way that made her lose her breath. By the time his gaze touched her mouth, she was shivery with anticipation. She clutched the collar of his shirt to pull him down to meet her.

His arms locked, resisting, when he found the gold chain around her neck. Gingerly, he slid his first finger between it and the skin at the high curve of her breast and lifted it, so the pearl drop rose from the V-cut neckline of her plum-satin blouse.

His eyes crawled back to hers.

"I've been thinking about you," she whispered.

He made a low noise.

Her chest rose and fell swiftly. She wished she could catch her breath. He made it difficult. "And I've missed you," she admitted.

He tensed. Then he lowered to his knees. His arms spanned her waist, and he tugged her to the edge of her chair.

When he buried his face in her throat and pressed his front to hers in a seamless embrace, she melted. Spreading her fingers through his hair, she latched on.

She couldn't handle him like this—urgent, tender, sweet. It disarmed her.

She swallowed. "Did something happen?"

His lips pursed against her skin. His breath across the damp circle left by his mouth made her skin hum all over. "I have to go back to Sedona."

"Why?" she asked, pulling back far enough to scan his face.

He stiffened. "I think I know who killed Allison."

"CJ Knight?" she asked.

"He was taking private lessons. I confirmed that. But I think I've been looking in the wrong place."

"Talk it through with me," she invited.

He eased back some, his hands lowering to her outer thighs. "*KB* is Kim Blankenship. Allison went to her bungalow for a lesson the day she died. But I don't think it's her either."

"Then who?" Laura asked.

His eyes hardened. *"DG."*

"You know who that is?"

"I think it stands for Doug DeGraw."

She squinted past the thumping behind her temples. "Isn't that CJ Knight's manager?"

"Yes."

"What makes you think he's guilty?"

"Other than that he's a complete and utter douchebag?" Noah drawled.

She sighed, nodded. "Yes."

"He was trying to flex on one woman. Ariana."

"Fitzgibbons," she said, plucking the name out of her

memory files. "She's a new television personality. Beautiful, smiley, bubbly—"

"Like my sister."

She stopped. "They look similar," she granted.

Noah swore. "She's a dead ringer for Allison. And she knows things about spiritualism and symbolism. I felt like I wasn't just looking at Allison. I felt like I was talking to her, too."

"Noah," she whispered. "I can understand how that must have felt. I know how it would have affected me. But is the fact that Doug DeGraw was hitting on Ariana Fitzgibbons the only reason you believe he killed Allison?"

"No," he said vehemently. "He saw the bracelet. He recognized it."

When he lifted his arm, she saw the evil-eye pendant around his wrist. "How do you know he recognized it? Did he say something?"

"Yeah." Noah's jaw locked from the strain. His hands gripped the arms of the chair again. His knuckles whitened. "He said he knew a woman who wore one. He said she was a real peach. I could've killed him on the spot."

"Okay," she said soothingly, laying her hands across his shoulders. "Let's just take a minute." For all his wrath, she could feel the grief emanating off him and she wanted to hold him until those waves came to shore. "I don't think you're in any condition to drive back to Sedona tonight." When he started to refuse, she spoke over him. "There's rain coming in. The roads will be wet, possibly icy. And it's after six—too late for you to make any headway."

"I need to nail this guy," he told her. "I need to look into his history, his record, his behavior—"

"Come home with me." She touched his face. "We'll soak in the pool, order dinner, then turn in before nine.

That way, you can be up and out the door first thing in the morning. And you'll have the whole day to do whatever it is you need to do."

His frantic gaze raced over her. "It's him, Laura. He's the one who took Allison's life. He must've lured her to his bungalow, drugged her, then…"

A sob wavered out of her. She shook her head quickly. "Stop. Please, stop."

He released a long, ragged breath, dropping his head. "I still want to kill him. Crabtree was right. If I find something on DeGraw, I'll need to hand the arrest over to Fulton. If it's me… I don't know if I have what it takes not to put a bullet in him."

Her hands gentled on his face. She kissed the broad plane of his cheek. Then the space between his eyes before placing both palms around the back of his head and drawing him against her once more. "It's okay," she said, blinking back tears. "It's going to be okay."

He didn't pull away. They remained that way, still in the upheaval, for a while.

"Noah?" she whispered.

"Hmm?"

"Will you?" she asked. "Come home with me?"

He shoveled out a breath. Then he nodded, reluctantly.

When he stood, he extended a hand. She took it and let him pull her to her feet. Switching off the lamp on her desk, she grabbed her purse. On their way out, she stopped to lock the door.

"You lock your office but not your front door," he grumbled.

She stuffed the keys in her purse and reached for the handle of the glass door that led out of L Building. He beat her to it, shouldering it open and propping it until she'd passed through. He took her hand. "Wait."

She stopped moving. At the sight of his frown returning, she gave in. "I'll start locking my front door if it bothers you that much."

"Yes," he said with a nod. "But there's something else."

She was stunned when he gathered both her hands in his. As his thumbs stroked her knuckles in fast repetitions, she tried to read him. "What is it?"

"Promise me, Pearl," he murmured. "Promise me you won't approach DeGraw while I'm off property. I can't leave you here if I think you'll put yourself in harm's way for even a second."

She nodded. "All right."

"You promise?" he pressed.

"I promise." Unable to watch the conflict clash on the inside of him, she raised her lips to his.

As he inclined his head toward hers and his hand cupped the back of her head, he let it be soft—let himself be, drawing out her sigh with a head-to-toe shudder.

He took her home, where they soaked in the pool. He remained close to her as she reclined on the steps. It was easy with him, she thought, not to cut through the water but to rest and let the moment stretch.

She offered to order in, but he found pesto, grape tomatoes, green beans, tortellini and chicken in her fridge. As she sat with her wine and watched him throw it all together in a pan over the stove, she saw someone channeling his demons. Filling another glass, she took it to him. He stopped long enough to clink it to hers, holding her gaze as he took the first sip. She did the same, then rubbed the bones that had been etched on the left side of his spine, leaving the right side blank.

She half expected to feel the inscribed tears in the flesh that separated the unmarked side of his back from the tattoos as she ran her fingers across his vertebrae. Warm, smooth skin greeted them instead, and she marveled again over the level of artistry he'd placed upon his body.

Noah mixed and flipped the contents of the pan so that the pesto coated everything.

He'd stirred, mixed and flipped her, Laura mused. He'd come at her like a demolition expert, knocking down walls, making a mess, hauling complete sections of those walls out.

He'd rearranged things.

Allison had called Laura a "classic Taurus," no more open to change than she was to heartbreak. *It's why you won't play with risk*, she'd told her.

Laura had shrugged that off. *Risk is overrated.*

*Maybe*, Allison had replied. Her wise eyes had flickered knowingly. *I'm just afraid that when you find someone who's right for you—really right for you—you'll shy away from the risk and lose the chance to get everything you've ever wanted.*

The sentiment had made Laura reevaluate everything. What if she'd already done that? What if she'd missed her shot because the risk scared her?

She and Noah were so different. Night and day, as a matter of fact. But as she watched the hair on the back of his head fan through her fingertips, as the tense line of his body eased and he lifted his face to the ceiling briefly to dig into her touch, she caught her lower lip between her teeth.

Could they be this different and this right for each other all at once? All the candles he lit inside her just by being whispered *yes*.

"You keep this up and I'm going to burn the first dinner I prep for you," he noted.

*The first?* Her heart leaped. She swallowed all the deeper questions and asked, "What's your sign?"

"What sign?"

"Your astrological sign," she clarified. When he gave her a long sideways look, she let a slow grin play across her mouth. "Come on. With a sister like Allison, how could you not know?"

"Please tell me you don't put as much stock in that as she did," he groaned.

"Not really," she said. "But it's a fun question. And I'm curious. You were born in November."

"You remember that?"

"Of course I do," she murmured.

He lifted the wineglass, taking a break to study her.

She smiled. "November either makes you a Scorpio or a Sagittarius. Which is it?"

Ever the man of mystery, he chose not to answer and took a long sip instead. Then he picked up the spatula and continued to stir. "I'm not a wine drinker. But this one's fine."

"It is," she agreed. "It's a rare vintage. One I've been saving."

He raised a brow. "For me?"

Why did he think he was worthy of so little? "Yes," she said, moving closer. "And after we eat, I'm going to find out how it tastes on your tongue."

The spatula clattered to a halt and his eyes fired. The tension hardened his features, but it had nothing to do with anger this time and everything to do with what they had made the last time their bodies had come together in a fit of urgency. He remembered that clash, she saw, and its sensational conclusion every bit as much as she did.

"Is that right?" he ventured.

She saw the smile turn up the corners of his eyes even as his mouth remained in a firm, forbidding line. "How much longer?" she asked.

"Not long," he guessed. He cursed. "Too long."

She wondered if his body had responded as eagerly as hers was. Crossing one foot over the other, she tried to tamp down on it. By pressing her thighs together, she only fanned the flame. She ran her hand over the small of his back, just above the line of the towel he'd wrapped around his hips, and made herself step away. "I'm going to change."

She made it to the corner before he spoke up again. "Scorpio."

She glanced back in surprise. His head was low, intent on the work of his hands. And she grinned because she saw the pop of color in the flesh leading from his collarbone to his ear.

His body *had* responded, and she could think of nothing more than unknotting his towel and letting dinner burn.

Taking a steadying breath, she said, "Of course you are."

In her bedroom, she opened the top drawer and pulled out the black nightie she'd bought online on impulse a few nights before. Lifting it by the straps, she considered. She hadn't thought she'd have the nerve to wear it for him. She'd thrown out all her nighties after the fiasco with Quentin, deciding she wouldn't need sexy finery again.

Carrying the gown into the bathroom, she closed the door after letting Sebastian follow her inside. She discarded her towel and the wet bathing suit underneath and hopped into the shower.

When she came back out, tying the belt of a black silk robe that had lived at the back of her closet for some time, the smell of pesto hit her. She followed the seductive aroma to the dining room table, where he had already plated dinner for them.

She stared at the candle he'd found on her side table in the center of the dining set. "My goodness," she said, at a loss for anything else.

He topped off her wine. "From the moment we met, I knew you were the candlelit-dinner type."

He pulled out a chair for her. Inwardly, she sighed. The hard man in the towel, quietly and devastatingly courteous, had no idea how irresistible he was. "Thank you," she said, turning her mouth up to his for a breathy kiss.

His eyes remained closed when she pulled back. His head followed hers as she lowered her heels to the floor. "You smell good. You always smell good." When his eyes opened, they were unfocused. "I could eat you alive."

"Tortellini first," she insisted.

He dropped his gaze to the silk covering her. "Are you wearing anything under that?"

*Later*, she cautioned herself when, again, adrenaline and desire surged. "All good things," she whispered before she lowered to the seat, tucking the robe around her legs when it parted over her thighs.

He pulled out the chair next to hers. Lifting her glass, she drank before lowering it back to the table and picking up her knife and fork. "This looks excellent."

"It'll get you by."

"Mmm," she said after the first bite. The different flavors gelled. Together, they were perfectly delectable. "Noah. This is fantastic."

"I just threw things together in the pan."

She jabbed her fork in his direction. "Modesty doesn't suit you. I watched you make this. You'll take credit for it."

"Or?" he asked and popped a long green bean into his mouth, chewing.

She reached for the bottle of wine. "I could pour this fine vintage over your head."

"You'll taste it on the rest of me, then," he said darkly. Wonderfully.

Images hit her brain, inciting more answers from her body.

"What's it going to be, Colton?" he asked, amused, when she didn't let go of the bottle. The delicious light of challenge smoldered behind his eyes.

*Jesus.* Did he play with fire often? Because he was good at it. She placed the bottle back on the table. "Fortify yourself," she told him, nodding at his plate. "You're going to need it."

Shaking his head, he muttered, "A little over an hour ago, I didn't think there was anything that could make me forget what's going to happen tomorrow. But you could make me forget the world if you put your mind to it."

That had been her goal. Hadn't it? Now she could only think about wanting him in her bed again. He'd been there since that first night they'd made love. He'd slept beside her. But this time, she wanted more. To make him forget, yes. But also because…

Because she *needed* him. "Eat," she said. It was the only safe word she knew.

They cleaned their plates, and he cleared them. She polished off her wine. Before he could think about washing dishes, she took his hand. "Follow me?" she asked, grabbing the soft faux fur blanket draped over the back of the couch.

As she led him to the back door, he said, "Anywhere," before sliding the glass panel open for both of them.

She held that inside her, letting it feed her, as she led

him around the chairs and pool to the path that tumbled down one flagstone at a time to the base of the natural hill her bungalow dominated.

The sound of trickling water led her. Little lights on either side of the path would be turned off soon in adherence to Dark Sky Community guidelines. The stargazing party would leave soon in the Jeeps provided by the resort, with the blankets and hot cocoa offered during cooler nights. The chill in the air was sharp.

"Is there a stream here?" he asked as the tumble of water grew louder.

"When I was a kid, it was a river," she told him. "This is all that's left." A small swath of moonlight shimmied over stones as water hurried across them. "My mother would walk here every morning. Sometimes she would bring me and the boys. But mostly this was her spot."

"Is that why you built your place at the top of the hill?"

"Yes," she said. "It was my way of feeling close to her."

His hand didn't leave hers as they stood listening to the water babble. "Do you find that fades...more and more as the years go on?" he asked quietly.

Her eyes sought his silhouette. As they adjusted to the dark, she carved him out of the night. Hooded brow, firm jaw, solid as the mountains that held the sky. "Yes," she admitted.

He nodded slightly. "So do I."

She tightened her hold on him, bringing his attention to her. As his feet shuffled to face her, she let go to reach for the belt of the robe.

He stopped her. "You'll freeze."

"It's why I brought the blanket," she said. "Will you hold it?"

He took the furry coverlet. Anticipation high, she untied the knot.

She wished she could see him better, but the moon was behind him. Knowing it bathed her, she parted the silk and let it slip from her shoulders.

She heard his breath tear out of him. Trailing her fingers over the low-cut neckline and transparent lace, she followed the cascade of silk to her navel. "What do you think?"

"I knew you'd drive me wild."

Intrigued, she planted the heel of her hand against the granite slab of his chest. "You feel okay to me."

"Laura, I—"

She bit her lip when he stopped. "Yes?" she breathed, wanting to hear exactly what he'd censored himself from saying. She waited long enough that she shivered.

"You are cold," he confirmed. He swung the blanket around her shoulders. "Let's go back to the house."

"No." With her hand still on his chest, she backed him up to the large chaise underneath a collapsed red umbrella.

He went down hard, grunting. She knelt on the thick cushion. It was cold, too.

They'd warm it, she knew.

She felt his hands close around the blanket on her shoulders. Using it, he brought her against the heat of his chest and rolled her beneath him.

She did taste the wine on his tongue. She tasted herself there, too, as she lay beneath him, shivering not from the cold anymore but the storm of worshipping open-mouthed kisses. They started somewhere around her instep and spread to the back of her knee, up the inside of her thigh, between them where he lingered, using lips, tongue and beard to push her over the edge. Then his kisses continued over her hips, navel, breasts, to the bridge of her collarbone where he found the pearl. He sipped the delicate ridge of her jaw, and at last took her mouth.

She'd brought him here to seduce him. The thick fur blanket lay heavy over their tangled forms as he joined with her. Long, deep strokes built fresh waves of sensation. The cold didn't penetrate the lovely languid haze of his loving, and she knew she was the one who had been completely, utterly seduced.

"Look at me."

Her eyes had rolled back into her head. She made her lashes lift.

His face was half shadow, half light. His hips rocked against hers in an unbroken rhythm and she found she had swallowed the fire. It burned so good, she wanted to bathe in it.

His mouth parted hers. His eyes remained fixed. "Again," he breathed into her.

She shook her head slightly even as the next climax gathered steam. His hand was between them, coaxing her at the point where their bodies met. She was trembling all over, a string about to break even as his touch made her pliant and soft for him.

His chin bobbed in a listless nod. "Do it," he bade, need bearing the words through his teeth.

She didn't have it in her to shy away. And she realized she'd thrown caution with him to the wind days ago. She burned, feeling like a phoenix as she let the firestorm take her. All of her.

He groaned, long, low, satisfied. "That's right," he whispered and added, "Stay with me," when she pooled beneath him. "Stay with me," he said again, quickening.

The base of his erection pitched against the bed of nerves at her center, and she dropped the crown of her head back, gasping at the assault of unending pleasure. He had to stop. She was going to catch fire.

No one… No one had ever brought her this close to blind rapture. No one had made her bare her soul like this before.

"Noah."

His response hummed across her lips as his brows came together.

Ardor painted his face, and she moaned. "I'm yours."

He swore. The word blew through the night as he buried himself to the hilt. His body locked, arcing like a current, and he slammed his eyes closed, suspended in the rush.

When his muscles released, he made a noise like a man drowning. She raised her hands to him, stroking as his lungs whistled through several respirations and his heart knocked like a ram against hers. Lifting her legs, she crossed her ankles at the small of his back and dragged his mouth back to hers, not ready to give up the link.

"I'm crushing you," he said when he caught his breath at last.

"No."

"Laura, baby. I'm heavy."

*Baby.* Her smile was as soft as the blanket. "You're perfect, Noah Steele."

He stilled in her embrace. It even seemed like he stopped breathing.

"A little while," she sighed soothingly, running her nails lightly over his upper arms. "Let's stay just like this a little while longer."

He made another noise, this one of assent.

Eventually…eventually, she agreed they had to get out of the cold. And when he wrapped her in the blanket and carried her back up the flagstone steps to her house, she was speechless.

## *Chapter 17*

Mariposa's anniversary always felt bittersweet. Twenty-two years ago, Annabeth Colton had escaped Los Angeles for Red Rock Country, where she'd purchased the hotel.

Today was cause for both celebration and reflection. As Laura went about her duties, she couldn't help but wonder whether Mariposa reflected her mother's vision two decades prior. For Annabeth, it had been both home and a place of hope and renewal.

Laura tried to focus on that and not everything she had learned from Noah the night before.

When CJ Knight and Doug DeGraw crossed her path, however, she thought even Noah would agree the mission verged on impossible.

"Ms. Colton," the actor called out, forcing her to stop on the path to S Building. "I hear there's going to be a show tonight."

"Yes," she replied. "We'll have music and canapés in the rock labyrinth from six to seven this evening, with fireworks to follow. Will you be joining us?"

"Wouldn't miss it," CJ asserted.

Laura looked at Doug. "And you, Mr. DeGraw?"

"If it's better than the excursion yesterday and today's massage." Doug rolled both shoulders back in a discomfited manner. "I wonder why Mariposa is the go-to destination for the rich and famous. I can't find much to recommend it."

As Laura's face fell, CJ cleared his throat. "Come on, Doug. You don't mean that." To Laura, he offered an apologetic smile. "I enjoyed the horseback excursion, and my massage was more than satisfactory. We're booked for lunch at Annabeth. I've told Doug your chef never disappoints."

She returned the smile. "I'm glad you think so." Uncomfortable, she looked at Doug again. "Is there anything I can do to make your stay more enjoyable, Mr. DeGraw?"

He raised a discerning brow. "You wouldn't know what bungalow Ariana Fitzgibbons is staying in, would you?"

"I'm afraid I can't divulge that information," she told him when she regained her voice. "It's against our policy to invade the privacy of our guests."

"Pity," Doug drawled. His mouth turned down at the corners, dissatisfied. "I guess I'll have to find out myself."

"I'd advise you not to do so," she cautioned.

Doug gave a small laugh. "Can't anyone around here take a joke?"

As he walked away, limping slightly on his right leg, CJ's smile deteriorated. He lowered his voice. "I'm sorry. He isn't normally like this. I've noticed he's been out of sorts lately. He practically begged me not to come back here."

She tried to appear as unaffected as possible. "Red Rock Country doesn't agree with everyone."

"I'm not sure how," CJ noted. "I get that Doug's a city guy. He's LA to the bone. But there's nothing I don't love about this part of the country."

"I'm happy to hear it," she said truthfully. "If there's anything you or your manager can think of to make your stay better, please let me know. I'll see to it."

"I appreciate it, Ms. Colton," he returned before hurrying to catch up with Doug.

Laura rubbed her hands across the surface of her arms. The chill had gone deep into her bones despite the desert sun doing its best to ward off the nip of late winter. Thunder rolled in the distance. She looked out across the ridge.

Steel wool storm clouds converged in the east, washing away everything except the foreboding that had been with her since Noah had kissed her goodbye in the wee hours of the morning. He had thought she was still asleep as he'd bent over her still form and skimmed his lips across the point of her bare shoulder before brushing the hair from her neck to repeat the motion there.

She'd wanted to turn onto her back then, ring her arms around him and roll him into the sheets with her. But she'd kept her eyes closed as he'd kissed her cheek and lingered there, his hand moving down her spine to rest warmly in the curve of her hip.

He spooked so easily when he was like that—tender and unguarded. She'd continued to feign sleep, absorbing the sweetness and tranquility.

It wasn't a simple thing, giving her heart to a man who could so easily break it. And yet, in that moment, she'd had no choice. She'd given it as she never had before. Freely.

Laura stared those storm clouds down, daring them to intrude on tonight's festivities. She wanted to follow Doug, track his movements, make sure he stayed far away from Ariana Fitzgibbons and every other woman at Mariposa.

"Come on, Noah," she whispered desperately before continuing to S Building.

The storm split and spread its quilting across the sky. Sunset burned ombré shades across, so the clouds glowed terra-cotta and apricot one moment, then orange and mauve the next. At last, the day died in a somber cast of mulberry, inspiring a round of applause from the multitude of guests who gathered at the rock labyrinth over steak and blue cheese bruschetta bites and spicy blue crab tapas.

"And that wasn't even the part we planned," Joshua said, amused, as he passed Laura a tall glass of champagne.

"No," she said. She sipped. "You cleaned up well."

"Thank you," he replied, running a hand down the front of his blue button-down. He'd popped the first few buttons on the collar, but the shirt was pressed, and he'd combed his hair back from his face, leaving his striking features to be admired by all and sundry. He glanced over at her. "Let's not pretend I'm the one turning heads tonight."

She peered down the front of the glittering, long-sleeved cocktail dress she'd donned. Its color brought to mind champagne bubbles, and its open back from the waist up made her aware of the swift decline in temperature. "A girl needs to shine now and then," she mused.

Joshua's lips curled knowingly as his champagne hovered inches from them. "If Steele were here, he'd swallow his tongue."

The thought brought out a full-fledged grin. "Perhaps that was the idea. It might've worked if he'd made it on time."

Joshua raised his wrist to peek at his watch. "He could still make it."

"I've learned not to hold my breath."

Joshua sipped, swallowed and looked at her contemplatively.

She narrowed her eyes. "What is it, Josh?"

"Is there something you want to tell me?" he asked. "About you and Fender Bender?"

"What makes you think there is?" she asked, tensing.

Joshua lowered the glass. "Because I looked him up. Noah Steele has never played for Fast Lane."

Her smile fled swiftly.

"How could he when he's been working for the Sedona police for seven years?"

*Oh, no.* "Josh," she began.

He stopped her with "Is he really even your boyfriend?"

She couldn't miss the light of hurt beyond the forced jocularity on his face. "No. Yes." Closing her eyes quickly, she shook her head. "I don't know. I—"

"How could you not know?" he asked, bewildered.

"I don't know how to explain," she tried to tell him, but he was on a roll.

"Is this about Allison?" he asked. "Is that why he's here? Did he manipulate you into being part of his cover?"

"He didn't *make* me do anything," she argued. "It was my idea."

"So he's not the reason you've been lying to me all this time?" he asked. "You decided that on your own?"

"I'm sorry." She grabbed his arm before he could walk away. "I couldn't tell you. He needed intimate knowledge of Mariposa's staff and guests. He needed to know the resort from the ground up, every operation, inside and outside."

"I knew he was hiding something," Joshua muttered. "I just didn't think you were in on it. We've always told each other *everything*, Laura."

"I know," she said, forcing herself to look him in the eye, however much the accusation in his wounded. "I'm so sorry."

"What's going on?" Adam asked.

Joshua pointed. "Our sister's been keeping things from us."

"About?" Adam prompted.

"Steele," Joshua said. "He's a cop."

"I know."

Joshua stared, aghast. "You know?"

"Yes," Adam said.

"So you've both been keeping things from me."

"Mariposa had to continue as usual," Adam stated, not missing a beat, "with no one the wiser except Laura and myself."

"Why not me?" Joshua asked. "You didn't think you could trust me?"

"Of course we trust you," Laura told him.

"But you have a tendency to wear your heart on your sleeve," Adam informed him. "You also party and social-ize more extensively than the two of us. I'm sure you would have had every intention of keeping Steele's actual reasons for being here to yourself. But it would have been all too easy to let something slip."

Joshua's jaw worked as he digested the information. His accusing gaze sought Laura again. "He spent the night with you."

Adam shifted uncomfortably beside her. Awkwardness pressed against her. It clung like shrink-wrap. "He did," she said.

"You don't think that's taking your role a little too seri-ously?" Joshua questioned.

She swallowed when the taste of anger coated her mouth. "I'm not going to take that—from you or anyone else. I don't have to explain what Noah and I have to either of you."

"I'm not asking," Adam pointed out.

"Not now," she granted. "But you have questioned it."

"Because I thought you would get hurt."

"I'm in love with him," she blurted. "If we're being honest, I might as well throw it out there. I've fallen in love with him and we're all going to have to come to terms with that."

Neither of her brothers seemed to know what to say anymore. Laura was relieved by the reprieve, though she sensed this wasn't over. They would need to discuss this more at another time and place. She and Adam would need to address Joshua's hurt. He would need to know the full details of Noah's investigation. There was no going back, no hiding anything from him anymore.

"He's making an arrest soon," she told them both.

"When?" Joshua asked. "Tonight?"

"I don't know precisely," she said. "I haven't heard from him since this morning. But he's gathering evidence to secure a warrant. Soon, he'll go, and this will all be over." There was relief and dread in the finality of that. With luck, Allison's killer would be locked away for good.

But Noah would be leaving Mariposa.

"Who?" Adam asked quietly.

She searched the crowd for the person she couldn't deny she had been keeping tabs on since the party began. She located him over at the buffet table, not far from CJ. "I'm afraid I can't say. Not without Noah's authorization."

Joshua wasn't heartened by the news. "Fantastic. I can't believe I actually liked the guy. I can't believe I trusted him with you."

Laura glanced around quickly to make sure no one would overhear. Then she hissed, "Allison was his sister!"

"What?" Joshua exclaimed.

"She was his sister," she repeated. "He needed help. I gave it—for her."

Joshua stepped back. He pinched the skin at the bridge of his nose, closing his eyes. "This is a lot to process."

"Then take a beat," Adam advised. "We'll speak about

this, however much you need to. But come back when you're ready to do so civilly."

Joshua dropped his hand. He glanced in Laura's direction but didn't quite meet her eye. "I've said some things tonight I'm going to regret later."

"Adam's right," Laura said. She tried swallowing the guilt and hurt. Together, they formed a knot that was anything but small. "We'll talk more when you're ready."

He lifted his empty glass. "I need another."

As he moved off, Laura dropped her face into her hand. "Oh, God, Adam. He's so angry at me."

"He's angry at us."

"I made you keep this from him," she reminded him. "You didn't have to take any of the blame."

"I may not understand all the reasons you did this," Adam explained. "But I will never not stand beside you. I thought you knew that."

His ferocity was something to behold. She wanted to tell him she loved him—that she was sorry that he had to weather Joshua's resentment and accusations, too.

Before she could put any of that into words, Erica said, "Excuse me?" In a black cocktail dress and heels, she looked elegant, but her beauty was subdued by the frown playing at her mouth.

"Yes, Erica?" Adam asked kindly.

"They're ready for your speech," she said, gesturing to the stage.

"Right." Adam downed the last of his champagne. He took the note cards Erica had at the ready, then straightened his collar and tie. "Wish me luck?"

"You always bring down the house," Laura murmured. "But good luck."

He gave her a single nod before taking the steps to the bandstand two at a time.

"I was wondering if I could speak to you," Erica said to Laura. Embarrassment and hesitancy battled for purchase on her face.

"Certainly," Laura told her, trying to inject some measure of cheer into her voice. It didn't work as well as she'd hoped.

"I heard a rumor," Erica said. "About the investigation."

"What kind of rumor?" Laura asked.

Erica coaxed the words out, paling as she did so. "They say that CJ Knight is a suspect."

Laura pressed her lips together, wondering what exactly to say. "He may be," she said, hesitant.

Erica shook her head. "That isn't right. I mean, you see, I…" Releasing a breath, she lifted a trembling hand to her head. "He has an alibi."

"He does?" Laura asked, surprised.

"Yes," she decided. "I lied to you and to Joshua. I'm not entirely sure what came over me that night. The night Allison was killed."

"You were with him," Laura intoned.

"I was with him," Erica agreed with a nod. "CJ and I… were intimate. It happened in his bungalow. So he couldn't have done it. He couldn't have killed Allison. And he wouldn't have. He may be the one-night-stand kind of guy. But he's not the type of man who would murder someone."

Laura set her champagne aside. She placed her hand considerately on Erica's arm. "You need to tell the police. You'll have to in order to clear Mr. Knight of all suspicion."

Erica absorbed this news. Her eyes widened, but she nodded slightly. "Of course."

Laura squeezed her arm gently. "It's a good thing you're doing, Erica."

"Do you think Adam will fire me?" she whispered faintly.

"It hasn't interfered with your ability to do your job," Laura noted. "I think we can all vouch for that. I'll speak with Adam, and we'll see about moving forward from this once the investigation's over."

Erica nodded. "Thank you, Laura—for being so understanding."

Laura simply nodded. As Erica slipped away, Laura looked around. She found Joshua near the bar, talking to Valerie. Adam was at center stage, cuing the band for his speech. Alexis and Tallulah stood shoulder to shoulder as they chatted with Greg and Tallulah's nephew, Mato, who held a tray of canapés on an upraised palm.

She spied CJ Knight at last as he spoke with Knox and Kim Blankenship.

If CJ had been occupied with Erica at the time of Allison's death, Noah was right. Guilt now lay squarely at the feet of...

"Ms. Colton."

The chill started at the base of her neck. It trickled down her spine as she pivoted on her heels to confront Doug DeGraw. He wore a suit in charcoal gray with a black shirt underneath. He'd gone without a tie, and the shirt was buttoned to his throat. His Adam's apple jutted over its neat collar and his cool smile turned her blood to ice.

"Mr. DeGraw," she greeted him. "I see you decided to join us. How was your lunch at Annabeth?"

"Superb."

She forced a smile. "Mr. Knight is correct. Our chef rarely disappoints."

"The food was all right," he said with a wave of his hand. "It was the company that was divine."

Her brows came together. "The company?"

"I slipped the maître d' a fifty. He seated CJ and me next to Ms. Fitzgibbons's table."

The smugness of his grin…the light that entered his eyes… They made Laura take a steadying breath. "Is that so?"

"Yes." He took a step toward her while Adam spoke into the mic on stage and those around them quieted. "You needn't worry. Ariana knows she will benefit from the attention of a man like me. And she's more than willing to take it."

Her lips numbed, and she realized she was pressing them hard together. "What did you do to her?"

"Do?" He chuckled. "Nothing she didn't ask for. In her own way." With a wink, he slithered off to stand with CJ and the others.

Laura's heart drummed. She barely resisted the urge to place her hand over her mouth as she searched the crowd desperately for the red hair of Ariana Fitzgibbons.

When she couldn't find her, she walked briskly to Roland. When he leaned down to hear what she wanted to say, she kept her voice low. "Doug DeGraw. Do you know who he is?"

"CJ Knight's manager," he said.

She nodded. "Can you keep an eye on him for me?"

"Yes."

"If you see him leave the party, I'm going to need you to call me on my cell phone," she explained. "Immediately. Can you do that?"

"Of course I can." His wide forehead creased. "Should I be concerned about anyone's safety?"

"Not at this time," she said, again looking around, wishing Ariana's face would pop out of the crowd. "The moment DeGraw exits the rock labyrinth…"

"I'll place the call," he finished. "You have my word."

"Thank you," she murmured, then walked away as Adam's speech wrapped to the roused clatter of applause.


"Ms. Fitzgibbons?" Laura called. She knocked again on the door of Ariana's bungalow, louder this time. "Ms. Fitzgibbons!"

No answer came. The windows remained dark. Laura cupped her hands around her face to peer through the nearest one.

A shaft of moonlight revealed an empty couch and table.

If Ariana had returned to the bungalow before sunset, she would have left a light burning before she'd departed again.

Trying not to panic, Laura sprinted along the path to the VIP bungalows.

When she reached Bungalow Two, where she knew Doug was staying on CJ's dime, she slowed.

Noah had made her promise not to approach a suspect. That promise made her hesitate on the doorstep.

She wasn't approaching a suspect, she reasoned. Doug was back at the rock labyrinth, where she knew Roland would watch him.

Raising her fist, she knocked on the door. When she heard nothing inside, she pressed her ear to the door, willing her pulse to stop knocking so that she may better hear a call for help.

When none came, she peered through the window. The blackout curtains had been drawn.

Frustrated, she tore open her beaded handbag and extracted her master key. If Ariana was in there and she wasn't answering, Laura could only assume she had been drugged, like Allison. That maybe she, too, had been given too much and was…

She swiped the master key. The lock chirped and a green light blinked. Laura pushed the door open and stepped inside.

She switched on the light beside the door.

There was no sign of a struggle. As she shut the door behind her, she peered at the couch. The cushions weren't mussed. A pair of men's shoes sat tidily near the door to the patio. There was a glass of wine, unfinished, on the kitchen counter.

Laura stared at the last sips of dark red wine. She saw the faint impression of lips on the rim. No lipstick.

Through the glass door, the pool sat undisturbed. Folded towels lay in the corner on a raised surface, compliments of Housekeeping. Laura counted one, two, three. None of them had been used.

She twitched the curtain back in place. There was no sign of a woman here. No sign that anything nefarious had taken place.

She eyed the short passage to the bedroom and clutched her handbag tighter.

If she could find proof…if she could help Noah nail Doug DeGraw…this would all be over. Allison's killer would be caught.

Laura stepped toward the bedroom door. It was open. She turned on the overhead light, illuminating the white linens on the bed.

She scanned the space, wondering where to start. Doug's toiletry bag lay on the dresser. His suitcase was open on the rack near the bathroom.

She searched all the outside pockets first, then lay a

hand flat between folded shirts. After running her hand around the inside rim to no avail, she checked the toiletry bag. Careful not to disorganize the high-end men's products she found inside, she shifted them one by one. Nothing hid underneath them except a sample sleeve of under-eye cream.

She stepped back, making sure everything looked exactly as it had before she'd begun her search. Frowning, she turned a slow circle.

Where else would a guilty man hide evidence of wrongdoing?

She opened the drawer on the nightstand. Nothing there—not a single dust mote.

The corner of the sheet stuck out kitty-corner underneath the coverlet. It had slipped from its holding under the mattress.

*...under the mattress...*

Hadn't Fulton found Dayton Ferraday's drug stash under the mattress or inside it?

She went down on her knees. Like she had with the shirts, she reached underneath the mattress and felt around.

Her hand met something cold. It rolled, then tinkled against something else. She grabbed the thin item and pulled it out into the light.

The vial was translucent, but she could see the liquid within. On the side, there was a label.

*Fentanyl.*

Holding her breath, she reached underneath the mattress and found the other vial and a ten-milliliter syringe, empty and capped. It looked like the kind used for insulin.

She placed them on top of the bed and dug into her bag. Remembering to breathe, she pulled out her cell phone and stood. When she unlocked the screen to place the call to Noah, she paused.

She'd missed a call—from Roland.

She checked the time stamp. He'd tried calling ten minutes ago.

*It hasn't rung*, she thought.

She checked her notification settings and her heart dropped.

After exiting the party, she'd forgotten to take her phone off Silent.

*Don't panic*, she coached herself. She'd simply take a picture of the evidence, then replace it and slip safely out of Doug's bungalow.

Quickly, she framed the vials and syringe in her camera view. She tapped the screen when it tried focusing on the fibers of the comforter underneath and ignored the sound of her heartbeat in her ears.

She snapped a couple of pictures, then stuffed her phone back in her bag. Replacing the vials, she left the covers on the bed as they should be. Then she stood and took two steps to the door before an item on the floor made her stop.

It lay innocently enough underneath the hook where Doug had hung his overcoat. A leather string with an evil-eye pendant.

Laura bent down to retrieve it. She raised it to get a better look and her lips trembled.

It must've fallen from the pocket of his coat without his knowing.

A sob rose as she studied the evil eye. Unlike the one she had given Noah, Allison's was light green. She'd once told Laura it granted her success in dreams, good health and contentment.

Laura felt a whisper of air across the bare skin of her back and the hairs on her arms and neck stood on end.

Before she could turn, he took her down at the waist.

She met the wall with a clatter, knocking the lamp over on the bedside table. The impact knocked the wind out of her.

Fingers raked through her hair and drove her face into the wall.

A dull gray film slanted across her vision. Her ears rang. She blinked, trying to bring everything back into focus as he spun her roughly around.

It took several seconds for Doug's face to solidify in front of her.

"Ms. Colton," he said with a sneer.

She saw his fist raised to strike. Before he could swing, she took up the fallen lamp on the bedside table. The lampshade fell. She arced the neck of the lamp toward his face and threw her weight into it.

It hit him. The bulb shattered and he toppled sideways on a shout.

She made a break for it, fumbling for the door.

She slipped in the hall. Her heel came off. She left it, scrambling to her feet as his footsteps chased her.

She ran out of Bungalow Two, screaming.

# Chapter 18

Fireworks crackled and thundered. Their lights sparkled across the path to L Building, illuminating her escape route in intermittent bursts.

She melded into the manicured hedges and cacti that lined the path, willing the rocks under her feet not to give her away. She'd lost her other heel. The sharp edges of stones bit into the undersides of her feet. She didn't slow. With her knowledge of Mariposa, she could locate help before he found her.

There was blood in her mouth. She'd bitten her tongue when he'd mashed her face into the wall. She swallowed it and kept going. Something dripped across her lips. She licked them and tasted blood there, too. Reaching up, she swiped the space above them. It came away wet and warm.

Her nose was bleeding. The pulse of pain around the bridge alerted her to the damage there.

Her fist was still knotted around Allison's bracelet. She hadn't lost it in the altercation.

She wouldn't lose it, she determined as she pushed on. The roof of L Building was visible through the foliage. She could see the lights of the pool. Her heart lifted. She was almost there. Someone would be there. Someone had to be.

First, she had to cross the open pathway. She glanced around. Hearing no footsteps, she made a break for it.

A cut on the bottom of her foot slowed her, but she half sprinted for the shape of the first pool cabana—the one where they'd found Allison.

Before she could reach it, fingers dug into her arm. She fought them, reaching for escape.

Doug shoved her off the path into the rocks on the other side. Her hands and knees scraped across them.

He covered her mouth before she could scream. "You couldn't leave it alone, could you? Couldn't live and let live?"

His hand covered her nose. She fought for air, her nails digging into his hand. Desperate, she threw her head back into his face.

He grunted. His hold loosened.

She turned over, scrambling away from him. Her back met the long stalk of a cactus plant. Its fine needles dug into the exposed skin of her back.

Doug was on her in a flash. She did scream now—before he could silence her.

He struck her across the face. The shock of the blow silenced her, as did the fingers he wrapped around her throat. The pressure he exerted made little rockets of flame blossom before her eyes. Her ankles kicked against the rocks. The stones scattered, preventing her from gaining purchase. Again, she clawed at his hand. The bracelet dropped.

He glanced down at it, then back up at her. "I don't like killing," he groaned as he watched her struggle. He shook his head to emphasize the point. "I never meant to kill anyone. If she'd been willing…if she'd just spread her legs for me…I wouldn't have had to subdue her. I wouldn't have given her too much."

Her lungs burned. Her eyes went blind.

"It was such a waste," he muttered. "Wasn't it? I hate thinking about it. Just as I'm going to hate thinking about you, Ms. Colton. Such a beautiful waste."

She fought to stay conscious. She fought to see something other than the whiteout she found when her eyes rolled back. Still, her kicking slowed and she hooked her hands over his arm because they'd fallen away from his fingers. The ocean roared in her ears. It was so loud, it drowned his words.

His grip fumbled away from her. His weight lifted. She gasped, choked, wheezed and coughed. As she fell sideways across the rocks, she reached for her neck, where the phantom hold of Doug's fingers stayed even as she took a breath that raked across her airways.

In the light from the path and the stunning bright lights screaming into the sky—the fireworks' grand finale—she saw two figures, one on top of the other, struggling on the ground.

Her hearing sharpened with the whistle and boom of rockets overhead and shouting. The haze around her vision broke and she realized what she was seeing.

Noah, his face a mask of fury, arced his fist down to meet Doug's face again and again.

Someone else—Detective Fulton—raced forward to pull Noah off. Noah fought him. Fulton didn't let go.

Doug stayed on the ground, curling in on himself. His face was a mess of blood. He didn't get up.

Noah shrugged Fulton off him. Rocks slid underneath his feet as he scrambled over them. He crouched, his hand going to the back of her head. "Laura."

She was afraid to speak. Her throat felt bruised. Sucking air in and out in careful repetitions, she watched his features sharpen.

There was fury there. But more, there was desperate fear. "Hey," he said. "Can you hear me?"

She gave a faint nod.

He blew out a breath, then cradled her to him. She closed her eyes because the cold had gone deep into her bones. She didn't know if it was the temperature or nearly being choked to death, but she lay still, absorbing the heat of him as he held her.

He pulled away. His gaze seized on her throat. "I need to get you to the hospital," he said gruffly.

She opened her mouth, but the words got trapped behind the pain. Looking around over the rocks, she fumbled a hand over them, searching.

She found the little braided cord and lifted it.

When she offered it, he took it from her and raised it to the light. At the sight of the evil eye, he stilled. "Where did you find this?" he asked.

Afraid, she locked her lips together.

He searched her face. Then he shook his head. "You didn't."

She lifted her chin in a half nod. A tear slipped past her guard. She wished she could look away. Then she wouldn't have to watch his disbelief meld into disappointment.

"Laura," he said. "You promised. You *promised* me."

His voice broke and her stomach twisted. *I had to*, she wanted to tell him.

His grimace was complete. It went through her. As he looked away, closing his hand around the evil eye, she felt it as keenly as a knife.

Noah spent an hour at the police station, watching Doug DeGraw be questioned, booked and processed. Even if he couldn't be the one leading him through it, he needed to watch, just as he needed to hear the bars roll into place as the man who admitted to killing Allison was locked in a cell.

An accident, he'd claimed. Allison had shown up at his bungalow after dark for his private yoga lesson. When she didn't respond to his attempts at seduction, he dosed her with fentanyl and waited for the drug to take effect before having his way with her.

"After, she didn't come around like the others do," Doug had claimed. "She just lay there. She didn't breathe. I checked and realized her pulse wasn't right. It was too slow. I tried to make her come around. She just lay there. Lay there and died."

"You handled yourself well," Captain Crabtree told Noah after they both watched Doug sign a confession.

"He's beat to hell," Noah pointed out, surveying the damage he'd done to Doug's face.

"You saved Laura Colton's life."

And nearly killed the man who'd almost taken it. If not for Fulton, Noah knew he would have done worse. Each of the knuckles of his right hand ached like a sore tooth from the impact with Doug's nose, jaw and cheekbone. "I've still got a job on Monday?"

"You closed the case," Crabtree noted.

Noah had spent the entire day on the phone, tracking victims in the wind. He'd finally found one—a twenty-three-year-old colleague of Doug's who had quit her job a year ago and moved to Tallahassee to live with her folks. She'd been reluctant to talk, and Noah had thought he would have to fly to Florida to speak with her face-to-face. But then she'd broken, and the story had come out. Doug had drugged and raped her, too, similarly.

There were others, Noah knew. A half-dozen women

Doug had sedated and terrorized. Noah would find them all. He would bury the man for hurting them, for killing Allison and for nearly killing Laura.

"He tried to frame CJ Knight," Noah said. "He assumed calling him away from Mariposa soon after Allison's death would throw suspicion on him. It might have worked, too, had Erica Pike not come forward."

"Knight was here while you were in interrogation. He confirmed he was with Ms. Pike during the time in question, but not much more."

"What did he have to say about his manager being the killer?" Noah asked.

"He was in shock. He didn't seem to know what to say."

"I should've seen it sooner," Noah muttered. "It was Doug's office who refused to return my calls, not Knight directly."

"You were pretty deep in the reeds on this one," Crabtree said knowingly. "But Fulton didn't see it any faster than you did. I'd like to give you both credit for the arrest."

"All that matters is that this scumbag is going away forever."

"Now you can focus on laying your sister to rest. And you'll take some time off."

Noah closed his eyes. He needed to let Allison go. He knew that. And Crabtree was right. It was time. "Yes, sir."

The hospital was five minutes from the SPD. Despite the cold and the sleet that fell sideways, he walked there.

"Laura Colton," he said to the woman at the information desk.

"It's after visiting hours."

He dug into his pocket before placing his badge on the desk for her to see.

She frowned. "One moment," she said before tapping

the screen in front of her. "Ms. Colton is in recovery. Room twenty-four."

"Thanks," he said before exiting the atrium and following the corridors to the Recovery ward. She wasn't in surgery, he consoled himself. Or the ER. Which meant she was going to be okay.

He'd heard her scream. As he'd followed Fulton across the pool area on the way to Bungalow Two, he'd heard her call for help. At first, he'd thought it had been coming from the pool cabana.

Like Allison, he'd thought, frantic. Then he'd discovered the couple grappling in the dark off the path behind it. He'd seen Doug on top of Laura, his hands around her throat, and he'd nearly screamed himself hoarse.

Noah passed the door to number twenty-four. He halted and backtracked, the soles of his boots squeaking on the clean linoleum.

Through the window, he could see her brothers, one on either side of her. Joshua was hunkered down beside her in bed. Her head nestled on his shoulder while Adam sat on the bed's edge, his arm across the top of her pillows, head low over hers.

Noah thought about walking away, leaving them alone. They were family. A proper one. And a proper family took care of their own.

He watched as his hand rose to knock.

Adam lifted his head as the others stirred. He motioned for them to stay where they were as he stood and crossed to the door. When it opened, he looked at Noah. More, he looked through him before blinking and seeming to come to his senses. "Oh," he said. "It's you."

"Can I come in?" Noah asked.

Adam ran a hand through his hair. It wasn't as neat as it usually was. "Are you here on police business?"

He should have said yes. What came out was "No."

Adam nodded and stepped aside.

Joshua sat up as Noah entered. Noah looked past him to Laura. She had raised herself up on her elbows. He could see the cut on her mouth, the red mark around the bridge of her nose, the fading bruise on her temple, and the shadows of hands on her throat that would soon fly their colors, too. She looked weary around the eyes, but clarity rang true in them.

Joshua rose and moved into Noah's path to the bed. When Noah only sized him up, Joshua offered him a hand.

"What's this?" Noah asked cautiously.

"I'd like to shake hands with Allison's brother," Joshua said.

The others must have told baby brother everything, Noah realized. He reached out and took Joshua's hand.

The man squeezed his. "If you hadn't gotten to her in time…"

Noah had thought along the same lines. If he and Fulton had been a minute behind… If he'd spent any longer on the phone tracking Doug's victims…

"You lost your sister," Joshua said, "and saved mine. I won't forget that."

"Nor will I," Adam added. "We owe you an immense debt of gratitude."

He didn't want their gratitude. He didn't want Joshua's idea of a truce. He'd spent the better part of the evening chiding himself for working after hours. If he'd been with Laura at the party, she wouldn't have felt compelled to run off into the night and…

He saw Doug's hands around her throat again. He heard

her choking. His hands balled into fists and he felt the quaver go straight through as fear lanced him.

"May I speak with her?" he asked. "Alone."

"She's tired," Joshua began.

"It's all right, Josh," came the small, hoarse sound of her voice.

Joshua reached up to scrub his temples. Then he turned and went back to the bed. "A few minutes," he allowed, leaning down for a hug. "Then we all need to get some sleep."

"You don't have to sleep here," she told him. "Either of you."

"You don't have to talk," Adam replied as he, too, came forward. Joshua stepped back and Adam lowered a kiss to the top of her head. "Rest your throat. We'll be right outside the door."

"Definitely not listening," Joshua said with a halfhearted, ironic twist of his mouth.

Noah waited until they'd both left. When the latch clicked shut behind them, he approached the bed. Then he halted, conflicted. "I have a couple of questions."

She sat up a bit more. Wincing, she lay back on the pillows.

It nearly broke him to see her struggle.

She spoke haltingly, fighting the rawness of her throat. "You *are* here on police business."

"Your brother's right," he said. "Don't try to talk."

She tilted her head. "Questions require answers."

"Just nod," he told her. "Or shake your head. That's all the answer I need."

She sighed and, slowly, subsided into a nod.

"Ariana Fitzgibbons has been located. It seems Doug was just yanking your chain when he claimed he'd done something to her. She left Mariposa for Sedona after lunch with a friend she made during yesterday's trail ride. They spent the afternoon shopping and caught dinner after."

Laura's lips folded as she spun the hospital band on her wrist. She tried clearing her throat and closed her eyes. When she opened them again, there was a pained, wet sheen over them. "I'm glad she's all right."

It was a miracle Laura was, he thought. Digging in his pocket, he pulled out Allison's bracelet and held it up. She watched it swing from his hand.

"Did you find this in Doug DeGraw's bungalow?"

She hesitated. Then she inclined her head.

"You went to his bungalow?" When she nodded, he wanted to stop. He didn't want to know—didn't want to have to replay it in his head repeatedly. "Did you go there alone?"

Laura's eyes were heavy-lidded with fatigue and swimming in regret as she nodded again.

"Did you find anything else in Doug's bungalow?" At her nod, he said, "Drugs?" She nodded once more. He wanted to raise his voice as the storm inside him built. Desperate, scared, angry storm clouds he couldn't lasso. He had to work to keep his next question cool and flat. "Do you remember last night?"

Tears came into her eyes again. For the first time, she turned them away from him.

He gripped the bottom rail of the bed. "I need your answer."

She nodded.

"You remember promising me you wouldn't put yourself at risk?" he asked. "You remember looking me in the eye and giving me your word before you took me home with you and made love with me for the rest of the night?"

Lips taut together, she nodded. A tear slipped down her cheek.

His heart twisted. And it hurt. It hurt so much, he couldn't breathe. "I trusted you," he said in a whisper.

"I'm sorry," she whispered back. "I thought… I thought he hurt her. Like Allison."

He wanted to go to her. He wanted to slip inside the bed with her and hold her all night—until the storm quieted. Until he could breathe right again.

The early bruising on her throat glared at him. She'd made a promise. He'd needed her to keep it. He'd relied on her word. She'd broken it and nearly died before he could get to her.

He turned away.

"Where are you going?" she asked as he made a break for the door.

He wrapped his hand around the handle. Christ, he couldn't breathe. It was exactly as it had been in the autopsy room when he'd viewed Allison's lifeless body for the first time. He felt a part of his mind detach, float away. He wanted to follow it. But his body anchored him. His lungs strained, his chest felt tight and his head spun. Panic sank in. "I need some time."

"I'm okay."

He looked back and felt the quaver go to his knees. He heard the pounding of his heart in his ears. "You're not," he argued. "I can still see him choking you and hear you fighting for air. And I can't do this. Not until that gets quieter. I need time."

"How much time?" she asked.

"I don't know," he replied. He looked away from the tears falling freely down her face now. He had to get out of there before he split in two. "I don't know," he said again, at a loss. He snatched the door open.

"Noah," she called.

"Get some rest," he replied. Then he was out the door. He bypassed Adam and Joshua and their questions, needing to walk until he could no longer feel fear locking up the muscles around his lungs.

# Chapter 19

Laura had never seen so many orchids in her life. Most were rooted in pretty pots. The colors ranged from warm to cool. Some clashed, like the one with blue petals and pink centers.

Allison would have loved the symbolism. Laura tried to remember what each color meant. Red for strength. Purple for dignity. Orange for boldness. Yellow for friendship and new beginnings. Being surrounded by them would have made her friend happy.

Laura held that certainty in her chest as the memorial service came to a close. The setting of nature's cathedral—cloudless, open blue sky above, the carpet of earth beneath—brought to mind Allison's teachings of mindfulness and inner strength. *Sky above us. Earth below us. Fire within us.*

Allison's fire had been extinguished. And those who loved her, who came to pay their respects, had to learn to live without her—to move on. It was as simple and as hard as that.

Laura waited in line with her brothers to lay a rose on Allison's coffin. Over a hundred people had come to pay their respects from Sedona, Mariposa and across the country—yoga and meditation students, her friends and, of course, her brother, who had sat alone in the first row.

Alexis met Laura on the green. "It was nice, wasn't it?"

"Yes," Laura said. "Funerals are never easy, but this one made the last few weeks better somehow."

"It reminds me she's at peace," Alexis explained.

"She is," Laura murmured.

Alexis searched the crowd. "If you're looking for a tall, dark and handsome detective, he's doing well to avoid people over there."

She saw Noah's lone figure and her heart gave a squeeze.

"You know you could have let me in on your secret," Alexis told her.

Alexis wasn't accusing or unhappy with her. Still, the guilt came for Laura. "I know. I never thought for a second you would give me or Noah away. And I wasn't thinking clearly enough to realize how the lies would hurt others." She found Joshua mingling, grave-faced, with some former Mariposa guests. "I regret that now."

"Tell me one thing," Alexis said. "That conversation we had at Annabeth—next to those poor shrimp?"

Laura thought about it, then closed her eyes. "Oh. The shrimp."

"You talked about you and Noah spending the night together. Was that part of the act?"

Laura shook her head silently.

"So the two of you really…" Alexis trailed off when Laura nodded. "But he's over there. And you're over here."

"Precisely," Laura said with a weary sigh.

"What happened?" Alexis asked.

Laura felt relieved she was free to tell Alexis everything. Still, she found it hard to explain what had gone wrong the night Doug was arrested. "I broke a promise to him."

"What kind of promise?"

Laura shifted her feet. Her heels poked through the bed of grass, making her reposition them for balance. "He lost

Allison in the worst way possible. And before that, he lost his mother similarly. He doesn't get close to people because he's afraid of losing them."

Alexis's eyes strayed to the marks on Laura's neck that were visible above her knotted black scarf. "He almost lost you, like he lost them."

"I promised him the night before I wouldn't confront Doug like I did Roger and Dayton Ferraday," Laura admitted.

"Why did you?" Alexis asked.

"I thought he was going to hurt someone else or already had. It was the same way when Tallulah told me that Bella had been hurt. I didn't think."

"You went into mama-bear mode." Alexis nodded. "I get it."

"Those men brought terror, rape and murder into my home," Laura said. "They brought it into a place where those things were never meant to exist."

"Have you told the man this?" Alexis asked.

"We haven't spoken since the hospital. He said he needed time."

"Allison would take this moment to remind us that time is fleeting," Alexis said, "and there's no time like the present."

"She would," Laura admitted.

"Is that Bella?" Alexis pointed her out in the crowd.

Laura shaded her eyes with her hand and waved when she spotted the young woman standing close at Tallulah's side. "Yes."

"Is it true she's coming back to Mariposa?" Alexis asked.

"Not yet," Laura said. "She still needs to heal. But I think she will, eventually. Tallulah won't be happy unless she has her under her wing. And I think Bella's learning how strong she really is."

"We'll all take care of her," Alexis asserted. "Not just Tallulah."

Laura couldn't agree more. "Are we still on for Taco Tuesday?"

"Absolutely," Alexis confirmed. "The Tipsy Tacos' owner called to say they're planting a tree in Allison's name in the courtyard where they're opening up the space for outdoor dining."

"I love that," Laura declared.

Adam and Joshua walked to them. "We're going to pay our respects to Noah," Joshua told Laura. "Want to come?"

She took Adam's arm when he offered it. "Of course." To Alexis, she said, "We'll talk later."

"You know it," Alexis returned.

As the three Coltons ventured closer to the tree line, Laura watched Noah. She knew the moment he spotted them. He didn't so much stiffen as still—like a deer in the headlights. Laura felt her stomach flutter with nerves.

Sensing her agitation, Adam whispered, "Steady on, Lou," and curled his hand around hers.

She fought the inclination to lean on his solid form, especially as the distance to Noah shrank to inches and, suddenly, they were face-to-face.

"It was a beautiful service," Joshua told him.

"You did well," Adam pointed out.

Noah looked past them to where the coffin stood. "Thanks," he replied. Sliding his hands into the pockets of his black suit jacket, he shrugged. "I'm not sure what I'm going to do with all the orchids."

"You could take some home and donate the others to the hospital or nursing homes," Joshua suggested. He glanced at Laura and Adam in question. "Didn't we do that when Mom…?"

"That's right." Laura smiled at him softly. "We did."

Noah cleared his throat. "You guys reached out to help, and I refused it. I just want you to know I appreciate the offer."

"We're going to miss her," Joshua said. "Allison was the kind of light the world needs."

Noah lowered his head and nodded. "She was."

Laura could hardly stand to watch his shoulders rise and fall over a series of hard breaths.

"We're dedicating the plaque to her in the meditation garden tomorrow evening at six," Adam said quietly. "You should come. The plan is to light a paper lantern and let it fly. Laura and Alexis will light it. We'd like you to be the one who releases it."

Noah kept his head down. He bobbed it in a solitary nod. "I can do that."

Joshua reached out. He grabbed Noah's shoulder. "You need anything, Detective, call me. Penny's available whenever you need a long country drive. I can accompany you as a guide…or as a friend."

Noah looked at him with the light of surprise. "Thank you."

Adam reached out to shake his hand. "I'm holding on to Allison's fund. I don't care if it's now or thirty years from now. If you think of something you'd like to do in her name, all you need to do is let me know."

"I'll remember," Noah pledged.

Adam looked at Laura. "You need a minute?"

She nodded. "Please."

"We'll wait by the car," Joshua told her before he and Adam strolled off.

Noah ran his eyes over her. He pulled a long breath in through the nose, his chest inflating. "You look stunning," he said on the exhalation.

She lifted a hand to the neck of her dress. "That's sweet of you."

He glanced around at the lingering mourners, unsure what to say or do.

Laura reached out, then stopped. "Are you all right?" she asked.

"No."

He didn't dress it up or deflect. That was something.

"What can I do?" she asked. He hadn't accepted help with the service. He would hardly lean on her now, she knew. Still, she had to ask.

"You're here," he replied simply.

"Of course I am," she murmured.

"Let me look at you a minute," he requested after some thought. "Would that be okay?"

She nodded. "More than okay."

He took a step back. His eyes didn't dapple over her. They reached. The yearning in them, the necessity, made her heart stutter. They started at her feet before winding up the path of her skirt to her waist, her navel, her bodice, before landing on the bruising that hadn't yet faded from her neck. He blinked several times, lingering there, before circling her face.

She saw so many things in him, and they matched what was inside her—regret, need, longing, hesitation… There was so much she wanted to say to him. *I miss you. I love you.*

*Please, lean on me. Just…lean.*

Her breath rushed out. "Noah."

He muttered a curse. "Part of me wants to chase these people off so I can have a single moment alone with you."

A match touched the dry tinder inside her. Hope flared as the fire caught.

"What would you do with that moment?"

His tungsten-green eyes spanned her face. They landed on her mouth as he answered quietly. "Beg."

Her breath caught. "No."

"Yes," he argued. "I told you I needed time. But I should've called. I should've checked on you."

She smiled knowingly. "Adam told me you called him to check on me. Every day."

"I should've grown a pair and called you," he grumbled.

"Why didn't you?" she asked. The distance had convinced her he didn't want this—whatever they'd made between them. And it had hurt—more than the bruises on her throat.

"Because I'm a goddamn coward," he said plainly. He paused, considering. Then he closed the distance to her. "You still want to know my secrets, Laura?"

She could smell the light touch of cologne he'd put on his skin. The flame popped, lighting little fires everywhere else inside her to catch and grow, too. "Yes," she breathed.

"I'm hands down, one hundred percent, head over heels in love with you," he said.

She closed her eyes. "You don't have to—"

"I do," he asserted. "I didn't call. Not because I couldn't move past what happened the night of the arrest. I didn't call because I've been grappling with the fact that you are the only woman in this world that I want. You're the only person I want next to me. And I don't deserve you, because what kind of man walks away from Laura Colton? What kind of man runs from the chance to be yours?"

"It's okay—"

"No, it's not."

"But it is," she said, bringing her hands up to his lapels. She traced them with her palms, caressing him as his lungs rose and fell under them. "We're both here now. You're saying these things. And you won't walk out again. Will you?"

He gripped her wrist. He didn't pull her away. Instead, he touched his brow to hers. "No." He ground out the word. "I won't walk out again."

They stood together as a strong breeze swept across the cemetery, lifting flowers and hats into the air. Laura felt the skirt of her maxidress flapping around them like wings, but she didn't move.

As the wind died down in increments, she said, "Tell me another secret."

He made a noise. After a moment, he answered. "I used to braid her hair when she was too little to do it herself."

She smiled at the image. "Softy."

"Yeah," he admitted. "She was the only person who knew that side of me—until you."

"Say more things," she requested.

He thought about it for a second. Then he lifted his wrist, pulling back the cuff of his jacket sleeve. Here, she'd noticed he carried a solitary feather on the inside of his arm. "This was my first tattoo. It's my favorite."

"You *do* have a favorite," she mused, touching it.

He nodded, his head low over hers as she traced the feather's shaft. She heard his slow inhalation and knew he was smelling her hair. "It's for my mother."

"Oh, Noah," she sighed.

"Every Christmas, I drive up to Washington and retrace my steps with her there. I go to the coast and hole up in a cabin we used to rent in the summer. I don't have anything of hers. We didn't have much. And everything that was hers got lost after she was killed. I only have memories. Every year, I'm afraid I lose more. I go to the cabin to remember, because if I don't, did she really even exist?"

"Yes," Laura assured him. "You're proof of that. Not just because you're here. Because you are the man you are—the kind that would take care of a little girl who had no one. The kind who puts bad guys behind bars and who does your sister and your mother proud every day."

He turned his lips to her cheek and kissed her softly. Lingering.

"I want this," she told him, her hands grabbing his lapels. "I want you. And if you try to tell me again that someone like you doesn't deserve me, I've got some ideas how my brothers can alter that line of thinking."

"Coyotes?"

"There's a gorge, too," she added. "What do you say, Detective?"

He scanned her, and his eyes were so tender they made all those little fires inside her hum. "I'm going to keep calling you Pearl," he warned.

"I'm used to it."

He nudged the pearl drop on the end of the gold necklace she hadn't taken off since he'd put it there. "My pearl."

When he said it like that, she shuddered and understood. "Do you want me? Do you want this?"

"Yes," he said, finite. "I want you. *All* of you."

She brought her hands up to his face. "Then you should know," she said, "I'm hands down…" She canted her head at an angle. "One hundred percent…" She skimmed a kiss across his mouth. "Head over heels in love with you, too."

His hands caught in the belt of her dress. "Come home with me," he said, whispering the words across her mouth.